A NEW ENGLAND BILLIONAIRES BOOK

The Billionaire's Assistant

A NEW ENGLAND BILLIONAIRES BOOK

For Halina...

The real Zuzanna.
It takes an amazing woman to mold a real man.

Content Warning:

This novel contains profanity, discussions of childhood trauma/violence, & sexually graphic descriptions.

Kira

"Kira! In my office."

"But—"

"*Now!*" Andrew hollers across the store before pushing the lopsided frames up his nose by the bridge. Pocked with acne and soft in the middle, the twenty-two-year-old points to the door in the rear like an infuriated parent sending a child to its room.

I can't help but laugh at how alarmingly serious this twerp takes everything. I've got almost half a decade on him, yet he insists on talking to me like I'm eight years old.

I can't believe this is real life.

I exhale a heavy sigh, slumping my shoulders. I dump the armful of sweaters in my clutches haphazardly on a display shelf in a gnarled pile of hideous yarn that should frankly be *burned*, not sold.

"Come in. Shut the door behind you," he orders.

My eyes bulge. I am fully aware of what this means. It isn't the first time I've heard it.

Or... even the *second.*

Several shoppers gawk as I walk the mile, their faces fraught with shock and curiosity. I

1

storm through the store, clenching my hands tight by my sides.

"*What*, Andrew? What *now?*"

"That's a hell of a way to talk to your manager."

"*Assistant* manager." I glower at him, wondering how long it's been since this weasel's gotten laid.

Not like I have room to talk...

"Sheena says you haven't been informing customers about the March promo when you're working the register."

"No one wants to be bombarded by a long spiel about a dumb deal that's happening in three weeks. I keep telling you it's too early for anyone to care. You tell people when the promotion is *happening*. Not damn-near a month *before*."

"You tell people whatever corporate *tells* you to, *whenever* corporate tells you to. I don't make the rules. I just *adhere* to them, which any employee seeking longevity here would be *wise* to do."

"Who the hell wants *longevity* at *The Sweater Hut?*" I scoff.

"*I* do, for one," Andrew growls, not an ounce of sarcasm in his stern voice. "And curb your language, for God's sake. Don't be insubordinate to your superior."

"*Insubordinate to my superior?*" I grind my teeth. "*Whatever.* I'm not going to feed your

Napoleonic complex. I'm going back out on the floor."

"No. You're not. We're not done here."

"Yes, we are." I breeze through the doorway, past Sheena, who is pretending to organize cardigans on a rack near the office, clearly there to eavesdrop.

"You can go back to work, Sheena. Nothing more to see here."

"I wasn't—"

"*Spare me.*" I shoot her a pissed-off glance.

"Hey," Andrew hollers from his desk.

"Hey, *what?*" I roll my eyes.

"You want to disrespect me, that's one thing. But you do it to another employee… no. Not on my watch. You're fired. Grab your stuff." He looks to Sheena. "If she doesn't leave, call mall security."

"Yes, sir," Sheena barks dutifully. I could swear I see her salute him like a soldier out of the corner of my eye as I brush past her.

Andrew shuts the office door hard.

I stop for a moment to breathe, soaking in the sudden left-turn my life has just taken. I pinch my eyes together, annoyed, and draw deep breaths. When they finally open, Sheena's pompous mug is there. Her wrinkled eyes are squinted slivers from the shit-eating grin on her face, crow's feet on full display.

"Take a picture, it'll last longer," I mutter.

"Oh, g*row up,*" Sheena fires back, proud of herself. "Your attitude is trash, Kira."

"Oh, shut *up*, Sheena," I grumble and roll my head back to glare at her.

"No one's gonna hire you in this economy. Not with your track record," she taunts gleefully.

The comment stings more than it should.

"You're an immature *child*," she adds.

"Well, at least I'm not *boring*. I'd rather cut an overgrown lawn with *fingernail clippers* than listen to you tell me another dumb story about your blind cat's diabetes."

Sheena laughs haughtily as I gather my tattered purse and worn romance paperback from beneath the counter.

"Buh-bye," she sings, clutching the standing metal detector with both arms like she's auditioning for the role of Mary Poppins.

"*Eat a dick,* Sheena." It's the last thing I say before I flip her the bird and make my way out of this prison of folded, retail garbage, leaving my insulted former co-worker *literally* clutching her pearls.

"You *what?!*" Cassandra runs a hand through her blonde locks, stressed by my news.

"It's not that big a deal, Cass!" I groan and plop onto the sagging couch, a housewarming gift from Cassandra's father when we got the place together a few years ago.

"Not that big a deal?!" She whips around to face me, pointing a finger. "I can't believe this. You always do this."

"*What?!* I don't always do *anything.*" I throw my hands up.

It's my day to be dumped on by everyone, I suppose. *Pile it on.*

"This is last spring all over again... when you got that legal assistant job for that defense attorney. It paid damn good. You had it for, what, *five months?*"

"The guy wanted me to stare at pictures of porn on his computer all the time. He'd visit Daytona every month and come back with pictures. It was the itty-bitty-titty-parade for an hour straight, *every* time. I'm sorry, Cass, but I don't wanna study the finest inverted areolas Florida's *Busted Spoke Bar* has to offer over my morning coffee. Frankly, he could've been sued for that kind of harassment."

After a pause, I snicker. "Can you imagine how wild *that* would have been? To sue a *lawyer*?"

Cassandra's eyes turn fierce. "What is *wrong* with you?"

"What?! Nothing's wrong with *me*. Andrew was the one being the prick."

"Do you *know* how many people have a prick boss in this world, Kira?" She stares at me, expectant, waiting for an obvious answer to spew forth from my lips. "The *overwhelming majority*."

"You're blowin' this all *way* out of proportion. It's freakin' *retail*."

"It was a *job*. You know... the thing you have to have to make *rent?*"

I chew my thumbnail; a bad, nervous habit I've battled for over a decade. "I don't need a mother, Cass. I've done just fine without one for *many* years." I pick up the remote and aim it at the TV.

Cassandra darts in the path of it, blocking the television. "Maybe you *do* need a mother right now because you're acting like a *child*. Ask Andrew for your job back." She throws her hands up. "No. *Beg*."

"I'd rather unclog the toilets on the Metro full time. And you have seen those things. They're horrific." I shake my head, swinging my wavy, blonde tresses in defiance. I'm way too proud, too *stubborn* to beg anyone... for any*thing*.

Cassandra exhales, searching for the strength to say what is on her mind.

"*What?*" I roll my eyes. "Spit it out already."

"...I need you out by the end of the month."

Her words hit me like a wrecking ball, smashing me to bits with every syllable.

"What?! I know you're pissed, but—"

"You're damned right I'm pissed. You're never gonna learn. I always felt bad for you for what happened to your family, but you know what? We aren't eleven-year-old little white-trash kids running around your Uncle Dan's trailer park anymore. We're *adults*. We're both gonna be *thirty* in a few years." She lowers her voice. "George wants to move in together after the wedding, and, honestly, Kira, I want that, too. So March first, when he and I are back from Maui, I don't care where you go, but it can't be here. Time to *grow up.*"

Ahhh, the theme of the day.

A hard lump forms in my throat as Cassandra storms off. I chuck the remote onto the coffee table beside my bare feet and debate whether I should pour a bowl of value-brand fruity pebbles for dinner or just go to bed with my book and do a hard-restart on this day.

As I'm giving both options thoughtful consideration, Cassandra's Maine Coon, leaps onto the couch and strides just out of arm's reach, a subtle pro-move for creatures like us who manage to artfully dodge physical affection like bullets in *The Matrix*.

"*You* still love me though. Right, Gandalf?" I ask as if the cat wouldn't immediately use my face for a scratching-post if I died in my sleep tonight.

He stands, presents his butthole, gives me a long, steely-eyed stare, and saunters off with grace.

Alrighty… *I'm batting a thousand tonight.*

3

Eric

"How long until it comes off?" I grit my molars, tensing my jaw so hard it aches. With everything going on, with our accounts in total disarray after my procedure last month, I need a win.

James stares sideways at my sling-encased arm as if it'll whisper the answer to him. The morning light pouring through the window hits the contours of his face, outlining him like an onyx sculpture.

"Don't say another week. I've already been in it for a month. Please," I plead.

"Another *week*? Eric, you're going to need it for another *four*, at *least*. Even then, you'll be healing for a few more months. This wasn't an *ingrown toenail*. This was *surgery*. A rotator cuff takes *months* to fully heal, longer if you don't keep it immobilized. As bad as the damage was, you're lucky you're only in this. It could have been, frankly, way worse. It could have been pins and plaster."

I pick up a mesh wastebasket beside my chair with my right hand and hurl it at the wall, striking a framed award for some bullshit accolade I never cared for. As it crashes down, along with crumpled paper hail, it also takes the

9

certificate beneath it, as cannon fodder. Both smash to bits atop my seventy-thousand-dollar imported, Tuscan area rug.

The Nigerian doctor flashes his brilliant set of teeth. He knows I'd never hurt another human. He's done nothing but *rib me* about being a fucking *softie* since college.

"Feel better?"

"No," I huff.

What if Bella saw me acting like this? That's *all* the ammo Tawny would need to usurp the place in my daughter's life that I earned by simply *not abandoning her.*

Pull your shit together, Eric.

"James, please. There's got to be *something* you can do."

"No, but there's something that *you* can do."

"*Anything.*" I turn to him.

"Let… it… *heal.*" He fights the urge to snicker. "Look, Eric, I don't have you in this appalling thing just so I can gain an advantage in racquetball."

I laugh, sliding my rough fingertips over the smooth glass of the desk before settling into my seat. "You *sure* about that?"

James looks at the ceiling and laughs, shaking his head.

I groan. "Ugh, I can't do *shit* with this thing on. You know how hard it is to make a freaking *sandwich* in this?"

"Oh, *please*, Eric. You haven't had to make yourself a *sandwich* since you gambled on that first, big crypto bubble. Lucky for *you*, you have a dedicated Parisian at your beck-and-call specializing in gourmet panini artistry."

"I don't hear *you* complaining about the *spoils* of that bubble." A grin creeps onto my face. "Rob and I made you a boatload, too."

"Oh, I'm *aware*, but you're proving my point *for* me. With as much money as I have, do you think I walk around, like, playing doctor just to make you miserable? It's a nice day out. I could be stringing up my rods and stocking the yacht for spring, man."

"Honestly, I don't have a *clue* why you still work or make house calls now that you mention it."

"The same reason you didn't buy some small island in the Bahamas and retire after you day-traders broke that gaming stock and '*stuck it to the options-trading trust-fund pricks*' or... whatever the hell you did. *I still don't fully understand it.*"

"We didn't *break* it, it still exists. It's down right now, but we—"

"Eric, I don't want the details about how the sausage gets made any more than you want a detailed account of Mrs. Cranston's labial warts."

"Ewww, *what*?" I make a sour face.

He waggles his eyebrows with a grin.

"Wait, isn't it a HIPPA violation for you to tell me that?"

"Only if Cranston *really* has a lumpy crotch." James adjusts one of his cuff-links. "And there's only one *sure* way you'll ever find out for yourself if I'm lying."

I feign gagging. "Hard pass. She's three hundred years old."

"It's a few more weeks, Eric. Then, the sling comes off once and for all."

"I can't even put on one of my damned *suits* for a video conference. What is the point of having tailored Armani if I have to woo investors wearing a *Guy Harvey* Hawaiian-shirt that says *'Life's a Beach'* because it takes forty minutes to wrench my arm into anything more complicated?" I motion to the hideous collection of jumping marlins spattered across the one I'm wearing.

"Don't do video conferences then. Or be a baller and straight-up *Hugh Hefner* that shit with some kind of dope-ass robe. Now *that's* a power move!" He waves his pink palm and shakes his head. "Nah, Salko, that's not even like *#firstworldproblems* anymore. That's like *#BezosMusk*-I-got-space-shuttles-for-toys problems."

James picks up his travel bag and opens the glass door to my office. "Which, if you get one of those, I got dibs on a front-row seat for the second launch. You're gonna want yourself a doctor who makes house calls when you filthy-rich dum-dums colonize Mars."

"James, you'd have a spot in the front row on the *first* launch, I promise."

"*Hell* naw. Gotta see you guys go up and come *back* safe before I strap into that sumbitch. I've heard that Bowie song *way* too many times. I ain't tryna radio to Major Tom." His hand slides over the handle of the glass door to my office. He glances back with sincerity. "It's one month. You can do that standin' on your head. I believe in you."

I nod. *He's right.*

"Until then, spend a little of that *crypt-dough* and hire yourself an assistant or something. Someone to help shoulder the burden, no pun intended." He grins. "We just hired this young kid, couldn't be more than twenty, to help with the filing and scheduling at the practice. He's been a godsend."

"How'd you find *him?* Just like, put an ad out in the paper?"

"Jesus, Eric. How old *are* you? Nobody takes an ad out in a paper anymore. That hasn't been a thing for about a decade. In fact, are you still getting *paper newspapers?*"

"No," I lie.

"Get with the times, Eric. There's apps for *all* that stuff now. We got our guy off that *ConneCT* app. Worth a shot."

I nod and stare at my sling. "Yeah, I'll put Rob on it. He's better with all the techy stuff. I barely know how to work my phone half the time."

"Oy, the irony of making a *literal* fortune off tech stocks and being unable to figure out smartphone apps. *What a time to be alive.*"

"Remmy, where did you *hear* about this app?" I ask, thumbing through my phone, reading blocks of text through the spider web of cracks. My face basks in the blue-tinged light of my screen.

"Who fuckin' knows." He spins my chair to face the mirror, grabs a comb from a ledge of sparkling metal tools, and runs it skillfully through my hair. It slides like a tiny, grinding skateboard through my sandy waves.

"If you don't want your cut to look like *ass*, you'll put that vintage Android *down*."

"I'm desperate, Remmy. Why do you think I'm spending my last twenty bucks here at a salon? It's so I can be *presentable. Employable*."

"First off," He points with the tool, "you know *damn well* you don't have a twenty in your purse. You probably ain't in years. Second, how much do you think a salon cut *costs?* This ain't *BudgetCuts*, honey. We don't do no twenty-dollar haircuts here. I do this for you on the sly. You're my little charity case." He bobbles in a sassy way and sighs. "Shit, girl, you always *did* have a beer-bottle pocket, even back in high school."

I laugh. "Beer-bottle-pocket? What does that even *mean*?"

He playfully yells at my face, "You *broke*, honey-child. You ain't never had a pot to piss in, and, love, you ain't never *gonna* at this rate."

"Why is everyone so obsessed with money lately? Jesus *Christ*."

He pats the short, dark curls on his head with the heel of his palm. "Green makes the *world* go 'round, baby. Don't you want nice things? A car that ain't held together by bread-ties an' hope? A fancy dress that forces men to gasp when you walk into an expensive restaurant? And what about *jewelry?*"

"Rem, what would I even be doing in an *expensive restaurant?* I grew up dumpster-diving for food and stealing books from the local library just to have something to *do* on the weekends. I had second-hand *everything*. And guess what? I turned out juuuuust fine."

Remmy makes an exaggerated expression of displeasure. He reminds me of a ten dollar boardwalk caricature. "Mmmm-hmmm. Keep tellin' yourself that, honey."

He spritzes my hair again and jerks my face toward the mirror before running the comb through again. As he trades it for his shiny shears, my head tilts down again so I can scroll through job listings.

"Can you at least hold it up in front of your face so I don't give you some whack-ass cut?"

I hoist the phone up and straighten my posture, skimming through the various classifieds. "Vet Tech. Damn, this one pays real good." I frown. "Oh. Never-mind. That's a *lot* of qualifications. Wow. My *Lord*, how hard can trimming a dog's *toenails* be?"

Remmy expertly trims my split-ends with quiet chops. "You gotta know how to to express anal glands, too."

I wince and scroll on. "Thanks for making that one sting less."

"It's what I'm here for," he jests.

"What about this one? Stock-person at the Stratford *Shop-and-Go*."

"Sounds like a lateral move from folding sweaters, if I'm bein' honest."

"Yeah." I favorite it and keep scrolling. Suddenly, a listing catches my attention. "Personal Assistant. Temporary Position. Greenwich."

"Greenwich ain't a bad commute from here," Remmy shrugs. "That's a rich-ass town."

"Yeah, the CR-V might be able to handle that if I take back roads and go slow," I say as I read on. "Basic home and small office errands, light childcare duties… Seems like it's like a glorified coffee-runner-slash-babysitter. I could do that."

My eyes bulge, and I shoot forward, forcefully yanking my hair from Remmy's hand.

"Are you *crazy? Girl!*" He yanks my shoulders back with a forceful tug, shooting me a threatening look in the mirror.

"Holy crap!" I exclaim looking at the ad. "*God.* Look at what it *pays!*" I'm equally astounded and skeptical as I shove the phone up to Remmy's face.

I am trying not to get my hopes up. It *has* to be a typo.

"Jesus, Kira." His eyes widen, too. "Apply! Like… *now.* Shit, ask if they need their own personal hair-dresser."

I laugh. I can't hit the application button fast enough.

At this point, what have I got to lose?

5

Rob studies my attire as I sit down. I already sense I'm being judged for my lowly place in the fringe of polite society.

"How are you with kids?" he asks, rubbing his clean-shaven face.

"*Fantastic*," I lie.

The truth is, I haven't been around many since I was one myself. And although everyone accuses me of acting like a child, I have no idea how it would translate to being responsible for a real, live, breathing one in today's world.

But hell, *fake it til' you make it,* they say.

"Excellent. Part of your duties, if hired, would be to help with the day-to-day activities, scheduling, and transportation of a nine-year-old. That a problem?"

"Not at all."

The kid, no. Not a problem… I think.

Transporting anything of value in my dented-can-of-a-vehicle...

That's another story. But I'll cross that bridge when I come to it.

"This child *does* have an *impairment* which can be, um, *obnoxious* at times. At least, in my opinion."

I nod, acting like I'm not alight with curiosity, even though I am. I wait for him to volunteer the information.

"She has Tourette's Syndrome."

"Oh! Well, I wouldn't call that an *impairment*—"

"She doesn't curse or blurt things out like in the movies, but when she gets stressed, her tics are really noticeable. She'll repeat words or sounds on a loop. Is that…" he leans forward, "a problem?"

"Not at all. I actually have experience with that. My younger brother had it."

Finally, something that isn't a lie.

"Outstanding. How are you with filing and errand-running and such?"

"Phenomenal. I don't wanna come off as too *braggy*, but I've been proficient with my ABCs since kindergarten." I point at myself and laugh. "Destined for *greatness*, this one."

Rob laughs. I think I'm winning him over, disarming him with my odd humor. I side-eye the heap of printed resumes and feel my smile wane. I think about the money this gig pays and feel a renewed sense of vigor.

I *want* this job. Even if it's only temporary.

"What about cooking and cleaning and all that?" I ask, leaning back in the sumptuous office chair across the chrome-trimmed desk from him. I try not to let it show in my face that I'm, frankly, shit at both. I live off a steady diet of sale-priced value-brand cereal and nuke-able, sodium-laden frozen dinners.

I haven't used a pot or pan in months. The last time I scrubbed a baseboard was...

Oh God, have I ever *scrubbed a baseboard?*

"Oh, *no, no, no,*" he shakes his head. "Salko's got a cleaning staff, chef, pool service, gardener... the whole nine. This would predominantly entail light receptionist-type duties and basic childcare. You'd be, just, running the rugrat to karate, therapy, filling prescriptions, answering phones, post office runs... that sorta thing."

"Love it."

I do.

I got this. Someone with *half* my intelligence could do this. I'm going to shine.

"Excellent. It's only a temporary position. Eric only plans to keep someone on until he's out of his sling in about a month or so."

"Perhaps in that time, I'll make myself so essential, he keeps me full-time." I smile.

"Yeah, good luck with *that.* I wouldn't hold your breath. It's going to be a struggle just getting him to let you help, I'm sure. He doesn't like *change.*" He smirks.

"Same. I haven't upgraded phones since right after they started putting the internet on 'em." I pull my cracked smartphone from my purse to show him how ancient the model is. The damn thing could qualify as an antique. "Heck, until I found out about this app, I was buying newspapers for the classifieds."

Rob doesn't laugh. Instead, he gives me a strange look I can't decipher.

"Sounds like you and Salko will be *quite* the match." I could *swear* he rolls his eyes a little when he says it. He clears his throat. "So, why did your recent employment terminate at," he stares at the paper for a long time before glancing at me, "*The Sweater Barn?*"

I erupt in a nervous chuckle and cover my mouth. I'm suddenly mortified about the embarrassingly-shitty jobs populating my resume.

"I know. I had my *dream job*, and I *blew it*," I joke, shaking my fist at the sky.

It's Rob's turn to laugh now.

"You want the truth?" I shrug.

"Wouldn't have asked if I didn't."

"I'm *sushi*." I correct my slouching posture.

"Beg your pardon?"

"I'm an *acquired taste*. I'm a spicy salmon roll. Not everyone likes me, but the ones who *do*, they grow to *love* me. Andrew, captain of the U.S.S Sweater-Barn, he wanted *unsalted french fries*. He wants someone tasteless, terrible, and yet widely palatable that won't stand out from the rest of the pack. Unfortunately, I don't really *do* bland."

"I see that." His eyebrows bob and he exhales hard. "Personally, I never understood the appeal of sushi, myself."

I can't tell if it's a jab at me directly or a diss on the heavenly flavor combo of nori, rice, and raw fish.

"...But Salko friggin' loves the stuff, so," he leans back into his leather, ergonomic throne. "If your criminal and driving record come back clean—"

"They *will*." I offer an apologetic look for cutting him off.

He smirks, "Then, when would you be able to start?"

"*Yesterday,*" I say with a smile.

6

I study the GPS location on my phone held in place by an old, busted cradle that I've had to tape together and tie to my air conditioning vents with fishing string.

This can't be the right place.

Idling roughly next to the intercom box, I stare up at the massive wrought-iron gate before me. On either side, sits a large matching black horse head bust, each with coal-colored eyes and patina staring down at me.

Beyond the gate, a capacious manor is the center-piece of the massive spread of land surrounding it. The building is two, gargantuan stories, each with a wraparound porch. Ornate Roman columns stud the front of the enormous estate. The house is flanked by orchards full of huge, dormant fruit trees and manicured, stone-wall gardens mounded with mulch. The path of grass and melting snow between the house and orchard looks like it crawls onward for a solid mile.

I can't imagine what its like to own so much property. Or... *any*, for that matter. The only thing I've ever owned is the rattling hunk of junk I'm sitting in.

In this moment, I feel extremely under-dressed. Maine Coon hair clings to the cheap material of my clothes no matter how many times I've lint-rolled this morning. I've had this button-down blouse since high school and the white tank beneath it still had the sticker on it two hours ago. And my shoes... let's just say, they've seen better decades.

I take a deep breath, straighten my posture, and press the button on the intercom. As I wait for a response, my eyes trace the long, bendy path I'd travelled up from the main thoroughfare in the side-mirror.

Is all of that property part of this estate, too? Rob never said anything about reporting to a damned *mansion*. Although, I guess I *should* have had a clue by the pay rate and the fact that Rob said this guy had a chef...

Honestly, I didn't even realize there *were* any mansions in Connecticut outside of the Gillette Castle in East Haddam.

"Hello?" A man's gruff voice sounds from the box.

I jolt against my torn upholstery, taken off-guard. "Oh, um, hi. I don't know if I'm in the right place or not. I was given this address, *at least I think it was this address,* by a man named Rob Samson. I answered an ad about—"

BNNNNNNNNNNNNNNN! A prison-like buzzer sounds and the gates quietly groan open, welcoming my beat-up, silver SUV like two hydraulic open arms.

25

I nod appreciatively at the call box as if it can somehow see me and creep up the driveway.

7

Eric

When I open the door, I'm not sure what to expect. All I know is that it sure *isn't* the woman standing in front of me with the mahogany-tinted, gold, aviator glasses glinting in the sun. My eyes can't help but follow the graceful curve of her face and neck down to her unbuttoned blue shirt and the white camisole hugging her petite frame.

Her pearl-white teeth make an appearance as she smiles gently, tipping her glasses to look at me with a set of *striking*, green eyes.

"Hi. Are you Mr. Salko?" Her voice is smooth. She sticks out her hand to shake mine. Her nails are un-manicured with chipped, colorful polish. The plastic, beaded bracelet around her wrist clinks together with the movement like a Newton's Cradle.

I shake her hand. It's so warm. "You must be Ms. Blumquist."

"In the flesh." She flashes another brilliant, yet mischievous smile, one that has trouble written all over it. I don't know why, but she looks like she's no stranger to breaking rules.

"Call me Kira. Or Ree-Ree. Or *Hey-you-whats-her-face*. I'll answer to pretty much anything."

Did she just say to call her Ree-Ree? Is Rob fucking with me? I feel like this is a prank.

She stuffs her hand into the back pocket of her pants, which were tight even beforehand.

I can't put my finger on why, but something about her feels like a tumultuous storm on my doorstep, rumbling, ready to shake my very foundation.

She looks around. Her wild, blonde locks trail so soft and light, like dandelion seeds in a spring breeze. "This is a really nice place. Reminds me of, like, a *castle*. You royalty or something?"

I laugh a little. Not a lot, because it's a ridiculous thing to say. And because I feel tense in her presence.

"Nope. It's just a house."

She scoffs, with a smile, "Yeah. One big enough for *ten* families. I bet the place I grew up in is the same square footage as your master bath in there."

"Doubtful. Unless, of course, you lived in an RV."

"Not too far off. *Single-wide.*"

Single-wide? Is that a joke? Please say that's a joke. Where in the hell did Rob even find Ree-Ree, the blonde from the trailer park?

I'm feeling like this is a huge mistake. I don't know this woman and here I am about to

28

allow her in my home… my *sanctuary*… and, more importantly, around *Bella.*

I eyeball the clunker in the heated driveway and fight hard to not make a disgusted face. If that thing were a *building*, it would be *condemned.*

"Is it cool to park there?"

"No, staff parking is around back," I say, watching the undercarriage of her disaster-on-wheels drip fluids onto my power-washed concrete.

"Here. Give me the keys. I'll ask Jacques to park it for you."

"That's alright. She's kind of… a *beast* to get started." She looks embarrassed, but the blush in her cheeks suits her. "Just point me to where I need to put 'er and I'll limp this monster on over."

Limp? Ugh, charming.

Sweet Jesus, what have I done?

I clench my molars. "Follow the path around back to where the road forks. Take a right there and it'll take you right to the lot behind the house. You'll see a couple of other cars there. A BMW and a Rav4, probably. I'll go through and let you in through the rear door."

"Do I get a full tour of this place?" She asks, looking giddy at the prospect.

Yeah, one that ends right back out at your sad excuse for a vehicle…

But my mouth says, "Sure."

She flashes me an arresting smile, one that momentarily overrides all of my compounding doubts. She's captivating, no doubt about it. Charismatic, too.

It doesn't matter though. I shake the fleeting thought from my mind.

She's the help.

The staff's cars are lined up in a tidy row in the back, each making me feel even more inadequate by my mortifying excuse for transportation.

I hop out and slam the rusty door shut. The hinges squeal.

I can't stop thinking about how strong Eric's damn hand was when he shook mine. I thought my palm was going to crumble to dust. I thought he was going to be some old dude in a cast or something who couldn't tie his own shoes without hiring someone.

…Not some gorgeous thirty-something with a chiseled jaw, waves of silken hair, and an arm like a *quarterback.*

The double doors in the rear of the house swing open. He stands there, in tailored dress slacks, shined shoes, a white dress shirt that shows off his toned physique, and a blue mesh arm sling.

I can't believe I didn't soak him in as a *whole* earlier. There's something about his intense, light-brown irises that have me… *entranced.* Thank God I'm wearing my sunglasses. The *last* thing I need is to be branded as some sort of perv for gawking.

It's just… *he's easy on the eyes.*

I can tell, even beneath the material of his coordinated ensemble, he must take great care of his body. Despite his left arm being in a sling, he has the biceps and shoulders of an athlete. The muscles tug at the tailored fabric of his shirt, clinging in all the right places.

I throw my leather satchel on my shoulder and try to hold my hand in such a way that it obscures the gouge running down the side of it like a scar. It's stitched together like Frankenstein's monster, but it was my father's and I refuse to concede when people claims it's on its last legs.

"You can use this entrance when you arrive in the future. I'll get your phone number today and text you the key code. It changes daily so no need trying to memorize it," he says in a stern tone.

I nod, catching a glimpse of the spacious room beyond the doors where the high, vaulted ceilings are accented with rustic cypress beams overhead.

"Come. I'll give you a quickie tour." He motions for me to follow as the doors click shut behind us.

All I can think about is the fact that the only kind of quickie I want with this guy does not involve much of a *tour.* Except maybe to the *bedroom.*

Down, Kira…

He walks me briskly through the house and my eyes drift down to the way his slacks cling to the curves of his muscular thighs and perfect butt. I wonder for a moment if he's a boxers-kinda-guy, but judging from his slightly uptight and uncomfortable introduction, I'm guessing he's stark-white tighty-whiteys all day. With the kind of money he has, he probably wears them once and throws them away.

"This is Jacques, the chef. Anything you want from 8:00 a.m. to 6:00 p.m., just ask him. Especially pasta, he's a wizard with anything pastry or noodle-related."

It's cute to see Mr. Salko so excited about something, even if only for a moment. Judging by his physique, I never would have imagined it would be about *food*. Gourmet or not.

Jacques waves a flower-coated hand above the lump of fresh dough he's been hand-kneading on the massive marble countertop. He wraps it in plastic wrap and scrubs up in the giant sink.

As we make our way through, I look around, in awe. The walls are fitted with top of the line ovens and vent-hoods. There's a brushed-metal refrigerator and upright freezer flanking the glass stove-top. The surfaces glimmer. Other than the workspace in front of Jacques, the room is immaculate.

"You got a specialty?" I grin.

"French cuisine," Jacques says with zest and zero hesitation. His French accent is strong. "Obviously."

"Ooooh, *cuisine française?*" The words slip from my lips.

"*Tu parles français?*"

"*Oui. Un peu.*" I hold my fingers up and pinch a small gap of air. Then I tell him, in French, that I spent a few weeks in Paris after high school.

"*Tres bon,*" he replies with a grin.

My leering eyes are drawn to the colorful array of fresh, chopped vegetables and peeled garlic that occupies the massive cutting board beside him. It looks like something out of a commercial, vibrant and evenly-chopped.

I catch a whiff of boiling poultry and I salivate. It looks like he's in the middle of making chicken pot pie from scratch. The heavenly aroma fills the massive kitchen, one nearly the size of the entire apartment I share with Cassandra.

"How's your *coq a vin*?"

"To *die* for. I learn it from a chef in Montmartre. He was… one of the best."

"*Mmmmm.* That's my favorite." I smile. "Hey, let's talk Montmartre sometime."

"I look forward to it."

"*Tres bon.*" I'm a bit rusty with my pronunciations, but speaking it takes me back to one of the most amazing trips of my entire life. I scrimped and saved for years to get there. And going, despite odds so stacked against me, has always been something I've been proud of.

Mr. Salko stares at us blankly for a moment and then waves me away. My tour continues through a labyrinth of spacious rooms, including a full home gym, large indoor tennis court, a warm glass-enclosed conservatory filled with tropical plants and a heated pool, a den, a walk-in humidor, a lounge full of puzzles and board games, a dining room that seats twenty, a children's play room with an assortment of stuffed animals and large toys.

We continue through his decadent estate past Bella's bedroom and a closed master suite that I can only imagine is just as palatial inside. The mystery of its size and decor bites at my mind and thoughts race as to how sterile and plain it probably looks.

***

I fight the almost overpowering urge to lightly chew my thumbnail on the couch in the lounge. It's a luxurious, tufted one that I'm certain cost more than all the mismatched second-hand furniture I've ever owned *combined*. It looks posh, like it's something one would use to drop the designer's name into conversation to one-up someone.

Oh, you think your Rosenberg ottoman is all the rage? Wait until you feast your eyes on the studded Thurman *settee I had imported from this quaint little shop in Germany. You can't sit on it because the bottom is made out of hand-woven wicker, but it makes a* phenomenal *conversation piece.*

Jacques enters the room, placing a charcuterie board full of crackers, deli meats, and various cheeses on a glass coffee table before us. The cubes and slices are carefully arranged like something out of a magazine for gourmands. A slice of brie oozes out of the sides of its crust onto the wood. My mouth waters but I fight the urge to launch myself at it in an effort to appear like I have even a *modicum* of restraint. My empty stomach groans.

"I put some imported camembert on there for you. I cannot recommend it highly enough," Jacques says, one arm tucked obediently behind his back like a formal servant. He winks.

"Thank you, Jacques. That'll be all." Eric nods and Jacques swiftly retreats out of the room.

Eric turns his intense gaze to me.

This is the first chance I've really been able to study his masculine face and all of its perfectly-angled edges. His jaw tenses as he settles into his chair, exuding a quiet sexiness. His eyes flash in the morning sun oozing in from massive windows through the blinds. They're extraordinary, flecked with amber and gold in a way that catches light like I've never seen before.

"How was your commute this morning, Ms. Blumquist?"

The way he says my name sounds so distanced and formal. The way a random gynecologist might say it.

"It wasn't bad. I live in Bridgeport, so its not a bad drive." Now I feel like I'm talking to a gyno, making that awkward-as-hell conversation to pass the time while he's between my legs.

Only *this* guy… I kind of wish he *was*.

That butt? *You could bounce a quarter off it…*

"I'm glad. Yeah, Rob said you didn't live far." He picks up a small circle of Genoa salami, rolls it carefully, and nibbles off half of it. "So throughout the day, you'll be assisting me with some work tasks, filing and all of that. This afternoon, when you meet Bella after school," he hesitates, like he's trying to figure out the right words. "You'll notice that she's got something of a nervous tic."

"Yeah, Rob mentioned she has Tourette's in the interview."

Eric tries to hide the sour look on his face but fails. "She's in the process of seeing a specialist about it right now. She has regular appointments with a counselor on Tuesdays and Fridays. I'll be sure to get you a schedule of the location and times. One of your duties will be to take her to those."

"Not a problem," I chirp quickly to inspire some confidence. I want him to know that I understand the needs of the position, even if I don't fully, yet. I want to keep this gig as long as possible. Even being temporary, the money would go a long way toward an apartment of my own.

"Honestly, Tourette's isn't a big deal unless you make it one. My little brother had it. You get used to it. Honestly, I didn't even notice it after a while." I finally cave and pluck a small pie-slice of brie from the charcuterie board.

It's divine. Even without a cracker. It melts on my tongue and my eyes flutter.

My new employer snickers at my reaction to the snack and shakes his head.

Ah, crap. He already thinks I'm weird.

"I'm thrilled to hear you have some experience, because it can get… *rough* sometimes. I don't always know how to deal with it. I used to think it just happened when she was nervous or felt put on-the-spot, but now it gets to the point that when she's doing something as simple as watching TV, she looks like she is getting electrocuted or prodded with a stun-gun or something. It gets to the point that I don't even remember what I'm watching ten minutes in. I'm too busy watching her."

"I know you're probably worried, but I assure you, it won't bother me in the slightest. Unless she's shouting the n-word over and over in public or something, we're golden."

Eric laughs so hard he starts to snort. He covers his face and his reaction makes me erupt in my own laughter.

I'm not that funny, but his laugh is honestly quite adorable. I find myself fighting the urge to make him do it again.

The moment he's shaking his head with his eyes closed, I seize the opportunity to sneak a handful of cheese cubes off the board and stuff several into my mouth. I suddenly wonder what level of laughter I'd need to get him to to be able to swipe that pink slice of prosciutto that's right there... *just staring me in the face.*

"Wow, I can't remember the last time I laughed like that," he confesses. "No. I *doubt* she'd *ever* do something like that."

I swallow, trying to not sound like my mouth is crammed full of dairy. "Great. Then, it's all gravy."

"My wife always made a mountain out of it. Insisted on her being on neuroleptics and all that."

I feel the wind disappear from my sails. Though I knew I'd never have a chance with a man of his social stature and wealth, I thought there might be at least a little wiggle-room for at least some harmless flirting.

But I guess it's not a shock. He's rich and ripped and, my God, those eyes...

They're mesmerizing. There's no way someone like him stays on the market for more than a minute before some affluent somebody swoops in at some million-dollar endangered species fundraiser and gobbles him up.

Still, it's a shame. The man *is* a bit of an Adonis and, frankly, the customers and staff I've been around at *The Sweater Barn*... let's just say that's not a pool I was *ever* going to swim in.

He winces hard, pressing his masculine lips into a flat line. The pink flush of embarrassment spreads across his sculpted cheekbones. "Ew, I just did it again, didn't I?"

"Hmmm?" I secretly think about the last of the cheese melting in my palm, hoping he will, once again, look away long enough for me to hork it down. "Did *what* again?"

"Ugh. Called her my *wife*." He shakes his head and looks up at the ceiling, disappointed in his choice of words. It's just enough time for me to pop the rest of the cubes in my mouth.

"Ugh," he groans, "old habits die hard, don't they?"

I don't speak. I only smile. Partly because I have a mouth full of delicious room-temperature Havarti, and partly because…

I don't know what the hell he's talking about.

"*She's* not… *we're* not." He waves his hands again, looking anxious and flustered.

"Mr. Salko,"I swallow so hard my eyes tear up, "it's honestly *none* of my business. Respectfully, sir, I'm here to make your life easier, not judge anyone's life choices. Trust me, I have my own…" my hands swim around through the air, "*stuff*."

He nods and nervously grabs the slice of prosciutto I've been eyeing like a patient Doberman. He rolls it up and stress-eats it. He wipes his hands on the cloth napkin peeking out from beneath the two-toned board and flashes a smile, taking me off-guard with the sudden zing of attraction I feel.

Be good, Kiraaaaaa…

I avert his gaze and look around the room, taking in all of the Italian-inspired decor, expensive-looking art, and luxurious furnishings.

I feel so *out of place,* like I'm *beneath* it all.

"Come. Let me get you acquainted with the office and give you the run-down in there."

For a second, I think he said he'd give me a *rub-down.* My eyes bulge and my face grows hot like I just ate a Carolina Reaper raw. I soon realize that I didn't hear him correctly.

As I follow him through a maze of impressionistic paintings and walls topped with ornate crown-molding, staring at a backside worthy of it's own featured month on a sexy calendar, I just keep imagining that ultra-strong hand of his massaging the tension right out of my neck.

Why is he just... *staring* at me? Those honey-colored eyes sizzle holes into my skin. It's hard to concentrate when he's looking at me like this.

My eyes flit across the typed paperwork about Bella's therapy sessions, homework, and extra-curricular activities like karate, Mandarin lessons, piano, and chess.

He's so... *organized.* Almost disgustingly so.

He's just handed me a packet. Everything is laid out for me, from GPS locations to an itinerary of daily tasks, to expected work attire, and scheduled snack times...

Literally everything. Everything is planned for her, almost to the *moment.* I'm surprised it doesn't have allotted times scheduled for his kid to take a piss.

I'll bet he is one of those guys who goes on vacation and has a minute-by-minute itinerary of everything he plans to do to *maximize the trip's potential.* He's clearly not the kind of guy who could enjoy a plastic chaise lounger by the beach, even for an hour.

Does he ever have any *fun?* Any *spontaneity?* I wonder when the last time he just got in the car and went on an unscheduled adventure… or went *camping*. Or rode a carnival ride.

What good is all that money if you live in a prison of your own design, trapped inside an Armani suit, shackled by ties and cuff links, whipped into a sort of stuffy submission by advisors, accountants, and the almighty buck?

And what about his *kid?*

I haven't even met her and I feel bad for her. She's doomed to have her first fender-bender in a Tesla-S going ludicrous speed in defiance. She will grow up accustomed to raw vegetables and kale smoothies, never understanding how a greasy cheeseburger, large fry, and ice-cold soda hits perfectly when you're in the right mood.

God, I should be reading this instead of letting my eyes drag across the page while I nod…

Mmmm-hmmm. Looks good. Yep, I'm totally reading all of this. Nope, not zoning out at all.

Oh God…

He's looking at me again with eyes that melt me like an ice cube in heated cast-iron.

I don't even think he's even *trying* to *be* sexy. I'll bet it's good genes. He probably didn't even take time to style and load product into that thick hair to get those perfect waves this morning. He probably didn't even spend more than a minute or two trimming his facial hair to make himself look virile and utterly masculine. This

43

guy probably woke up looking like he just walked off a shoot for *Surf* magazine.

I'll bet when he's wet, he looks *amazing…*

Jesus, Kira, focus!

10

Eric

Kira's laid-back, casual demeanor is a bit sexy, I must admit. The women I meet through our firm are all stuffy and posh, married to wealthy, emotionally unavailable men with limitless platinum cards. They're usually in drab skirts, pale blouses, and orthopedic shoes, and if you piled all of their shoulder pads atop each other, the stack would probably be taller than me.

Their expressions always lack that sparkle, that *joie de vivre*, that Kira has. Just seeing her talk to Jacques in the kitchen in another language with such exuberance, her lust for life and craving for a new adventure are obvious. It's refreshing.

I keep catching myself staring at her. Something in her eyes is positively wild, like an untamed mare.

But at the same time, I wonder, *can I have this woman around my daughter? What kind of influence is she going to have on Bella?* My child is like a *sponge,* soaking up everything in her vicinity.

Will I have to worry about inquiries like, "What's a *double-wide*, Daddy?"

How do I explain that?

While *I* may not have been born wealthy, this lifestyle is the only life *Bella'*s ever known. And, frankly, I'm fine with ours being the only world she's exposed to.

I would do anything to shield her from the grotesque realities of life. She's never had a transient berate her for pocket change. Or an alleged *friend* try to pilfer her client list. She's never had friends who were embarrassed to be seen with her in public because of her social status. She's never seen a man wearing a trash bag smacked with a baton in front of the gold-faced towers on 5th Avenue, a garish and lurid juxtaposition of income disparity in this country.

But I have. And I would never want that for her.

Bella's never eaten spaghetti-O's cold from a can before. She probably doesn't even know what fast food even *is*. And now I'm entrusting *Ree-Ree from the trailer park* with her? Tawny would have a total shit-fit if she could see this.

Actually, never mind.

Put that in the *pro* column.

I'm supposed to be reading through all of Kira's new-hire tax forms to ensure she didn't miss a signature, but it's like my eyes don't belong to me. They're not listening when I tell them to focus on the W-9. Instead, they're glued to her as she walks around my office, handling the awards on my shelves like a curious kid in a toy store.

As my eyes finally fall back to the page in my hand, I think about the women I'm usually around. No *joy*. No *passion*.

"What's in there?" she asks, pointing to the door caddy corner of my office, finger smooshed against the glass wall, leaving a print.

She whips her head to stare at me. I wish she would put her sunglasses back on.

Her eyes are *arresting*.

"You can go in. It's not locked," I mumble.

"Yeah?"

I nod.

She drifts into the hall, opens the other door, and gasps. "Hoooooly freaking s—"

I smile to myself. I think the same thing every time I walk in there, too.

I glance at the stock prices on my screen and the labels of the ten financial browser tabs and news sources that seem to stay perpetually open.

I sigh and rise from my desk. I'm not getting any work done right now. I brought her on to share the workload so that I could focus more, but I feel as if my day has absolutely derailed since the moment she drove that tired, leaking hunk onto my property.

"*Wow.*" Her voice wafts in as little more than a whisper from the vast room across the hall. "Are you for *real?*"

I chuckle.

Dammit, I wish she'd stop making me laugh. Earlier, in the living room, I think I snorted.

Fucking embarrassing…

As if on autopilot, I find myself drifting like a ghostly specter into the next room to follow. Her genuine sense of astonishment is endearing. I'm so used to being around stodgy adults who no longer find much to marvel at in this world beyond the almighty dollar.

But Kira's *different*.

This… feels like a problem.

I don't want to be distracted. Yet, here I am, watching my new hire make her way through the museum-like gallery of signed guitars in my music room.

"Does the *Hard Rock* know you're their number one competitor for autographed memorabilia?" Her bright eyes twinkle with the sun's reflection skipping off of my electric guitars. She places a finger with chipped glitter polish on my Slash-signed Fender, drags it along the edge, and then starts over on the next instrument.

This room houses a carefully curated ensemble of music-related rarities. The walls are lined with hanging guitars, carefully mounted on specialty neck hooks, many signed by famous artists. Lit glass cabinets populate some of the vast floor space, each featuring a collection of small instruments and artist memorabilia from the glitzy stage-wear of Neil Diamond to one of John Popper's harmonicas to one of the understated newsboy hats of Bob Dylan.

A gloss-black grand piano sits in one corner with its lid wide open as an opera singer's lips. In the corner across from it, a full drum kit sits in waiting, practically begging for someone to hammer away on it with the wooden drumsticks crisscrossed across the top of the dust-free floor Tom.

Colorful, plush couches and chairs are peppered throughout the room, each with amplifiers and neat cables at the base, ready to plug and play at a moment's notice.

Kira flashes a distant smile, one that shows she's miles away in a dream world full of nickel strings and flashy Sharpie-scribbled pick-guards. Her voice wafts back, "You play?"

"Guitar? Or…?"

"*Any.*"

"Yes. Piano, guitar, and a little drums. But none as much as I used to. Especially not *lately*." I look down at my arm in its hideous mesh sling. "You?"

She nods, wild blonde hair bobbing with every movement. "Guitar mostly, but I know just enough on the drums to be a little dangerous."

Of course, she does.

She speaks French and plays guitars and drums…. The next thing I know, she will tell me she also races and ask to take my Mercedes Black-Series Roadster out for a hundred-mile-an-hour leisurely spin.

She locks eyes with me, and I feel my cock stiffen beneath the fabric of my pants. I feel like a fucking pervert ogling her like this. She's just…

Stunning.

The more I look at her, the more I seem to find myself entranced. And now the rigidity in my slacks is making this slightly awkward. I step casually behind the glass cabinet and lean against it. Fortunately for me, it's one of the waist-high ones jewelers display their wares in.

"What do you play? Electric? Acoustic?" I wipe at the beveled crevice where the glass meets the metal frame, searching for dust, but it seems my housekeeper, Conchita, has been on her A-game.

"Mostly acoustic," she answers. "I used to sing in a couple of bands, too."

Of course, she did. Add that to the list, too. And I'll bet she has a voice like an early morning *songbird.*

"Any I might've heard of?" I ask, catching a glimpse of my sling in my reflection in the glass.

She scoffs as if the idea is ludicrous and bends over to examine a signed *Rolling Stone* I have laid out on the circular end table near the chair in which I usually practice my tablature.

I flex my jaw at the sight of her curvaceous ass presented in front of me and ease myself harder against the glass, hoping it will cool me through all the starch in my trousers.

Ugh, I feel like a horny-fucking-*teenager.*

"Doubt it. Not unless you're really big into the Bridgeport indie music scene." She flashes a mischievous grin.

I avert my gaze like she's Medusa so my growing problem isn't exacerbated. "Alas, I am not."

Hell, I can't even remember the last time I went to Bridgeport for fun.

She shrugs. "Nobody is."

I lean up against the display cabinet a little harder, willing my hard-on to go down. I try to think about how gross Bridgeport is instead of studying the lines of her body, which are making me feel strangely primal right now, like some horned-up caveman whose extinction is on the line.

I don't know why, but I can't seem to shake the momentary uninvited fantasy of her, stark naked, on that cushioned sofa next to her with nothing but the tiger-striped belly of my Gibson Custom Les Paul sandwiched between her bare, inviting thighs.

I swallow hard, jutting myself chaotically back into reality where, unfortunately, she's still fully clothed.

Her green eyes are staring almost *expectantly* at me.

Oh shit. Did she ask me a question while I was off in fucking la-la land?

"Hmmm?" I ask, hoping she thinks I just didn't hear her properly.

51

She beams, smiling brightly. "I didn't say anything."

I clear my throat. *Awkward.*

"Sorry, I just thought... I have trouble hearing sometimes."

Jesus Christ, why did I say that? That isn't even true. She's probably imagining me as some wrinkled old bastard who needs a hearing aid now.

Why do I even feel any need to impress her? She's bodacious and attractive, but she and I wouldn't work in a *million years*. Even with my dry spell nearing a year, she's not the kind of girl I would ever tangle with.

We're from different worlds.

"Anyway," I tilt my head to the side, and my neck erupts in a staccato symphony of pops, something that would have nauseated and annoyed Tawny. Kira doesn't seem to react to it.

"Are any of these for playing? Or are they all for decoration?" She points up to the wall of instruments, bodies glinting in the sun pouring in through the blind slats.

"The ones in the corner over there," I point to an area near the large picture window that overlooks the grounds. Beyond the glass, my concrete cherub fountain is wearing a toupee of untouched snow.

"All of those over there are for playing. The seven electrics and four acoustics."

"They're beautiful," she walks over to get a better look at them.

"Thanks."

She looks at her watch. It's a cheap one. Nylon band with a plastic electric-blue face. "Shoot, what time does your daughter come home?"

"Oh," I look at my brushed-metal Rolex. The smooth second-hand sweeps fluidly as if it's got somewhere more important to be than on the watch face. I curse myself silently for not paying closer attention to the time. "She should get out soon, actually."

"Sweet. I can't wait to meet her." She perks up, straightening her body until her firm breasts are once again out before her on display.

I'd bet a literal grand that they're sensitive as hell.

"She's still too short to sit in a regular seat. Do you have a booster in your vehicle for her?"

She looks at me blankly, as if I just asked the question in Latin instead of English.

"Oh, you want *me* to go pick her up?"

"Yes… that's… part of what I hired you for. Did Rob *not* go over the specifics with you?"

"He was a bit vague about the specifics." She pauses. "I assumed with a chef, a maid, a groundskeeper, and all that, you'd have a driver, too."

"No," I smile. "Normally, I pick her up from school, but lately, Rob's been doing it. I have a hard time steering with this thing on." I motion to my sling.

"I see."

"Is that... a problem?"

Why the hell is she acting so shocked about this?

"No," she says, but her voice is higher with a hint of alarm, making me uneasy. I furrow my brow, suddenly acutely aware that I don't know this woman from Adam. When it comes to my staff, I just am not great with personal deep dives. *I didn't even know where my chef was from until today.*

I waltz back toward the room's entrance.

"Will it be weird, though? Just showing up at a school and whisking a child away who's never met me? Hasn't she ever heard of, like, *stranger danger?*"

"Rob already put you on the pickup list at her school, but I'll text her cell and give you both a password."

"She's got a *cell?* Isn't she nine?"

"Of course." I just stare at her as if she's an alien.

She presses a few random keys on the piano. "So what's the password going to be?"

"*Sanok,*" I say without skipping a beat.

"What's... Sanok?" Her green eyes lock onto mine again, and the burst of lime coloring knocks the air out of my lungs.

"It's where Bella's *Babcia* is from. It's a city in Poland."

"Oh wow, you're Polish?"

"As a *pierogi.*"

She smiles, unsure what to say. It seems like she finally settles on: "Yes, sir, I need to borrow a loaner booster seat, if you don't mind."

Oh my God, the way she calls me *sir* is such a turn-on. It makes me feel dominant and dirty despite her meaning it in the most innocent way possible.

But then, I think about her leaking rust bucket outside and shudder at the thought of my precious Bella in its vibrating chassis as it *limps* back home.

"You know what, I'll get you keys to the Tesla. You can pick her up in that. There's a booster seat already in that one. It's her favorite of the vehicles anyway."

"The... *Tesla?*" She swallows hard as she follows me into the hallway, closing the door with reverence behind her, a simple act of respect that doesn't go unnoticed by me. "It's just, *wow*, a *Tesla.* Full disclosure, I have like the *bare-minimum* insurance."

No shit. I could have guessed that the moment your four-wheeled death trap sputtered into my life.

I sense her calm, cool demeanor waver for the first time all day.

"You'll be fine. Just don't get into an accident, and you're golden."

Her laugh is nervous. She looks like she's about to break out in hives. "Yeah, easy-peasy."

Kira

Waiting in line for Bella at the posh private elementary is a bizarre new experience for a dirty, little public school kid like me.

Not only have I never driven a vehicle younger than myself — and one worth more than my pathetic excuse for a "life savings," at that — but, until today, I've never even really *seen* a private school up close, only from drive-bys on main thoroughfares.

This place looks like a converted castle, gray brick with pristine, manicured grounds. Detailed, snow-capped designs line every window. Teachers and staff exit in suits and pencil skirts, swathed in pricey woolen long coats, clutching Prada bags worth more than several months of my rent. Brand new cars fill the U-shaped pick-up area, each glistening as if stored in a garage and regularly sprayed clean of road salts. There are sporty BMWs, Rivian trucks, sleek Mercedes, and classic Rolls Royce. One presumably "cool mom" even idles in a shimmering purple lifted Jeep behind me, one so clean it looks like it just sped off a showroom floor.

Kids spring from the building like rioting prison escapees, each eager to get the hell away from their concrete cell block. I was never a fan of school myself, so I can relate.

Mine was in a rough neighborhood. Highly diverse and perpetually cruel. It was nothing like this undulating sea of youthful Anglo-Saxons frolicking toward this line of parked trust-fund splurges.

No one ever picked me up in a Tesla, that's for damn sure.

Hell, I didn't even get to ride the *bus*. Instead, pennies were thrown at me from it daily while I waited for my uncle to come pick me up in his hideous El Camino, a car that was ancient and battered, even for *those* days.

But the joke was on them. Every week, those kids flung enough change at me that, when collected off the sidewalk, it was enough to exchange for a Snapple from the vending machine every Friday at lunch. Every time, I drank it with smug satisfaction from the lonesome corner where I sat with my plastic Pee-Wee Herman lunch box, eating some shitty sandwich that usually consisted of bologna, white bread, and mayo crammed into a re-used baggie.

I doubt any of these privileged kids will ever know how good they have it or how much harder and meaner the rest of the world can be outside of their wealthy little bubble.

My restless leg jiggles the Tesla as I scan the crowd, glancing frequently at the photo of Bella that Eric texted me.

Where are you, kid?

I'm anxious to return Miss Daisy to her ginormous real-life princess castle.

Suddenly, as the throng of children thins, a girl with shoulder-length golden locks finally shuffles out, gripping the straps of her backpack and nervously scanning the vehicles. Her eyes settle on the Tesla I'm in, and she stares pensively.

Bingo.

She takes a couple of nervous steps forward. She's slow and cautious, eyeing me like a potential kidnapper. I roll down the passenger window with the button and narrow my eyes above my sunglasses to get a better look.

It's her. I'm *reasonably* certain.

I cup a hand around my mouth and holler, "Bella?"

The girl's eyes blink wild. She tenses, and her head jerks toward her shoulder.

The twitch removes all doubts. *It's her.* I smile warmly.

She takes another hesitant step toward me, staying a safe distance away. She bends to look through the window at me and jerks her head subtly again.

"Hey," I utter in my most soothing voice, realizing how fucking bizarre this all is. I'm a stranger sent here to lure a kid in my car. My whole life, that has been ingrained as *kind of a big no-no.*

"You Bella?"

Instead of nodding, the young girl twitches again. She clutches her backpack straps as if she's rappelling down a cliff, and they're her only lifeline.

"I know this is weird, but your dad hired me. I'm here to pick you up."

"*Password*," she barks, trying to sound stern and brave but, instead, coming off like the frightened kid she is.

Oh fuck, what's the town again?

Sala... Sarno... oh, yeah...

"Sanok?" I ask it instead of saying it confidently. But then, I smile and add. "It's *Babcia's* hometown."

The word makes her shoulders sag with relief. A weight has just been visibly lifted off of her. She steps toward the car, and the woman in the grape Jeep lays on her horn.

Without thinking, I stick my hand out my window and flip her off. In the rearview, I see the woman's jaw drop, mouth agape.

Yeah, you just got flipped off, hun. You aren't impervious to shit like that up in your ivory tower, you rich...

Let it go, Kira. Don't embarrass the kid.

"C'mon, squirt, your chariot awaits." I motion with my head for her to hop in. She does, clicking herself into her booster seat like a pro.

The whole time, I stare daggers in the mirror at Purple Jeep Lady.

*****

Getting any conversation on this ride back is like pulling teeth. I watch her in the back, flinching and blinking in her seat. "Hey, little mouse, you comfy back there?"

Her twinkling eyes rise to meet mine in the mirror. "*Huh-huh*, why did you *huh*-call me *mouse?*"

"I like nicknames. They're more personal. I already know three women named Bella. But you're small and adorable and oh-so-quiet." I smile. "Like a *mouse*."

"My dad says, *huh-huh,* mice are *vermin.*" Her lids flutter, clearly nervous.

"Yeah, some people think that. Some think they're dirty or diseased, and all they do is damage shi… stuff."

Nice save, dumbass. Are you trying to get fired?

"...But mice are actually *incredibly* smart. I love 'em. I've had a bunch as pets over the years. I had one really sweet one that would sit in my shirt pocket for hours and just hang out with me."

That perks her up a little. "What was her name?"

"It was a *he*. His name was *Muchacho*." I say the word in a fast, playful way. Bella giggles like a character out of an animated kid's movie.

The sound is so hilarious that it instantly makes me laugh, too.

"*Huh-huh Mu-cha-cho*?"

"Yeah! *Muchacho*." I say it again fast, and yet again, she laughs. It's endearing as all hell. "He had a little plastic ball that I could put him in and twist the top, and he could run all around the house safely for hours. He loved that thing."

"Did he stink?"

"*Any* animal stinks if you don't clean up after it. But, no, I kept his bedding changed, and he didn't stink at all. He was my best little buddy."

"What happened to him?" She twitches again, milder this time. I notice she gets the whole sentence out without the verbal tic.

"Well, they only live for about two years. So, eventually, he died of old age. But I still miss him. I had another one after him. A girl named Missy. I taught her how to do some little tricks. She could roll little thread spools and stuff. She was really a smart little thing."

"*Huh-huh,* that's cool." She blinks super hard and then stares longingly out the window.

"What's wrong? You okay back there?" My eyes flit between the mirror and the gorgeous snow-dusted trees lining the curved road.

After a long silence, she says, "Dad won't let me have pets."

"No?"

"*Huh-huh-huh*, he says they're too much work." She sighs deeply, still staring out the window. She sounds like she's a stressed forty-year-old who just got done paying her surprisingly high bills for the month.

"They *can be* a lot of work, but they can be very rewarding, too."

"Mom said she was going to let me get a dog, but…" She trails off.

The light of the afternoon sun patters across her face, dappling her skin through bare trees. It illuminates her youthful eyes and makes her hair shimmer like spun gold.

"Well, don't leave me hanging with half a story!"

"She left." I can tell she's clenching her teeth. Her eyes have grown glossy with tears.

"Oh, I'm sorry," I say, suddenly feeling like I've swallowed a brick whole. The words hang in the air between us like a hot air balloon.

I want to know more because I'm nosy. I'm the type of girl who loves to hear about other people's drama. But this girl is not here for my entertainment. She's hurting, and it's obviously a sore subject.

I want to open my mouth and tell her that I can identify. I want to tell her I know what it's like not being able to spend time with either of my parents. I want to tell her that we are strong, kindred spirits, she and I. Both bonded in our own differing forms of tragedy and abandonment.

But I don't. Because I see a tear escape her eye and roll down her freckled little cheek. I close my lips tight and focus on the road.

Way to go, Kira. Five minutes into meeting this kid, and you've already made her fucking cry.

12

Eric

Bella wafts past my office door with a hardcore frown on her little face.

"Whoa!" I bark playfully from my desk, pretending to be stern. "Little-Miss, just *where* do you think you're goin'?"

She walks backward, coming back into view through the glass walls of my office. *"Beep-beep-beep-beep,"* she mutters, pretending to be a large piece of machinery backing up, and I can't help but laugh out loud. She saw it once and now does it all the time. It never fails to make me smile.

She drops her backpack to the floor like a breakaway parachute and races to me, embracing me in a tiny bear hug.

"Ow, ow, baby! Careful!" I hiss, motioning to the arm in the sling she's just crunched in her grip. "I love your cub hugs, but not so rough, okay? You want Daddy to *heal*, right?"

She nods, and those little brown eyes melt me. They're Tawny's through-and-through, that's for certain, but they're huge and full of life.

"Sorry," she says, pressing her twitching head into my dress shirt.

Kira comes into view and stands in the doorway, shimmying my key in her palm. Seeing her there suddenly feels like a shot of espresso buzzing through me. Her cool demeanor and clear eyes unknowingly demand my attention.

"How'd she do?" I ask.

"Oh, five-star passenger." Kira flashes a casual smile. "Highly recommend. Would Uber again."

Her sense of humor has taken me by surprise several times already today. I am not used to it. Rob and my clients are pretty much all business all the time.

And Tawny... I can't remember the last time she cracked a joke. Probably not since we got *engaged*.

"She said you won't let her have a pet, though. That was kind of a bummer."

I frown and pull Bella from my chest, studying her innocent eyes. "We talked about *why*, Bella. Animals are a *huge* responsibility. They're messy. They require a *lot* of attention."

Kira looks up at the custom light fixture hanging on a long chain above my desk from the vaulted ceiling like she's got something she wants to say but is biting her tongue. With a slight shake of her head in disagreement, her gaze tracks over to the stock ticker mounted on the wall facing me, trailing its ever-changing red abbreviations and unpredictable numbers across the four-foot-long LED screen.

"Something on your mind, Ms. Blumquist?" My tone is mildly hostile, but I can't help it. I feel defensive anytime someone wants to undermine me in front of my child.

"No, sir. I just think that a pet is a great way to *teach* a child responsibility while at the same time providing some companionship, that's all." She points to Bella. "From what I gather, Bella seems like she could use a friend."

Kira winks at Bella.

Part of me enjoys seeing someone other than myself, trying to protect my daughter's interest for once.

The other part of me fumes at the overstep. Her desire to tell me how to parent when she's been in my life all of seven hours is way out of line and not what I hired her for.

"Miss Kira was telling me about her mouse, Muchacho, in the car. She said he was a great pet and that she had another one named Missy that did tricks."

I try my best to speak calmly. "Bella, hun, if I were going to get you a *pet*, it wouldn't be a filthy rodent. They're *vermin*, honey. They carry Lyme Disease and Hantavirus."

"See?" She's looking at Kira now. "I told you."

Bella's eyes are sad, and it's breaking my heart to know that despite the wealth, I can't give her everything she wants in this world. But sometimes that's what a parent *has* to do.

I mean, suppose that thing *got out.* I can't have my home overrun with mice.

"Sure, wild ones, especially *here*, *do* carry Lyme disease. But I wasn't insinuating you should pluck some pest out of the gutter. I'm talking about fancy mice, the kind they sell in pet stores that have been bred to be handled."

"They're bred as *snake food.* Yes, I'm fully aware of the ones you are referring to, Ms. Blumquist."

I can feel Bella's neck and shoulder muscles tense beneath my arm. It will only get worse due to the tension in the room, so I remove it. I try to focus on Kira, but I can clearly see the repeated bob of my daughter's flaxen hair out of the corner of my eye.

"My apologies, Mr. Salko." Kira looks at the floor.

Even though I'm heated, the *Mr. Salko* from her lips gives me another *zing*.

I have an instantaneous flash to a fantasy world in which Bella scuttles off to her room so I can bend Kira over my desk, pull down those painted-on pants, and give her a lesson in manners.

But, alas, I'm launched back to reality as if from a slingshot as she speaks again.

"With all due respect, sir, she just said that her mom promised her a pet a while back, and she never got one. I didn't mean to tread on any toes with my comment."

I want to fold my arms across my chest, but my damned sling is in the way. Instead, I tap my obsidian-black glass desktop with the ends of my fingers and flex my jaw. "You were supposed to pick her up from school, not coordinate a plan to try to strong-arm me into caving on an animal."

She laughs like it's completely ridiculous and then reels herself in. "Strong-arm?" She clears her throat. "I just said it's a *bummer.*"

"Bella," I sigh, "do you have homework to do?"

Bella nods and blinks hard a few times. Her head twitches to the side.

"Okay, go get Jacques to make you a panini or something, and then go work on it in your room. I'll be in shortly to check on you after I finish work, okay?"

Bella grabs the top loop of her backpack and drags it noisily across the imported tile. Kira slides her fingers over my daughter's hair as she scurries out like she's known her forever.

Seemingly agitated, Kira crosses her arms, forcing her hefty breasts up into an accidental display of miraculous cleavage.

Where the hell does this girl get the nerve?

I don't need this shit. First day equals last day.

"I can help her with her homework if you'd like."

"No. Stay." I growl. I grab my golden Cartier ballpoint pen and rap it against the legal pad that contains my day's notes on electric vehicles, unemployment rates, gains, and losses. I can feel myself getting heated. "Come in. Shut the door behind you."

Her eyes widen. "Am I in trouble?" she asks, following the order.

I suddenly wonder what she's like in the bedroom.

Is she a good girl who obeys every command?

Or a bad girl, just as defiant out of clothes as she is in them?

"Have a seat." I point the pen to the chair opposite me, and she settles into it. "I don't think this is working out."

13

Kira

He looks at me like a stern parent and chews his lip. His words whirl in my head. This has got to be the fastest I've ever lost a job by a mile.

I perspire like I'm in the principal's office facing expulsion. I watch the reflection of the stock ticker in the glass behind him, a ghostly scroll of fire-engine-red numbers. None of it makes sense. It might as well be binary code.

KOS? Is that some sort of airport? NVAX? Sounds like an STD medicine? How the hell does anyone make sense of this stuff?

I guess if I knew, *I'd* be the one in the sprawling modern mansion adorned with various Italian imports and a French chef making me authentic *coq a vin* and not clinging to my shitty matchbox-of-a-room in Cassandra's apartment driving an SUV held together by zip-ties and luck.

"Look," he sighs and runs a hand through that impossibly lustrous hair of his. The look on his face reeks of internalized stress. His eyes say he's overwhelmed, though he barely let me *do* anything to help today.

"Let me stop you right there, if I may."

"You may *not*." He tries to stop me with the comment, but I continue anyway.

"Look, I get it. You don't want a rodent running around your house, and that's fine. That's *valid*. But please, Mr. Salko, I'm begging you not to fire me over one suggestion."

He's dead silent. I don't know him well enough to get any kind of read on him.

"I'm begging you, Mr. Salko. Please, just give me a *chance*, a full twenty-four hours, even." I tighten my grip on the arms of the chair and offer a sincere look, searching for mercy in his whiskey-colored eyes. I'm ready to grovel, hoping I don't have to stoop that low on my first, and possibly *last*, day. "I assure you, I'm one of the hardest workers you will ever meet."

He scoffs, staring with intensity. He doesn't blink.

"Look," I continue, "I never told her she *needed* a pet. Or even that she *should* have one. I told her that *I* had one. I had a lot of them, actually. I was a lonely kid. Having them through some," I pause, "*really* dark times enriched my life. Caring for something other than yourself gives you tools and strengths that school can't teach you. When something depends on you, you learn how to protect and nurture. No one knows that better than *you*, I'm sure. You're a single father who learned how to do those things with Bella. And doing so didn't ruin your life. You're actually *thriving*."

I must sound like a sap, but I mean it. In the few minutes I've seen them together, I can tell he is a doting, caring dad.

One like my *own* father was.

I would give *anything and everything* to have him back.

I lean forward and lock onto his captivating eyes. They're the color of dripping honey in the sun, and I find it hard to look away. "I've only known your daughter for an hour, but I *know* you love her. I can tell you want what's best for her. I promise you right now, I will never get in the way of that."

I wouldn't dare.

A girl needs her father.

I sit back and fold my arms. I look down and realize that it's making my cleavage heave above the hem of my camisole, and I subtly lower my arms, fairly certain he didn't notice.

Or if he did, he's the world's best poker player.

"I apologize if I stepped out of bounds. It's just that when she told me her mom promised her a pet before…" I don't know how to phrase the rest, so I move on. "My heart went out to her."

I feel a wave of emotion ebbing across my skin. "I have issues with my own mother, so it just hit a little close to home. I sincerely apologize."

The silence is painful. During it, I rehash an amalgamation of all of the shitty things my mother said and did during her swift descent. Nausea sets in as I remember that *those* memories were only the tip of the iceberg.

The way the mid-afternoon sun hits him, Eric looks like a sculpture that Michelangelo unearthed with a chisel from a hunk of unblemished marble. He sits perched with excellent posture in his ergonomic chair, still and quiet.

"Please, sir," I take a deep breath. I'm begging now. Ready to drop to the floor on my knees, hands pressed together like a Catholic, if needed. "I *need* this job. I promise that if you give me a shot, I could be the best assistant you've ever had."

"You're already the *only* assistant I've ever had."

"See? I've already proven I keep my promises," I jest. Then I erupt in a nervous laugh that I wish I could suck back into my mouth the very second it escapes my lips. I feel my cheeks blush with unadulterated embarrassment.

"Please, sir, allow me to help you," I motion to the doorway behind me, "*both.*"

After another stunningly long silence, in which we could both hear my always-hungry stomach rumble, he tries to fight his urge to laugh at the grumbling noise in my gut.

"You're still on probation."

"Understood." I nod, almost panting with relief. My face is solemn and serious, but inside, I'm grinning.

"I'm a bit high-strung right now. I'm bogged down and way behind. I'm still unsure what sort of tasks I should be delegating to you."

"Say the word. I'll help with anything. I'm here to lighten the workload and help you get back on track. Seriously, put me to work. I can handle it."

I mean it, too. This job pays more than my last two *combined*. Plus, it isn't *retail*.

"*Fine.*" He looks around the neat stacks of papers on his desk and thumbs through a pile. "There's a copier in the smaller office down the hall on the right. Make a copy of each of these new client applications. There are some empty files next to the filing cabinet and labels in the desk. Each one of the starting account balance sheets gets placed into a new, labeled hanging file. You know what? I can just get them mys—"

I jump to my feet, only now realizing that one of my shoestrings is undone. "Sir, please. I've got it." I hold my hand for the forms. "Am I labeling it with the account number or name?"

"Name. Last name first." He relinquishes them to me. "You'll see others in the cabinet the same way."

"Got it." I start toward the door. "Child's play. Easy-peasy. No problem. And after that?"

"After that… you can check in on Bella and see if she needs help with her homework. I'm going to handle some things that Rob just emailed me. I'll come to relieve you for the day in a bit."

"Great." I bow like a Japanese businessman and then blush at what an idiot I am.

Why did I do that?

He laughs as if it were a joke — *thank God!* — and I head toward the door. Near the glass wall, I kneel down and place the papers on the floor to tie my shoe. I hope he doesn't notice that the soles are ripped apart between the rubber and cheap fabric. If I can stay on the payroll long enough to collect an actual check, the first thing I'm buying is a new pair.

I look over my shoulder at him, and I'll be damned if that gorgeous, grumpy bastard isn't staring straight in the direction of my ass. His eyes dart to his computer screen immediately, trying his best to hide the fact that he was leering.

I stand and hold the papers up. "I'll get these filed for you, sir."

"Thanks." His eyes are now locked on his email, over-correcting for having been caught mid-stare.

I smile as I leave the room. I've had bosses leer before...

But never one that looked like him...

14

Eric

With another account set up, notes made, and a few tax documents filed online, I lean back in my chair and glance down at my sling. I hate this thing with a passion. It's *hideous* and puts an obnoxious barrier between me and my bespoke tailored suits with my signature high gorges and wide lapels, forcing me to dress like some dickhead about to drag a cooler of canned beer onto his dinky deep-V Crestliner while yelling something like, "*Get 'er done.*"

This sling also serves as a symbol of *weakness*. I have always been able to handle my business, until now. I built a successful firm from the ground up. The only person whose help I've ever needed was *Rob's* to expand the business and my *father*, God rest his soul, whose massive financial gamble on me ultimately gave us the leg-up we needed to build our thriving day-trading empire.

Though I wasn't lucky enough to be *born* with some trust fund, I at least had family who believed in me. And that belief paid off one-hundred fold.

But now, this mesh piece of navy-blue fabric with its cushioned nylon strap represents *helplessness*, needing other people to do just about everything but *wipe my ass* for me.

Ever since Tawny ditched us — a selfish act that I will NEVER be able to wrap my head around no matter *how* many times that whack-job tries to explain her reasoning—Bella's had to fend for herself in a lot of ways.

I can't be a father *and* a mother. I can only do my best, which lately feels like it is not quite enough.

I marvel at how all of those single mothers in the world somehow manage to rear well-adjusted children, ones who turn out to be an *asset* to society. Many of whom have more physically demanding jobs than mine. I can't fathom how the hell they *do it*.

I feel like before Tawny ran off to go "find herself," I had a lot more time with Bella. Or at least it was *quality*. *Fun* time. Time spent *spoiling* her and watching that goddamned live-action talking *duck* movie from the 80s that she'd watch on a loop if I let her.

I stand and roll my chair out, studying how erratic electric vehicle stock prices are behaving in the after-hours, after tonight's favorable earnings call. I finally sigh and put my computer to sleep for the evening.

I have a feeling that tomorrow will start a bit bearish at the bell, and I mentally prepare myself for a wild morning of trades to take full advantage of the extreme volatility.

I shut the office lights off and head into the hall. I turn and check my *ridiculous* shirt in the reflection of the glass. This isn't something I make a habit of doing, *preening* like this. *Peacocking* for the help. But knowing I'm about to see Kira...

No, keep it formal...

Ms. Blumquist...

It's as if I *care* what this woman thinks of how I look, which is, frankly, insane. She's an employee, here to help. Nothing more.

She could *never* be anything more.

Yeah, that's it...

Keep repeating it until eventually you believe *it.*

"*Huh-huh*, you're pretty good at that." Bella packs away some papers, eyeing me like a boss who can't believe her employee turned out to be *capable*. It's the same surprised look Rob had when I explained I'm proficient in setting up and working accounting spreadsheets, a skill acquired from an old job.

"*Huh-huh-huh,* now that's done," Bella winces hard in tandem with her vocal tic. I ignore it without another thought.

"I *huh-huh-huh* think I just have one more packet. Don't worry, it's a short one."

Please don't be math, please don't be math, please, for the love of GOD…

Don't… be… math.

That's the thought swimming around like a dense koi fish in my brain as Bella rifles through her tiny backpack in search of her workbook.

I watch the faces of the unicorns on it malform and ripple like they're underwater, mocking me, laughing their little unicorn laughs and saying…

Not just *math, Kira.*
Common core.

You might as well be trying to teach Bella Arabic…

"*Huh-huh-huh*-here it is." Bella produces a stapled stack of papers with a volcano on it and sliced-away sections of earth revealing different layers of core and rock.

Yessss. Science. I got this!

As I'm doing a happy dance in my mind, a quiet knock sounds. Our heads whirl in unison. I study the door for a moment. It's gigantic.

Dear God, how did I only just notice how gigantic that door is? Who even needs a freaking door that large? Yao Ming would say, damn, that's tall! You'd need a ladder just to hang a robe on the damned thing!

Eric's smiling face peeks in through the crack. "Ladies."

He smiles warmly, a completely different side to him than I've seen the rest of the day. He spent most of the morning grinding his molars and tensing his chiseled jaw into an angular work of art. With regular stress like that, it's astounding that the man has any hair left, much less the Pantene commercial swath of silky waves he has.

No, this must be *off-duty Eric*. There's a new depth to him that's only shown its head since Bella's appearance, a softness reserved for her. As a woman without a father figure, it honestly warms my heart to see it.

He glances at his watch and speaks softly, "Ladies, it is almost six o'clock."

"Oh!" I jolt as if being zapped by static. "I will take that as my cue and skedaddle and let you guys enjoy your evenin'."

"*Huh-huh-huh*, awwww." Bella's shoulders slump, and she plops the packet down on the squat activities desk at the footboard of her hot-pink bed, a bunk-style bed where each story is twice the width of mine. The top mattress is overtaken by an entire zoo of stuffed animals, all peering at us with black, plastic eyes.

Without thinking twice, I lovingly smooth Bella's dirty blonde hair and stand up.

I suddenly feel a little embarrassed over doing that as I remember that she is not related to me. It's something I used to constantly do to my little brother. Total habit.

No one seems to have noticed or taken offense, so I relax.

"*Huh-huh-huh-huh* you want to stay for dinner, Miss Kira?" Bella's wide, innocent eyes stare up at me chock-full of hope.

"Ohhhh, I don't think that would be a good idea, Bella. You and your dad should have some time together."

"Aw, we *always* have time together." She sighs and then twitches hard, jolting her shoulder to her ear. "You said we were going to build something."

I look at Eric and frown. "I told her that if we got her homework done in time, we'd break out that crazy thing of building blocks over there and build something together."

81

I point to an absurdly huge gumball machine full of plastic pieces in bold, primary colors. It's filled to the brim with every shape and size of block the company offers. With the price of those these days, that thing is holding a small fortune in molded bricks.

"Maybe tomorrow, sweetheart. It's time to wash up. Jacques made your favorite tonight."

Bellas's lips smack joyfully. "Mmmmmm, French onion soup!" She pretends she's slurping her own drool. I laugh a little too hard at her sudden burst of excitement.

"Not to rush you, but you'll want to get out and run for cover while you still can. It gives Bella the air-biscuits something fierce. She will be cutting the cheese all night. It's gonna smell like an onion bomb went off."

His look is so serious that I laugh until I snort. I cover my face, cheeks burning with embarrassment.

The smile on Eric's face is unreal. "Did you just... *snort?*"

"I can't... I...I..." I literally can't catch my breath. I'm still laughing. He's just been so stodgy all day, I just did not expect him to say that.

Neither of them is laughing, which makes it even funnier to me for some reason.

Then Bella finally exclaims, "It smells the same going *in* as it does when I blast off!"

I croak out another laugh, tears flooding my eyes.

I'm still mortified over the snort, but there's no way to laugh that hard *and* look sexy. Though, I am not entirely sure why that feels important.

He and I are from two different planets. Even our *doors* are different. The ones in my place are hanging off bent hinges, dinged, presumably from *Kyles* with fragile egos who rented the place before and used the drywall as an outlet for their bubbling toxic masculinity.

Eric's, however, are made of airplane-grade glass. Or when they're wooden, they're tall enough for a damned *giraffe* to walk through without ducking.

I've dumpster-dived for bread. He's got a chef that can prepare baguettes fresh daily.

Eric and I are from different planets.

"As tempting as it would be to stay and experience the detonation of Onion-heimer's atomic bomb, I think it's time for me to head home. I will see you tomorrow, Miss Bella."

Bella smiles at me. Eric puts a hand on her shoulder and manages a smile at me too, a gorgeous one that takes me off-guard, shooting a shiver of excitement through me.

"See you tomorrow, Miss Kira," Bella says in a small voice.

"Thanks for not firing me today." My smile is awkward; I can feel it.

Eric snickers a little, and his whiskey-colored eyes settle on mine, boring to my soul. His voice is warm and genuine. "See you tomorrow," he says.

Eric follows me to the back door, insisting on escorting me out like a gentleman. However, I have the sneaking suspicion that he just wants a few more moments to enjoy the view as he follows.

He plucks my jean jacket and scarf off of an Italian marble rack. "This is all you brought, correct? Seems like such a thin coat."

"I run hot," I say quickly.

It sounds like innuendo, though I mean it literally. I blush a little at the double entendre, knowing I'll draw more attention if I backpedal. I don't know what it is about this guy that makes me feel so thrown off, like I'm suddenly not cool or coordinated. I feel clumsy in every sense. I'm secretly hoping for smoother sailing tomorrow.

I slip into my jacket and step through the threshold into the cool, dusky air. He places an innocuous hand on the small of my back, just beneath the hem of my jacket. I am suddenly thoroughly aware of him, of his touch radiating through the fabric of my clothes into my skin.

"Oh, let me get your number before you go," he says once outside, removing his hand gently, "so I can text you the door codes in the morning."

I can see his breath as he stops beside me. Despite it being in the upper thirties, his smile makes me feel warm, the way drinking a hot toddy during a blizzard does.

84

Tensing from the sudden cold, he fishes his cell phone from the pocket of his starched slacks and fumbles the phone onto the concrete.

I gasp and cover my face instinctively. I can only imagine how much that thing costs.

He picks it up and tries to dust it off using his only free hand, rubbing it on his ridiculous Marlin-covered shirt.

"Is it okay?"

"Yeah, it's fine." His cheeks are pink. He looks a little flustered and embarrassed at the clumsy drop. He awkwardly tries to input my contact with one hand, bobbling the phone to and fro as he types with his large, masculine hands. "*Would you…?*" he whispers under his breath.

I pluck it softly out of his hand and smile as I take over, adding myself as a contact. I click the photo icon and use the front-facing camera to snap a picture of myself winking and shooting a finger gun. I save it as my contact icon.

He chuckles as he sees the new image of the dork on his payroll plastered on his phone.

I wink playfully and hand the phone back. "If I start getting unsolicited dick-pics from this number, I'm going to have to go to HR."

His cheeks grow redder, and he shakes his head. "You're looking at our HR department."

"Well, then."

I don't know what to say.

What the fuck?! Normally, I'd have some sort of witty comeback to that! What the hell was that? 'Well, then?!' Kira, you dum-dum!

85

"Worry not. This text thread will stay D-pic-free. That's a promise."

"Dang," I say as I open the door to my SUV, "that's the *second* bummer of the day."

What the fuuuuuuuck, Kira?!

Did you just actually say that? Please tell me that was just a thought.

Awww shit.

The way he is staring all wide-eyed like that... I most definitely said that out loud!

Fuck.

Play it off. Own that shit. And for God's sake, stop blushing!

"Drive safe, Ms. Blumquist. I'll see you tomorrow," he says, trying hard to contain his shock.

Inside the SUV, I huff air into my cupped palms, rub them together swiftly, shut my eyes tight, and whisper a quiet prayer into the frigid air. "Dear CR-V Gods, please let this old hunk'a junk start. Do *not* let me break down in this man's driveway. I have already made enough of an ass out of myself. *Amen.*"

I look out at the sky through my fogging window, freckled with stars in the indigo dusk from the lack of light pollution on his vast acreage. I turn the key. With a slow chug, the SUV struggles to turn over.

"C'mon. You got this."

I pet the sun-cracked dashboard with love and slide my fingertips across the CD player that hasn't worked since I bought it, one of many problems I inherited as its fifth owner.

I wipe some dust from the display panel, which reads 238,389 miles, many of which were mine. "*You can do it, love. I believe in you.*"

Finally, the engine roars to life.

I cheer, joyously slapping the steering wheel. "Yeah, baby! See? I knew you could do it."

It isn't until I've stopped cheering that I realize Jacques has also been watching from the partially-enclosed back patio the entire time. A cigarette hangs between his smiling lips. Smoke curls around his youthful face, and he laughs so hard that his shoulders are bobbing.

I offer an embarrassed wave to both men as I pull out of the spot to see a large oil stain where my vehicle had just been, marking my presence like a hideous, black graffiti signature that shouts *Kira wuz here.*

Dammit! In all my excitement this morning, I forgot to lay the cardboard down.

I brake, staring at it momentarily with a heavy sigh, and roll my window down.

"I'm so sorry! I forgot to put the cardboard down!"

Eric shakes his head and looks down at the stain. "I'll have it taken care of." He tries hard to hide his disapproval, but some leaks into his expression.

"I'll pay for the cleaning," I say, hoping to God that he doesn't hold me to that. I don't know if I have enough in my account.

He waves, nods at Jacques, who is snuffing out his butt in a crystal ashtray, and heads inside. I slink down in my seat, mortified, and drive away for the night.

"Cass, I wish you could've seen this place. I'm telling you, this friggin' *manor* was huge." My eyes bulge as I say the words in the doorway. I watch Cassandra bleach her hair over our sink, one installed in the seventies, marred by a dark web of cracks in the porcelain.

"Why don't you let Remmy do that?"

"Remmy's *expensive*."

"He doesn't charge *me*."

"Because he knows you don't have any *money*." She flashes a motherly look at me. "I don't *mooch*."

Cassandra and I *have* always been *fiercely* independent, a strong bonding force for us through the last ten years.

"Finish your story."

I start up again as if I had never derailed from the topic, "I don't know what I was expecting. A mansion, *sure*. He's a *gazillionaire*. But this was a house you could seriously get lost in. It reminded me of the Overlook Hotel, only if it were decorated by some award-winning decorator like… I dunno, *Belmonpan*."

"First," she holds up a gloved finger covered in white gel, "*Belmonpan* is a freaking *cartoon* character from a Seth MacFarlane show. He's not a *real* designer. Second, I just gotta know how that works in your mind. So, what? Does it go million, billion, trillion, *gazillion*? What did they *teach you* in public *school*, Kira?"

"Hey, not everyone was smart enough to go to a sticker school like you, okay?"

"*Magnet.*"

"What?"

"They're called *magnet* schools, you *yutz*. And the fact that you *don't know that* is part of the reason *why* you never got to *go* to a magnet school."

I blow a fart sound with my mouth.

Cass laughs. She always does when I act like a bored child. Deep down, I'm a kid at heart.

Shit, maybe that's why I bonded with Bella today more than her damn dad. And it would explain the craving I have to get back there and build something with those damn blocks…

I really wanted to do that today!

"Is he hot?"

"Who? *Eric?*"

"Oh, wow. You're on a first-name basis, huh? You don't have to call him Mr. Something?"

"I don't *have* to call anyone Mr. Anything. We were given first names for a reason."

"Yeah, but it's *respectful,* Kira," she nags, "Society is *full* of idiotic niceties that you must adhere to if you want to get anywhere in life."

90

"Why do I need to *get somewhere?* Why is everyone always trying to just *get somewhere* in life? Why can't I just be here? Like, right here? Enjoying *right now*. Living in *this* moment."

Cassandra rolls her eyes and stares up at the ceiling. "God, grant me *strength* with this one." She spreads some more frothy cream onto her brunette roots. "You didn't answer my question. You just did that thing you do where you ask another question instead of giving an answer."

"What question? Is he *hot? That's* what you want to know?"

"You're doing it again. See? That was *three* questions! Oh God, it's getting *worse.*"

"Okay, fine," I bob my head, avoiding eye contact, "Yes, he's... *good-looking.* He's young. Younger than I thought a billionaire could even be."

"I thought you said he was a *gazillionaire.* Now he's downgraded to simple *billionaire*?"

"Stocks are a fickle bitch, Cass. You can get downgraded to lowly billionaire like *that.*" I snap my fingers.

She ignores my silliness and presses on. "How old is he?"

"I don't know. Early... thirties, maybe?"

"Are you asking me or telling me?"

"Both.... *question mark?*" I shrug.

Cassandra laughs, bright and cheery.

I'm going to miss living with her. This sucks.

"What's he look like?"

The second she asks, I get lost in my memories of him. *Those golden flecks in his irises. The dreamy spice combination of his masculine cologne. Dark waves of thick hair I just want to run my fingers through like a human comb again and again. The tight, gym-toned ass you could eat lunch off of. And muscular arms made for cuddling during a freezing Nor'easter.*

"He's… *attractive*," I finally mutter with a shrug, downplaying the importance of the role he'll play in my mental fantasies tonight when my bedroom light flicks off and my vibrator revs into high gear.

"How's the kid?"

"Bella? She's fuckin' *awesome*."

"With a mouth like *that*, wow, what a role model you must be." She pulls a towel off the shower rod and drapes it over her shoulders.

"You know I'm not really a kid person, but she actually seems really sweet. I was helping her with her homework toward the end of the day."

"Sweet Christ, that child is *doomed*."

"Thanks for the vote of confidence." A huge grin spreads across my face. "I got to drive a Tesla."

"*What?!*" Cassandra's voice couldn't be any higher. "Seriously?"

"Yeah, he had me pick Bella up from school in it."

"Yeah, makes sense. No one would want to be seen in public with your rattletrap."

"*Rattletrap?*"

"Yeah, you know. Your shitbox."

"Do you even know how *jealous* you sound right now?" I joke. "You're just sad your vehicle doesn't have a fold-out table in the trunk like mine."

"And how many times have you actually *used* that table?"

I sigh, "*Anywayyyyy...*"

She chuckles. "Well, sounds like it was a solid first day." Cassandra checks her shimmery pink kimono to ensure none of the bleach has reached it.

I grimace comically. "I *did* almost get fired, I think."

"*Kiraaaaaa!*" Cassandra glares at me. "I'm sure I don't even *want* to know what you did. You are *such* a self-sabotager. You can't take anything seriously, can you?"

"There's more than enough to take seriously in life already, Cass. Not everything's gotta be life or death. Things aren't as extreme as you like to make them sound."

She's getting pissed now. "Go in there tomorrow and act right. Dress cute. *Schmooze* a little if you need to. Bring him some coffee or something."

What the...?

"Cass, he's got more money than *God*. I have, like, less than two grand to my name, and that's if I liquidate, like, *everything*. Why the hell would I buy him a damn thing?"

Cassandra points her french-tipped finger at me. "You have a month to get out of here. I'm *not* playing. After Hawaii, we're going to start trying for a kid."

"But... you've already *got* one." I pull the second towel off the rack and smack her in the butt with it.

Cassandra yelps. I rear back, twisting the towel to smack harder.

"Ow! Dammit, Kira! Put it... *put it down!*"

She lunges. I dodge.

"I said put the towel down. *Now!*" She stomps her bare foot on the ugly tile floor. I double over with laughter and fling it in her direction. She catches it midair with a half-smile.

"You're gonna be *great* at this whole mom thing," I mutter with a smile.

"Yeah, well, raising a twenty-six-year-old for the last few years has really whipped me into shape. What could a two-year-old do to me that *you* haven't already?"

"I mean, I didn't suck on your *boob*."

"Get out." Cassandra laughs, kicking the bathroom door closed.

I stand on the other side, giggling so hard I can barely form words.

"I... don't think... I've done that... since community college."

"Kira, you're disgusting," Cassandra's muffled giggles subside, and she barks an order through the door. "Go to bed."

17

Eric

I starfish in my California king, covered in the Egyptian cotton high-thread-count sheets Tawny bought with the black Amex a month before she skipped town.

I stir beneath the covers, agitated by images of Kira's mane of flaxen hair and jungle-green eyes glimmering with that hint of mischief. I recall the curves of her body, a form built for speed.

She's a Ferrari. A Goddess with a body worthy of worship and adoration and skin as smooth as fresh milk.

My lids feel heavy, and the side of my face settles into the pillow, but sleep feels miles away. A current of excitement buzzes through my nerve endings, and I feel like I downed a pot of strong coffee.

I pluck my phone off the magnetic charger and navigate through the menus until I'm staring at the contact picture she saved, studying the delicate curves of her face, ensnared by the lure of her lips. I look at the finger guns and snicker quietly. For a moment, I can't pry my eyes from those delicate hands, imagining them on me…

Don't be a creep. She's the help.

Jesus, Eric, don't go dipping your fucking Montblanc into company ink.

My cock stiffens at the thought of dipping anything in her.

I blame my ex-wife for my idiotic, teenage-fucking-horniness, this *maddening frustration.* It's been a long time since I've gotten any. Tawny skipped town over a year ago, and the divorce was finalized only a few months back. It had been at least six months before her *grand escape* that she ever shared so much as a *scone* with me, much less the depths of her body.

I slide my hand beneath the cool sheets, inside my boxer briefs, until my hand is gripped around my engorged cock, standing at attention at the thoughts of my new assistant.

Closing my eyes, I allow myself a moment to fantasize. It's summer, suffocating and muggy outside. I picture her curvaceous thighs, perfect ass, and heaving tits bursting out of a tight, red bikini as she glides out of my Olympic-sized swimming pool, soaked and fierce like some *Ridgemont High* babe.

I stroke myself to the thought of her body, sopping-wet, and those eyes staring at me, unblinking, tearing me apart with a look.

She walks up to me and presses her slick, hot skin against mine, and I pounce like a lion.

Starving, uncaged...

And it's feeding time.

If I close my eyes tight enough, I can almost feel her breath against my lips as I scoop her up forcefully in my arms, finally untethered from its mesh sling. She feels small there, in my imaginary grasp. I picture myself laying her down in the netted hammock strung to the Montmorency cherry trees, hovering above lush grass. She swings slightly, calves swaying over the ground like a dripping wind chime.

Before she can get situated, my lips are on her body, kissing her collarbones, running my lips along the hollow of her throat, lapping errant beads of chlorine from her skin with a pointed tongue. I can almost smell the faint scent of the cheap, flowery essential oils she wears, which mix mystifyingly well with her pheromones.

I travel south, taking one of her hardened nipples gently between my teeth through the spandex fabric of her triangular top, feeling the soft areola beneath respond to my touch.

She moans at the sensation, the *tease...*

The promise of *what's to come.*

I kneel reverently before the drenched deity, *my* deity. My hands travel up the smooth skin of her calf, her thigh until one is poised at the fabric-covered door to the paradise between her thighs.

I use my thumb to caress her tenderly through the fabric. With my other hand, I press her back into the netting, watching the ropes mark temporary diamonds across her pliable flesh.

I stroke myself harder, *faster*, as I imagine pulling the fabric of her string bikini bottom aside, rising higher on my knees, and sliding my middle finger inside the hot depths of her pussy. She gasps, and her head lays back until her damp hair brushes the grass. I burrow beneath the fabric until my lips and tongue join my finger in her slick nirvana.

I feel myself arrive at a point of no return, stroking my cock into a climax so hard that I want to growl out like an angry dog into the quiet night air. Instead, I grind my molars, feeling a pulse of cum paint the inside of my blue underwear white.

I sink down into my pillow with my hand still wrapped around my sensitive, spasming cock. Sweat beads across my face. My heart thumps wild in my chest, and my pulse pounds. A sense of relief floods every inch of my body.

My dick pulses angrily, thick in my loosened fist, like an animal in its death throes. I inhale deeply, unaware I'd been holding my breath for some time. Though clarity, sanity, and logic all make their slow, casual reappearance, I can't seem to shake the image of pleasuring Kira from my mind. I still feel that buzzing excitement like an infusion of caffeine.

I thought that jerking off would help me get to sleep, but with the thoughts swimming in my mind, I'm in for a long night — and at *least* one more round once I recover.

At this moment, I fantasize about firing her. I think about how much easier it would be if I just picked up my phone and sent a text telling her where to pick up the paycheck for her one and only day.

I have no desire to *abuse* my position as her employer. I have no desire to pursue a physical relationship with her... or anyone for that matter. No matter *how* fucking *sexy* she might be. And with the disparity in our social statuses, I certainly wouldn't be pursuing anything *beyond* physical, either.

Yes. There's no point in dragging this out. Late or not…

I reach awkwardly across the bed and pick up my phone again, wincing at the pain it inflicts on my healing shoulder. With my thumb swishing across the glass screen, I pull up her contact again.

I've got to end this before I start thinking with an unclear head again.

I don't really need help. This was Rob's idea, not mine.

I stare at the selfie in her contact picture, and the ghost of a smile creeps across my lips.

My heart is still racing from my orgasm, and now I'm staring right into those green eyes and that pearl-white smile, poised to text. Poised to tell her to go away for good…

But my eyes stay glued on her image for far too long.

My brain starts scheming to figure out the best way to prop up the photo on the phone against a nearby pillow so that I can free my only available hand for another round.

Every fiber of my being tells me *this isn't meant to be.*

But for *tonight…*

Fuck it.

A man can *dream*, can't he?

18

"Morning, Mr. Salko," I chirp as I slide in through the propped-open door to his office with a large cup of Dunkin' in each hand like some bubbly server.

"Please, call me Eric. Mr. Salko just sounds strange."

"Sorry, I was just trying to be professional, sir."

"You don't have to call me sir, either." He shakes his head. "Social niceties get exhausting."

I *freeze* as he says it. That's damn near verbatim what I said to Cassandra last night.

Great minds think alike.

He looks tired, almost drowsy, as his eyes drift from his computer screen to me.

"What's that?" He points to the cups.

"It's cool. It's called *coffee*. You see, there are trees called *coffee trees,* and they put out cherries. Now, *inside* that fruit is what's called a coffee *bean*. People collect a whole bunch of those, dry 'em out, and then grind 'em up and mix 'em with boiling water to create this potent go-go juice that simulates crack but is *alarmingly* legal."

He just stares up at me, no trace of a smile in his chiseled features. He sighs, presumably at my smart-ass nature. "I'm *aware*."

"I imported this batch *alllll* the way from a place called *Dunkin'*. Everyone up here in New England seems to have heard of it. You literally can't throw a rock without hitting one out there."

Again, he just stares at me.

I plop down in the chair across from him with a smile. "I thought I'd give it a go and double-fist these for a boost."

Oh God, what the hell did I just say? Double-fisting? Jesus, close your yap, Kira.

"Oh, so they're both for you?" He looks up at me from across his desk with an almost pathetic expression of desire for one of them. From the redness in his eyes, I can tell he needs it more than air right now.

So just for shits and giggles, I decide to tease him a little longer.

"Yeah, one's a hot coffee, one is an iced coffee. That way, if I start to burn my tongue, I can put ice on it, and if I start to get brain freeze, I can warm my mouth up in a jiff."

He snickers at my idiotic attempt to amuse him.

I don't know what it is about him laughing, but I have the sudden urge to make him do it again. I've always been a clown, but something about his professional exterior makes me feel like it's my *mission* to make him laugh again.

…As often as possible.

Hell, maybe if I can keep his spirits high, he'll keep me on the payroll for more than a couple of weeks.

I smile and finally offer up the hot coffee. He takes it, hoisting it into the air with a little life. "*Thank you.*"

"It's an Americana or some shit." I cover my mouth. "Sorry! Or some *crap*."

He laughs again, a little harder this time. Then, he takes a sip of the drink and moans with gratitude.

"I promise I will tone down the language. *Especially* around Bella."

"I'd appreciate it. I don't need her to expand her vocabulary with colorful, new phrases. Her teachers already aren't massive fans of Tawny and me because of some missed parent-teacher conferences." He stares down at the coffee and rubs a finger around the outer ring of the lid. "Wow. I haven't had one of these in a long time."

"I never know what to get, so if there's a kind you like more, let me know, and I'll buy that for you tomorrow."

"You don't have to do that. We have a five-thousand-dollar cappuccino machine in the kitchen."

"Five-thousa — " I close my slack jaw. "Then why don't you already have a coffee on your desk? *Hmm?* Mister-I'm-too-good-for-a-five-dollar-Americana?"

He rummages through a desk drawer and pulls out a zippered pouch.

"I don't have one in front of me because I gave Jacques the morning off to go to chemo with his mom, and I don't know how to work the machine."

He awkwardly struggles to open the rectangular bag, gripping it oddly due to the sling.

"Hold on a sec. Allow me." I extend my hand for it, and he reluctantly hands over the pouch. "You hired me to help, after all."

I hand back the unzipped pouch, noticing the huge wad of cash neatly piled inside. Eric rifles through the bills and tosses a ten-spot onto the desk.

"What's this?" I feel my head cock sideways like a dog who just heard a curious noise.

"That is called *currency*. The US government prints a whole bunch of those out and assigns them a somewhat arbitrary value that, as a *society*, we all then agree to abide by. You can use one of these to exchange for an almost unlimited number of goods and services."

Jesus, he's just as much of a smart-ass as I am.

"Ha-ha." I roll my eyes.

After a pause, he says, "It's called *reimbursement*."

The moment he says it, my cheeks redden, and my body hardens like hickory. I'm a proud person, stubborn as the day is long. This was supposed to be a gesture of *kindness*, a small offering toward building something bigger.

...A small step toward proving my worth and value around here. I don't have a lot to give.

And, yeah, sure, that five dollars I spent on his drink was all I had budgeted for dinner tonight, which *would* most likely consist of dollar-menu nuggets and a small fry. And, yeah, sure, he's a fucking *billionaire*, but taking that money defeats the entire *purpose.*

As much as it pains me to turn it down, I leave the cash where it is and press back into the luxurious chair I'm parked in. It swallows me up like a loving embrace from a favorite aunt.

"Okay, so let's get down to brass tacks. What's on the agenda today? Because, as fun as it is to watch you try to juggle a million tasks and do everything yourself, it would be *stellar* to get some marching orders upfront so I can actually do my job and, you know... *help you.*"

I swirl the contents of my iced coffee around in my plastic cup. I love the sound it makes.

"You seriously actually got an *iced* coffee in February? It's thirty-one degrees outside right now."

"*And?*" I mutter and then suck a bunch playfully through the orange straw, wincing at the icy goodness as it makes the back of my throat feel cold. "I told you. I run hot."

"You're a psychopath," he snickers wildly in disbelief and leans back in his chair. His light brown eyes glance between the stock ticker above my head, the ten dollar bill between us, and me.

"Fine," he finally says. "Let me set you up in the other office. You can help with some quarterlies coming up."

"*That's* the spirit." I grin.

"Get in the car, Mouse!" The Tesla's windows are fully rolled down. My feet are in the driver's seat, and I'm perched precariously with my butt on the door so that my head is over the giant sunroof. I could have waited for her from inside the car, but… hell, where's the fun in that?

Bella comes racing up, a big smile plastered on her face. Behind me, the purple Jeep sings me the song of its people with a whiny honk, complaining to whoever will listen almost as much as I imagine its owner does.

Once again, I flip Purple Jeep Lady off, this time with a broad pageant smile.

"You know, you can go around me, right? That thing's made for driving on all sorts of terrain. Sand, mountains… that little curb is a cakewalk," I holler.

"Tell your kid to hurry the hell up!" The bitchy woman with the asymmetrical bob seems furious, and I have the sudden urge to call her *Karen*. Although, I *won't* because I've actually known three *very* nice Karens, and this lady is a dick through and through.

"No, you take your sweet 'ol time, Bella. Don't listen to that wicked, old witch. She's just mad that her stylist fell asleep during her last haircut."

Bella snickers as she reaches the car.

Purple Jeep Lady is fuming.

Once Bella's clasped into her seat in the back, I slither in through the window and waggle my fingers at the chick behind me with a dramatic flourish. She lays on her horn again, and I decide it might be fun to sit for another ten or twenty seconds before taking off.

Bella's eyes stay locked over her shoulder on the Jeep.

"You fastened in, squirt?"

Bella nods, and I adjust my aviators.

"Good. I'm taking you on a little detour before we go home. Is that okay?"

She's hesitant. "Will Dad be mad?"

"No way. You let *me* handle that. Catch, Mouse." I lob a plastic package of frozen peas over my shoulder, and she grabs it midair.

She laughs, "Ew! What is this for?"

"You'll see."

Finally, after sufficient honking has fed my soul, I pump the gas pedal. I can see the rage burning in Purple Jeep Lady's eyes as we peel out of the school's U-shaped drive and away from this manicured, academic youth prison.

"Let's blow this Popsicle stand," I say as we glide down the gorgeous, winding Greenwich roads lined with blossoming displays of brilliant yellow forsythias that signal the nearby start of spring.

The air is brisk, and I'm surprised the small waterfall at Babcock Preserve is still liquid. It feels like everything around us should be frozen solid. Two swans, a smattering of gray geese, and one lone white duck glide across the placid water below the short ridge beneath Bella and I. Her breath fogs the air around us in dragon-like gusts, tiny nose red from the cold.

"*Huh-huh-huh-huh*, coooooooool!" A huge smile is broadcast across her face.

"*Des pois verts, s'il vous plaît.*" I hold my hand out.

She looks at me like I am from another planet. "*Huh-huh-huh*, what did you just say?"

"I said: *hand me the green peas, please.*"

"Is that French?" She hands me the bag of thawing veggies.

"Yep! Do you know any French?"

She shakes her head solemnly and then suddenly perks up, "But I do know some *Polksi*!"

"Whaaaaat? You do?" I rip open the bag, and it tears more easily than expected. Some of the peas explode into the air. "Oh, *shoot!*"

The birds flock to us, skating atop the glassy plane, excitedly flapping their wings as they dive and gobble the errant, green vegetables.

"I thought you were supposed to, *huh-huh,* feed birds *bread*," Bella says, eyebrows cocked at the waterfowl below.

"Bread is actually bad for birds. They can't really digest the gluten in it. Doesn't give them any nutrition. It just mucks up the water. They say stuff like *this* gives them nutrition, and it's easier for them to eat without dissolving, so it doesn't make the water all messy."

I hand the bag off to her, and she stares at me with great hesitation before finally taking it. "Why are we here?"

"Well, since your dad *understandably* doesn't want a pet in the house, maybe you can have one in the wild. This place is on our way back to your house, so we can swing by and visit them whenever you want."

Her eyes are full of gratitude when she finally looks up at me.

"I know it's not the same thing, but it's the best I can do." I smile down at her. "So feed 'em, talk to 'em, get to know 'em for a little bit, and then pick out a name for one. That way, we can come back occasionally and, if they're here, feed 'em again. Sound good?"

She nods and sniffles. I can't tell if she's on the verge of tears or if her nose is just running from the cold. Either way, a look of pure joy is etched into her little features.

"I'm gonna give you a few minutes with your new friends and send your dad a text so he doesn't worry, okay?"

"Okay." She's already taking off her glove to handle the peas better. Before her sits a captive audience of mature birds, clamoring over

110

each other through the cold mist of the tiny waterfall on our right.

I step back and pull out my phone. I snap a few photos of Bella giggling and the spray of frozen peas midair as it leaves her mitten-less palm. I follow it up with a wide shot of the scenic preserve around us. It feels like we are tucked deep into the woods, even though we are just a quick walk back to Eric's car.

I compile them into a text message.

> **KIRA: Made a pit stop on the way back. Bella is having a great time. Back in 15.**

I send Eric the pictures and stuff my phone in my pocket, rejoining Bella at the top of the ridge.

"So, that big white one right there, do you know what that is?"

"A swan?"

Dang, she's good. Then again, I have no friggin' *clue* what a nine-year-old knows or doesn't know. She's the first kid I've ever spent more than five minutes around since my brother.

"*Nailed it.*" I reach into the bag and throw a couple of peas at the geese. "Okay. Know what those gray guys are?"

"No. *Huh-huh,* but they sure are hungry fellas." She twitches a little as she tosses some peas at them, too. They gobble the green pellets up like little feathery piglets.

"Those are *geese*." I point to the small white bird, one who has been shoved off to the side numerous times because of his smaller body mass. "Know what that one is?"

"Yeah! A duck! He's my favorite." She beams. "Can I pick him as my pet?"

"Girl, you can pick whoever you want!" I look at the gleaming-white duck and nod. *I dig an underdog, too.* "What are you gonna name him?"

"Howard."

I laugh. *That's clever.* I was shocked that she had a vintage collectible of him on her dresser. He was way before her time.

"It's from one of my favorite movies."

"Oh, I know the one. It was one of my favorites, too, growing up. My parents used to hate that movie because I played it so much."

She looks up and locks eyes with me like a tiny, kindred spirit.

…Like she finally has a *friend*.

"Well, introduce yourself to Howard. See if he likes his name."

As she talks to the duck, I whip out my phone again and notice a text reply from Eric.

ERIC: I thought we agreed to keep this chat duck-pic free. ;)

I fight the urge to grin at his winking emoji.

112

KIRA: I never said I wouldn't send YOU hot shots of MY duck.

Eric sends back a laughing emoji.

I take a short video of Bella talking to Howard, the duck, and tossing him peas, giggling gleefully every time the greedy bird devours them.

He quacks, and she gasps, whipping her head at the camera. "He likes his name!"

I'm chuckling so hard at the genuinely surprised look on her face that I can't hold the camera steady.

I send Eric the video.

20

Eric

Receiving the pictures and videos of Bella with the ducks feels like my chest is filled with apple cider, all warm and sweet. Bella deserves the world, and it's broken my heart to see how few friends she's been able to make at her school. The obnoxious parent-teacher conferences are always the same. The staff always tells me that because of her Tourette's, she isn't well-liked. Sometimes, she's even picked on for it.

I can only imagine how much worse it would be at a public school like the one I went to.

I watch the video again, and I hear something I didn't on the first watch. Bella yells, "*Kaczka*," which means *duck* in Polish. It's hard to hide my smile when she says it.

While she did a fine enough job with the filing and spreadsheets this morning, the fact that Kira has taken this sort of initiative with Bella makes me think she might be worth keeping on the payroll for a few weeks. With Tawny out of the picture, it *would* be nice to have a female influence in Bella's life, especially one with experience with her disorder.

I hear the patter of small, energized feet racing down the Italian marble. I set my phone down just as Bella races into sight through the glass. She runs in, flings her backpack onto the chair opposite my desk in a wild flurry, and holds her hands out like she's being electrocuted, face contorted like a crazed madwoman.

Oh shit, is this a new tic? A new spasm she's developed?

Then, she yells, "Dad! That was awesome! I got to feed some birds! My duck, Howard—"

I hear her say the name, and I can't help but laugh. Of *course,* she would name him that. I realize now that she wasn't having a seizure… she was just *extremely* excited.

"He came up and ate peas right out of my hand!" She giggles. "It tickled!"

Kira rounds the corner with a smile and a wave. "*Cześć.*"

I don't believe my ears when she says it. Her pronunciation isn't great, but the Polish greeting takes me off-guard.

"*Cześć,*" I reply, stunned.

"Bella's been teaching me some Polish."

"Oh, she *is*, is she?"

"Yeah, she's surprisingly bilingual. So I figured, heck, let's go for *tri-lingual.* She's been picking up French like a sponge." She looks at Bella. "Tell him what you learned today."

"*Mon canard est mignon,*" Bella utters without a trace of *huh-huh.*

I'm *floored.*

115

...Not just at her surprising adeptness at a third language, but at the fact that her vocal tic seems to be at bay due to the thrill of it all.

I love seeing her like this, so full of life and zest.

I smile up at Kira. I can't help it. "What does that mean?"

"Tell your dad what it means."

"It means *my duck is cute.*"

"Wow, I don't know what to say." *I really don't.* I'm shocked and pleased on so many levels. If I knew Bella could be having this much fun, I'd have hired someone like Kira the *instant* that Tawny bolted.

Bella pulls off her hat, and Kira smooths down her fly-aways, all askew due to the static. Then she says, "Hey Bella, what do you say you hug your dad, and then we go work on your homework together so you and him can have time for a movie or somethin' tonight?"

"Okay!" She starts toward me and smiles. "I know *just* what I want to watch."

"Please, dear God, no. I can't take that movie again, Bella. We can rent something new."

Her shoulders sag. "Fine." She wraps her arms around me like a limp rag doll, and I squeeze her hard.

"I promise, we can stream something just as cool. I have a few ideas."

That perks her up. She runs back toward Kira.

"Hey, see if Jacques still has any croissants left. We need some brain food if we are going to tackle that geography thing you told me about in the car."

"Okay, Miss Kira!"

And she's off.

Kira's eyes bulge as she gently places the Tesla key on the desk before me. She scrunches her face anxiously. "Are you mad?"

"*Mad?*"

"That I took her to the preserve instead of bringing her straight home?"

I sit back in my chair. I want to laugh at how ridiculous it is. But I wouldn't dare. I want her to remember that I run the show around here.

"If you hadn't shown for a while, I'd have been mad. But the fact that you texted right away… I'm glad you took her."

"Did you see the video I sent? She was having a *blast!*"

"Yeah, I haven't seen her that excited in a long time. And did you hear her?" I rise in my chair and look around suspiciously as if I can somehow see through the walls with X-ray vision. I whisper, "Her little *huh-huh* thing… she didn't do it *once!*"

"I honestly haven't been paying attention to that, so I'll have to take your word on it." Kira snickers. "I'd temper your expectations, though. It's not like she's suddenly going to be cured of it because she fed some ducks or anything."

"I *know,* but just hearing her be so excited that she didn't do it…" I bobble my head and grimace. *I can't fucking believe what I'm about to do.* "Tomorrow…"

Just shut your mouth. It isn't too late, Eric…

"Go on. I'm curious now."

I wince. "Tomorrow, I need you to run an errand."

"Okay," she makes circles with her flattened hand, "what *kind* of errand?"

Don't do it, Eric.

"I want you to get her a pet."

Kira gasps the moment the words leave my mouth.

"Wait, what? Seriously?! Because I wasn't doing this so that you'd—"

"No, I know." I swipe my hands across the cushioned mat by my keyboard. "I thought about it a lot last night, and she doesn't really have any friends. She's a good kid. And, although I can't *stand* them, I think after seeing her with the birds…" I struggle to get the words out. "I just think, *mayyyybe* you might have a point."

Kira doesn't say anything for a moment. It's her turn to be flabbergasted. Finally, she says, "I think she will love it. And I think you'll be amazed at how well she does with it. What kind of animal are you thinking? Like a puppy or something?"

"No, I'd like it to be something that can be contained in her room. Preferably something that won't keep her up at night. Something small that doesn't like live a million years like a tortoise or a parrot or something."

"You got it. I'll try to keep her away from the rodents. I know how you feel about those."

"No, it's fine. Get her what she wants. Get her what makes her happy. I'll give you some money tomorrow so you can go out and get her the cage, accessories, and stuff. Whatever it needs. And then, the *animal*, obviously."

"With all due respect," she leans forward, "I would like permission to take her with me to pick out the animal. It's something she will, with any luck, have for at least a year or two. It's a commitment. I'd rather *her* pick out the one she wants if that's okay. I know that, for me, that was a really exciting part of it. I wouldn't want to rob her of that."

I nod. "Sure. Just don't say anything about it to her until then, alright? I want it to be a surprise."

"Copy that," she says and rises from the chair. She says something almost under her breath like she's a little choked up. "You're a good dad."

Without another word, she's gone, and it's just me, a streaming set of red numbers, and the warmth I feel from the genuine compliment.

21

Kira

Bird squawks fill the air, and I am hit with that too-familiar scent of every pet store I've ever been to. It's a pungent mix of cedar, pine, aquarium water, fur, and feathers that hits you like a playful smack in the face the second you walk in. That said, it's one of my favorite places in the world. Animals don't disappoint like humans do. The hardest part about being here today is avoiding the impulse to buy something living for myself.

You're here for her. You don't need another mouth to feed. You can barely afford to put food in your own.

"Alright, Squirt." I look down, and Bella's brown eyes are full of wonder. She looks like she just walked into Wonka's factory.

"Your dad is pretty awesome, you know that?"

"I know." She smiles and scans the store from the front door, twitching hard as she does her sweep. Then, she looks back at me again. "I know *you* like him, too."

"Of course. Mr. Salko seems like a very nice person."

"No, *huh-huh-huh,* I mean-*huh* you *like-like* him."

What the…?

"What makes you think that?"

"*Huh-huh-huh* 'cause 'a the way you look at him." She flinches, gazing out at the array of cages and accessories before her, and I feel like I'm really noticing her tics for the first time. "Your face turns all red."

"Enough stallin'." I clear my throat, anxious for a change in topic. "Time to go find you a new best friend."

"*Yessssss!*" she hisses, balling her hand into a fist.

"Now, what kind of little baby might be a good fit for you? Do you want something furry? Feathery? Scaly?"

She makes a face like she just smelled a fart.

"Don't give me that face. You should see how cute the little leopard geckos are. They look like they're smiling all the time."

"*Awww!*" She clutches the sides of her own face.

"They have *birds*, although you already have *Howard,* so I think you're pretty covered in the avian department."

"Yeah, I'm all set on birds. I'm, *huh-huh,* at *capacity.*"

I suddenly laugh so hard that an associate stops the inventory she's in the middle of to stare at me like I have a second head growing out of my neck.

"Let's see… they have ferrets. They are playful little sweethearts, but I will warn you, they can get pretty stinky. That smell will knock you out if you're not changing their cage constantly. I'm sure it's even worse than your *onion soup bombs*."

"Yikes, ewww, no thank you."

"You could get a fish. They're super easy to upkeep, and you—"

We shuffle through, and I motion to a wall of aquariums, each separated by dividers. Although the way some of their stock is floating near the filters it doesn't inspire a ton of confidence.

Although, I'm sure Eric would be pleased with that choice. Clean. Contained···

"I want a mouse." She's firm. Her chocolate irises scan the aisles intently for any sign of rodent enclosures.

"You want a *mouse?*"

"Yes. I want a *Muchacho*." The way she pronounces it is fast and silly, just like me. She's imitating me.

Suddenly, it hits me that my being here is not just a *temporary gig* for her. I am helping form her.

Holy crap, I am *shaping youth*.

Jesus-H-Christ, who would let me shape youth?! I'm a fucking child myself! I shouldn't be anyone's mentor.

For God's sake, I can barely fucking dress myself.

I snap out of my miniature freak-out as we drift to the spot beneath a giant banner that says: RODENTS.

"You want your own *Muchacho*, eh? Oh boy." I exhale deeply, knowing that Eric will not be pleased with the vermin of her choice when we return.

We make our way over to the glass enclosures. Bella isn't tall enough to see in the mouse cages without assistance. I scour the aisle and find an employee step stool tucked away. I drag it over so she can get high enough to peer straight in.

"*Awwwwwwww*." Her voice reflects off the glass back at me.

I know that sound. It's the same sound I make when I fall for a furry creature, too.

And from the look in her eyes, she's in love with all of them.

"Okay, looks like they have a few black ones, a few albino ones…"

"No. Not the albino ones. Their eyes, *huh-huh-huh*, scare me."

"Hmmm. Yeah, they do have a bit of a demonic look to 'em."

She gasps and covers her mouth, and I know she's found *the one*. He scurries into the light, and I can see his cream-colored coat. He's *adorable*. He walks right up to where Bella's face hovers near the glass. He puts a tiny, pink paw up against right by her nose and studies her.

Bella whips her head around to look at me. She's pouting, trying not to cry. "He's perfect."

"Yeah? You want him?" I raise my eyebrows.

She nods violently. "I'm gonna name him *huh-huh* Sernik."

"Sernik? That's a weird name," I tease.

"*Huh-huh,* it means *cheesecake* in Polski."

"Oooooh, wow, I see." I nod. "That's perfect." His coat is almost the *exact* shade of good New York cheesecake.

I wave for the employee breezing by. She holds up a finger as if to say: *one moment, please.*

"What's cheesecake in French?" Bella asks.

"*Le flan au fromage.*"

"*Le flan… au… huh-huh… fromage,*" she slowly repeats.

"Perfect. Nailed it." I high-five her.

"Sernik is easier to say than all *that,* though."

"You're right. It is. I think you've made a wise choice."

22

Kira

We put the finishing touches on Sernik's new multi-level wire cage. It was half off with the Pet-Points Loyalty coupon that I brought from home.

Despite a billionaire footing the bill, I abhor waste and have never been a fan of frivolous spending. I've had to dangle in commercial dumpsters just to reach fucking expired bread that's been thrown out just so I could *eat*.

Stuff like that, it changes you.

Along with some clearance bedding, we also grabbed a small school bus-shaped travel carrier and a bag of colorful papaya treats.

"In about a week, we will check Sernik's bedding. If it's starting to get a little smelly, I will teach you how to change it, okay?"

Bella nods, taking this all gravely serious like she's going to be tested on it.

Sernik pleads for release from his cardboard PetSavers carrier with a flurry of gentle scratches.

"So, let's do a check. Wheel?"

"*Huh-huh,* check!" Bella points at the bright red clip-on wheel in his cage.

"Food bowl?"

125

"*Huh-huh,* check! It's full of deeee-licious food, too." She twitches, smiling at the seeds and grains inside.

"Alright. *Bedding?*"

"*Obviously.*" She rolls her eyes.

"And what is the most important thing to ensure is always in this cage?"

She thinks for a moment. "The *mouse?*"

I laugh. "Okay, what's the *other* most important thing that should always be in his cage?"

"*Huh-huh,* um… water?"

"Bingo." I point to the full blue water bottle clipped to the cage. "If this gets empty for more than a few hours, Sernik can die, and we don't want that."

"Ohhhhhhhh, no. No, we don't." She shakes her head. Then, it is as if a switch flips in her, and she is suddenly super-excited. "Is it time? Can we let him out now?"

"Do you want to bring your dad in for this?"

"He doesn't like mice." She frowns.

"Yeah, but he might still like an invite. He really wanted you to have this even though he doesn't like them. He knew this would make you happy, and that's a very selfless thing to do."

Appreciate your father, kid.

Some of us aren't nearly as lucky.

"I think you should bring him in for this," I insist. "This is a big moment. Your family is growing today, even if only by a little furry bit."

126

She bolts out of the room in a flash so fast it makes my head spin. All I can hear is the soft scramble of the helpless creature in the box, and I smile at how good he's about to have it.

Not only is he not ending up in the belly of a python, but the little dude's got a double-decker cage, treats, a travel bus, a ball... you name it.

Ah, to be kept by a billionaire. I'd be lying if I didn't say I was jealous of the little guy.

Eric enters the room with his hand in Bella's, and I feel the air change. It's as if suddenly, the room feels charged, *electric*.

His hand leaves Bella's to rub his neck where the sling strap is pulling. He grimaces. It looks painful and irritated. Eventually, his tea-colored eyes lock onto mine.

"Looks like the entire welcoming committee is in attendance." He looks around, and his short waves of clean, mahogany-colored hair bob with the movement.

"Should I do a drum-roll or something," he asks. "You're not going to make me *hold* it or anything, are you?"

"No." Bella grabs the hole-punched box with the reverence of a clergyman carrying a reliquary through a church. The box stays steady and flat. She's being so gentle with it.

She tries to offer it up to me to do the honors.

"Oh no. I think *you* should be the one to welcome him home. Yours should be the first face he sees when you open the box."

"What if he jumps?"

"He won't. He's scared. He probably thinks you're about to *eat him* right now. These guys are on the bottom of the food chain. Pretty much everything eats a mouse. Cats, snakes, birds—"

"Huh-huh, birds?"

Eric jumps in. "Oh yeah, this thing is like a *Kit Kat* bar to an owl."

"Go on then. Don't be afraid. Just open the box, scoop him out gently, and put him in his cage."

"This cage is really nice, Bella," Eric says, trying to be encouraging. "This little fella is gonna be on an episode of MTV Cribs: Mouse Edition. All he needs is a pool."

"...And a Parisian chef, and a music room full of instruments," I jest, "and a walk-in *humidor*..."

"Oh, you saw that?" Eric smiles at me, and it feels like a flash of heat barrels through me. I try to regain my composure.

"Yeah, that humidor is bigger than the whole friggin *store* where I used to buy my Churchills."

"You smoke cigars?"

I wind my way around the other side of the cage and nod. "Occasionally. As a treat."

"Well, well, well. Learning something new about you every day." His grin is so sexy.

128

"Sernik, *huh-huh-huh,* welcome home, little buddy." She opens the top flap of the box as if she expects a ray of light to come shooting out from within. Inside sits the terrified little guy, just staring up at her. "It's okay. I'm not gonna hurt you," she coos lovingly.

"Remember how I told you to hold him." I'm leaning over the cage now, terrified she will panic and drop him. That's the *last* thing I need, for Eric to have to go on a mouse hunt with me. All the *I-told-you-sos…*

"You named him Sernik? Like, as in *cheesecake?*" Eric makes a confused face.

But his question is answered when Bella pulls the mouse out, and he glimpses its cream coloring.

The mouse stares up at Bella with giant black eyes, wrapping its multi-tonal tail around her thumb.

She places him in the cage ever-so-gently, and Eric and I breathe a quiet sigh of relief in unison as she secures the cage door.

Success.

As Sernik explores his new multi-story mansion, Bella sits infatuated, arms folded beneath her head, eyes wide with excitement as he silently roams every inch of his new home.

Through the bars, I see Eric's eyes staring at me. I'm frozen in place by his unblinking stare and that devilishly handsome face.

His lips move, and he mouths the words *thank you* with a smile.

He kisses Bella on her head, but she might as well be at the Brooklyn Zoo or the Norwalk Aquarium right now for how intently she watches her hairy new friend.

Seeing how Eric is with Bella makes me feel a longing I have stuffed deep inside myself.

I miss moments like this with my own father. I miss having a *family*. I haven't had that in *so long*.

In this moment, in this huge room with this loving father and his grateful child…

I have never felt more *alone* in my life.

23

Eric

I tap my Cartier pen on my legal pad with so much force that it rattles my iced water with lemon like a scene out of a Spielberg film. The waiter approaches and asks if I would like to order an appetizer while I wait. I decline. He bows respectfully and scuttles off to his next table.

Only a minute later, I see Rob's familiar face squeezing through the lunch crowd here at our usual steakhouse in New Rochelle. He nods from afar, approaches quickly, and slinks into the chair across from me.

"Oh my God, this fucking *traffic*." He splays both hands and slides them across the white linen to smooth it before finally looking up at me. "Sorry, Salko. Some asshole was trying to parallel-park and obviously had *no idea* how to do it… so I just had to *sit* and watch the travesty unfold with everyone behind me laying on their horns."

"It's fine," I say, eyes darting around for our waiter, "but I do have to get back in a bit. So, take a look at your menu before we start. I already know what I'm going to have."

"Of *course* you do." Rob scoffs.

"What's that supposed to mean?"

He leans back, wraps one arm around the back of his chair, and sighs. "It means *you like what you like*. It's not a bad thing."

"You're making it *sound* like a bad thing."

"No, it just means you're a creature of habit. You take the same vacation to Milan yearly even though you're richer than God and the world is your oyster. You wear the same brands. I'll bet that shirt is Dior, and if you could wear a jacket right now, it would probably be a navy or taupe *Brunello Cucinelli*. And at restaurants, you're no different. You always order the same things at the same places."

"No, I don't, not always."

"Let's see," he leans forward and eyes the menu, "we are at Leonardi's right now. You're going to have a scotch-and-soda, which you will quickly down and then wash back with about two cups of water, effectively killing any buzz you might have gotten."

I push my empty glass to the side, which contained just that a few minutes ago. I purse my lips and narrow my eyes a little.

"Then you will say you want to skip the appetizers. You'll insinuate that it is because you're somehow overweight by patting your stomach, but we both know you have a fuckin' six-pack under there."

I shift uncomfortably in my seat. I *was* planning to forgo appetizers.

Christ, am I really that *predictable?*

132

"Then, you'll order the filet mignon, which you will mispronounce as *mig-non*. You'll ask if they can substitute the mashed potatoes for asparagus or, if you're feeling real wild... *broccoli*."

"Shit." I lob my pen at the yellow pad and lean back. "No wonder Tawny left. I'm a broken record."

"Naw," Rob seems genuine. "You just don't step out of your comfort zone. You find something that works and just cruise at that altitude. It's fine. I'm just saying, try something new. Get out of that zone. Yeah, the fucking thirty-two-dollar Wagyu burger *might* be trash... but it might be ten times better than the filet, and you won't *ever* know that because you didn't give it a shot."

The waiter approaches, and Rob folds his menu closed.

"Welcome to Leonardi's! Can I start you off with a drink or an appetizer, sir? Another scotch and soda for you, sir?"

Rob's eyes flash with excitement, and he raises a finger to point at me but doesn't say a word.

I slump a little and reply sheepishly, "I think we're ready to order."

"What's something you recommend?" Rob shuts his menu and stares up at the young man in the starched apron.

"Drink-wise or food-wise?"

"Both."

133

Rob is *bold*. I'll give him that.

"For drinks, they make an *outstanding* dirty martini here."

"Hear that, Eric? *Outstanding*."

The waiter isn't sure if Rob is mocking him, and it's apparent in his slight hesitation to continue.

"I'll have one of those," Rob says with confidence. "And as for food, my good man?"

"The *Chicken Quattro Formaggi* is the best. We were in a couple of magazines last month because of it."

"Mmmm, what is that?" Rob is staring at him now, and his gaze is unintentionally intimidating. It's one of the reasons I love watching him deal with our more difficult clients, but man, I fucking *hate* being on the other *end* of that stare.

"It is a chicken breast that is stuffed with pecorino romano, mozzarella, fontina, & goat cheese with spinach, garlic, and sun-dried tomatoes. It's battered in a wine sauce over polenta. It's delicious."

"Jesus, kid, you had me at goat cheese." Rob hands his menu to the waiter, and all eyes turn to me.

"I'll have the filet *mignon*," I say slowly to ensure I pronounce it as Rob did. "And, is there any way to swap the mashed potatoes for some Brussels sprouts?"

"Of course, sir."

"*Chicken shiiiiit.*" Rob says it playfully, but I feel disappointed in myself.

"The filet mignon here is excellent."

I smile. *I already know. Rob's right. I've had it at least twenty times.*

As the waiter leaves, Rob kicks me in the shin with the toe of his Berluti derby shoe. "Why didn't you try the chicken thing with me?! That was the perfect opportunity to try something new."

"Rob, I didn't know what half of that stuff was."

"And you never will," Rob fires back, looking around in disappointment. "That's alright. Stay in your safe little box."

There is a stilted pause between us. I know he's right, but I have nothing to say in response.

Finally, Rob speaks again.

"How long did the doc say the sling's gotta stay on?"

"Couple more weeks, at least." I feel defeated as I look down at the dark blue felt-and-mesh monstrosity stealing all of the attention from the two-thousand-dollar shirt beneath it.

"At least you're in a sling. I broke my arm when I was 16, and I had to have that shit in one of those big plaster casts. Oh my *God,* did that thing fucking *reek* after a while? My arm got all pale and scrawny in it." Rob shivers.

"Yeah, it's still such a pain though. I'm awkward at everything. Typing is the worst. I go to do those reports, and I'm pecking like a chicken with my right hand." I mimic a rooster pecking at my legal pad, and Rob laughs. He spreads his arms to stretch. I've always admired his effortless confidence, especially in public. There's a reason he's usually the face of our business.

"Sooooooo…" He looks at me expectantly.

"So?"

I have no idea what he is alluding to.

"So, how's the assistant workin' out?" Rob helps himself to a sip of my water, and I stare at the glass momentarily.

"Kira? She's actually," I smile, "working out. It was a little rocky the first couple of days. Plus, I didn't really want to let her help—"

"*Control freak.*" He crunches some of the ice from my drink between his molars. With his near-black irises and the way he's gnashing, he reminds me of a shark.

"Yeah, I suppose I am. But the rest of the week, she stepped up to the plate, and she's been helping me with all the spreadsheets and errands and all that."

"Good. I mean, I know the surgery was necessary, but with all that shit so backed up on your end, I was getting a little… I dunno, worried."

I soak that in for a moment. I know being behind stressed me out, but I never really considered the toll it might be taking on Rob's end of the business.

"She's pretty careful, too, which I like. I spent two hours trying to find any error or typo in one of the spreadsheets she put together the other day, and I couldn't find anything."

"You didn't trust her to do it right?"

"Of *course* not. I barely trust *myself* to do it right, and I've been doing 'em for years." Forgetting about my injury, I shrug and then wince at the dull pain that radiates through my shoulder.

Rob snickers and downs half of my water in one go.

"She's great with Bella, too. She's taken a lot of initiative with her this last week or so, and they seem like they're bonding."

"That's good. Bella needs a woman in her life, and since you're *celibate* now…"

"I'm not fucking *celibate*." I snicker. "Jesus, I'm just not *dating*. There's a difference."

"Are you getting' any ass?"

I won't dignify that with an answer.

"…Then you're *celibate*."

"It's not like I've taken some *vow*."

"Look, it's fine. You need a boatload of time to get over Tawny, and I get that. But you're thirty-one years old, man. You're in your goddamn prime. You look like a fucking GQ model. You've got *Fuck-You money* and you're *still* letting that woman control your life."

"She isn't controlling anything. I don't even think about her."

"*Sure.*" He doesn't believe me.

"I don't. Not in a *longing* type of way. The only time I think of her, I get pissed off. I mean, forget about me… who runs off and fucking abandons their only *child*? I'm always waiting for the other shoe to drop and to have her pop back up."

"Yeah, I get that. She's always been a bit… insidious in that regard." He sighs with pride. "But that's why I thought you deserved a little eye candy."

I'm taken off-guard by the comment. "*What?*"

"You know, with Blumquist. She's smoking hot. The girl's a knockout. Perfect teeth. Nice little figure. And those tits… my *God*. As my father would say, she's built like a brick shithouse."

"Jesus, Rob, she's a *person*, not a horse you're looking to buy."

I don't know why it enrages me so much to hear Rob talk about Kira that way. I know I've only known Kira for a short time, but the more I've seen, the more she's growing on me. I feel something bubble up in me. Something that feels an awful lot like jealousy, which is an emotion I haven't felt in forever.

When I was with Tawny, toward the end, she was so disinterested in me that I almost *welcomed* the note she left saying she'd taken off to Tampa on a whim in search of, quote, *greener pastures*.

"I thought you hired her because she's qualified."

"I mean, she's an assistant handling the most generalized duties for a temporary fucking position. The qualifications are a spotless criminal history and a clean driving record. That's it. For what we were offering, people were coming out of the *woodwork*." He snickers. "Hell, we probably had sixty *qualified* applicants apply on the first day. But Blumquist was the hottest by a mile. I mean, Jesus, Eric, if *you* aren't trying to tap that, shit, let *me* know. I'm not a fuckin' *monk* like you. I'll take a run at 'er.""

The waiter arrives with Rob's martini. I want to stuff a hundred bucks in his apron right now just for interrupting this horrendous conversation.

I love Rob to death. He's been my best friend for years, but I'll be *damned* if the saying doesn't hold true. Opposites *do* attract.

He sets another water down, which I promptly slide over to my side of the table.

"Your food is coming right up." He nods at both of us.

"Great, thank you." I try to offer him a genuine smile, but I have a sour taste in my mouth over Rob talking about Kira like she's the same way he talked about a slab of Wagyu. She's not a *Fleshlight* with a pulse for our amusement. She's a *person*.

139

I suddenly feel just as bad for leering at her, stealing glances all week every time she hasn't been looking. Eyeing the curves of her body as she drifts around my home. And, Jesus, how many times have I looked at that *contact picture* on my phone?

I have no right to judge Rob. *I'm just as fucking bad.*

"Here, at least try it." He slides his martini to me.

I take a conservative sip, and my eyes widen. "Wow, that really is good."

"See what happens when you get adventurous and try new things?" He holds up his stemware to cheers. "To exciting new futures, whatever they may hold."

"I'll cheers to that." And I do. I may be successful in the eyes of an outsider, but inside, I feel like a hot mess, one that *is* stuck in a rut.

"Let's talk about the DeMeester account." I flip through my notebook to a page scribbled with some notes and grab my pen. "Talk to me, Rob. What the hell is going on with him? Why does he want to pull out?"

"Damien's flighty. I don't think he can hack it, honestly. He doesn't have the stomach for high risk, and I keep telling him that we can invest in something more stable, but he keeps insisting on volatile stocks. Now he's saying he wants to pull out of electric vehicles altogether."

"Yeah, but he's down like thirty-six grand right now on those. If he does that, he solidifies the losses."

"Eric, I know how the fucking market works. This isn't my first rodeo. You, of all people, should know that. I already gave him the whole spiel about how the market ebbs and flows and how it's not a loss unless you tuck tail and run. But he seems adamant."

"Did you tell him about how the earnings report goes sometimes? That's all this shit with Rivian is right now."

"Yeah, I even cited all the goddamned streaming services and shit that plunged after favorable earnings calls. It doesn't matter. He said he wants to withdraw a bunch of the money he's got in those to build a fucking addition onto his house. Said he's willing to eat shit to do so."

I growl. "*Fine*. I'll have Kira process him out and cut him his check."

I flip through some notes I scribbled on another page. "Let's talk penny stocks."

"Jesus, Eric, *again with the penny stocks?* We've been over this a hundred times. You've *got* to let that shit go. We don't dabble with that kind of startup shit anymore. That's way *too* high risk."

"It's stocks, Rob, it's *all* high risk. Wall Street is just classy Vegas."

Just then, a young man with a briefcase makes his way through the crowd, pushing through the closely-seated tables behind Rob. He looks right at me and waves.

I'm confused. I don't think I've ever seen this guy before.

"Eric!" He hollers and waves again.

Rob turns around in his booth and cocks a jet-black eyebrow at him. "Who the fuck is this?"

"Oh, thank God I caught you," the man exclaims, out of breath, as he reaches our table. He shoves his way into the seat beside me, perched on the very edge of it.

I look at his ill-fitting jacket with a button point that looks absurdly high for his physique. The stitching for his traditional English shoulder seam seems all wrong. The suit is dirt cheap, obviously not tailored.

"You're Eric Salko, right?" The stranger holds out a hand to shake mine.

I do, hesitantly and with a suspicious look plastered on my face. "*Yes...*"

"Great." He huffs, still out of breath.

"Can we… help you?" Rob asks, annoyed.

The man ignores his query. "So sorry I'm winded. I had to run. Parking out there is an absolute nightmare right now."

Rob scoffs and takes a long sip of his martini, never peeling his eyes away from this guy, even when I flash him a look that says: *What the hell is happening right now?*

The man sets his briefcase on the table, opens both clasps, and pulls out a manilla envelope. He hands it to me, and I take it. My heart nearly stops when I do. I realize what this is the minute I see the tiny white label stuck on it:

FROM THE LAW OFFICES OF GENTRY AND GENTRY.

"You've been served," he says. Without another word, he closes his briefcase and shuffles back out of the building.

I can't move.

I can't bear to look at this even though I know exactly what it probably is.

Gentry and Gentry were the law firm Tawny used for the divorce. And since that was finalized over six months ago, this can only be one thing…

"Oh, *fuck*." Rob's voice is reverent and horrified.

I'm frozen with this stupid folder in my hand. I want to rage. I want to overturn our table. I want to blow a blood vessel and let darkness take me. My molars grind. The already painful muscles in my neck and shoulders stiffen.

"Is… that what I think it is?" Rob's quiet now.

But I'm still too *stunned* to respond.

I feel Rob snatch the packet from my hands. He opens it and slides out the legal papers inside. He sighs deeply and stares at me with a look of alarm. *It's exactly what I feared, isn't it?*

Worst-case-scenario.

"Don't worry, Eric. I'll get the lawyers on this right away."

143

He tucks the pages back inside, and our waiter arrives with our food. He smiles at us, setting my sizzling filet in front of me. Even though I haven't had anything but a cappuccino and a scotch and soda since dinner last night, I find myself too anxious to touch it. I eye the seasoned juices glistening on the grade-A beef and the perfect sear of the halved roasted Brussels sprouts, and I feel physically ill, as if all of the blood has drained from my face.

"Thank you," Rob says to the waiter with a forced smile.

"I'll be back in a moment to see if you need anything else, okay?"

Rob nods, and the man walks off, leaving us in utter silence. Rob hands the packet back to me with a solemn look in his dark eyes. "I'm so sorry, Eric."

My head swims. I feel completely drained. *The soul-sucking vampire strikes again.* And this time, she's trying to sink her gel manicure into something much more important and valuable than half my assets…

She wants *Bella*.

I make my way through the maze of this manor toward Eric's office with several tote bags of office supplies, astounded by the amount of space this place has. I feel for the maid. Not because Eric and Bella are messy, but because you'd need an extension ladder just to clean the fans and chandeliers with these outrageously vaulted ceilings. There have to be a mile of baseboards in this place, not counting the other mysterious buildings peppering the property.

It must be nice to have money.

The moment I see Eric's open office door, I start talking. "Okay, so Bella is at her therapy appointment right now. I got the graph paper, ledgers, and the grid sheets. They were out of the brand of planner you want—"

I realize I'm not talking to anyone. The office is vacated. The computer and the laptop are both asleep. I set my bags down in the cushy chair in front of his desk, and I walk back out searching for Eric.

"*Hellooooo?*" I say quietly, in case he's on the phone or mid-nap.

No answer.

I wander around, past a giant glass wall with a bubbling hot tub and a massive, enclosed pool just beyond. It looks so inviting. It's lagoon-blue with a bridge leading over to a grotto bunched with a variety of live tropical plants. It looks like a miniature indoor island paradise in the middle of Connecticut.

I brush past the walk-in humidor and the small movie theater with reclining chairs that could seat around thirty people in front of its large projection screen, one flanked by vintage signs and movie posters, and an antique popcorn cart.

I walk past Bella's room and peek inside. It's silent, save for the whisper-quiet whir of Sernik's wheel. He's a blur, burning off energy as fast as his little cream-colored legs can manage.

I continue past rooms I didn't even realize were here before. I must have missed them on the tour. Ones that house an indoor basketball court and a library loaded with books in shelving that must be fifteen feet tall. It's even got one of those sliding ladders for accessing books on the upper shelves. Two huge, tufted chairs sit in the middle of the room on either side of a giant L-shaped couch. It looks as if the furniture is forming a smiley face. *I'd be smiling, too, if I were surrounded by that many books.*

I decide to try the kitchen. In the best-case scenario, Jacques will know where Eric is so I can squeeze in another task before I pick Bella back up from her therapy session. *Worst case, I can probably snag a fresh blueberry scone.*

In the kitchen, Jacques toils away over a sauce that makes my mouth water the instant the aroma hits me. There's garlic, butter, and a hint of fresh lemon… I want to drool at the smells constantly emanating from this room. If I lived here, I'd gain thirty pounds right off the bat in the first month, I'm sure of it.

"Hey, Jacques, seen Eric around?"

He looks over his shoulder with a devilish grin and shakes his head. "Nope."

"Do you know where he usually is around this time?"

"*Non, mon chérie.* I typically keep to the kitchen or the dining room when I'm here."

The way Jacques leers cracks me up. He reminds me of that cartoon skunk that's always trying to get laid. Harmless, but forward.

"Okay, thanks." I nod, but I don't leave.

His smile morphs into a full-blown belly laugh. He opens one of the wall ovens to his left and pulls me out fresh pastry.

I hold it in my fingers and curtsy. "*Merci beaucoup.*"

"*De rien.*" He nods.

I head away from the kitchen, scarfing down the delectable, flaky dessert, checking myself for crumbs as I carry on.

It suddenly dawns on me that I might know where Eric is. I shuffle through the halls again, ending my journey at the door of his music room.

It's comically tall and coated in black gloss. I knock gently and turn the handle. "Mr. Salko?"

Inside, he's sitting in the far corner next to the record player with canister headphones on. The dying light of the afternoon is seeping in through the curtains and lighting him so perfectly. He's like a work of art, a feature in a gallery, and I find myself taken aback by how attractive he is in this light.

I wish he weren't my boss. I suddenly wish he didn't have money like Bezos. I wish, instead, that he was just some random barfly I could spend a night in bed with. With a body like his and those dripping-honey-colored eyes that make me feel a little aroused every time they lock onto mine... we could've had some real fun together.

I'm snapped out of my horny thoughts of this dreamy man by the sight of him wiping the far side of his face and sniffling.

He clears his throat and removes his headphones, jostling the acoustic guitar lying across his lap. "Can I *help* you?"

It's the first time he's talked to me with that curtness since my first day when he tried to fire me. I'm taken aback by the gruff tone.

I watch him rub his neck beneath his sling strap so hard it looks like he might take skin with it. The flesh is agitated and red.

"I'm so sorry to interrupt, sir. I just wanted to let you know I was back with the supplies and had a bit of time for another task if needed before I go back and pick Bella up."

He looks a million miles away like I'm speaking a foreign language.

"*Oh*… okay." It's all he says.

I'm confused. "Want me to wait elsewhere and get out of your hair?"

His brown eyes look glassy. I just stand there for a moment, studying this new emotion in him. I steal a glance at the stack of papers and terracotta-colored envelope lying on the couch cushion beside him.

"No. You can come in. I was just listening to some music."

I point to his headphones. "I don't know if you know this yet, but you own this giant estate that no one is trying to nap in right now, and you can actually just… make noise."

He laughs a little and looks down at the guitar and then back up at me, and that's when I see it. *There is a sadness in his eyes.* A deep one.

I don't know what it is about seeing him like this, but it makes me want to drop-kick whoever made him feel this shitty. I have the sudden urge to wrap him up in a giant bear hug and squeeze until he isn't upset anymore.

If he were *mine*, I would be all over him right now, gently kissing away the hurt, embracing away the agony and strife.

"Play me something." I motion to the guitar in his lap and sit on the couch across from him, kicking my shoes onto the lush carpet. I pull my feet onto the couch until I'm nearly sitting on them. "One song. Music's good for the soul."

149

"I can't. It's too awkward with this damn sling. I can strum, but I can't hold down the frets. I don't have enough range of motion to even hold the neck right." He picks up the guitar again and offers it up to me. "You play *me* something."

I freeze a little. The look in his eyes is one of sad desperation, a micro-expression that says so much while also saying nothing at all.

"If you insist." I nod dutifully, and he settles into the cushions behind him. He sniffles again and clears his throat.

"Any requests?" I ask with a laugh. This whole thing is ridiculous, and my rusty singing is about to get me shit-canned. I can already hear Cassandra's nagging *told-you-so*.

"Play me something that makes you smile when you hear it."

My heart starts to race, pounding harder than when I used to perform for whole crowds in Bridgeport. My hands shake a little.

The moment he made the request, I knew the song. There's always one that comes to mind. It's one that my father used to play me when I was a little girl.

Back before life went to shit.

Before the ugliness of the world put its grotesque, sadistic stranglehold on my family.

Back before my father was taken from me.

My fingers start to play the John Denver song I've played a thousand times before. It's simple, and I have the chords memorized out of pure muscle memory.

"*Sunshine…*"

It was Dad's song. It makes me smile. But I forgot, until now, that it also makes me cry. My eyes are suddenly glassy now, too. "*On my shoulders… makes me happy…*"

25

Eric

As she quietly croons, her voice is like a pair of velvet arms cradling me. She has a voice like no one I've ever heard before.

The lyrics pour from her glossed lips with so much feeling that it wrenches my heart in my chest. I can imagine John Denver's approving gaze cast on her like the lowering sun pouring in through these sheers. The notes she hits make me want to break down and cry, but I staunchly refuse, clenching my jaw to fight the emotions overpowering me.

I see a tear roll from her cheek, and I want to wipe it away. I hear the quake of her voice as she fights her own demons. At this moment, I want to hold her in my arms and tell her that everything will be okay for her, even though I have no clue if it will.

As she strums the song's final notes, I feel a vast void of emptiness open inside me. I don't want her to stop. *Ever*. I wish I could live in this room and listen to her serenade me all night.

"That was beautiful," I say, but my voice is barely a whisper. "Thank you."

She hands the guitar back, and I place it on the stand.

"I never imagined you'd be a John Denver fan."

"He was my dad's favorite. He actually taught me how to play the guitar with *Take Me Home and Country Roads*. But that one was his favorite."

Was.

It's a heavy word that explains a lot about the tears in her eyes. I want to ask her more about him, but I don't want to pry.

Without thinking, I rub my neck and shoulder again. The sling is irritating me more than usual today. It feels like my arm weighs seventy pounds, and my shoulders and neck feel incredibly tense.

Without another word, Kira rises and walks behind the couch I'm on. I sense her presence close to me and feel my shoulders tense even more than I thought possible. I feel her fingers ever-so-gently slide beneath the strap of my sling, and I jolt.

"Oh, sorry, did I hurt you?" Her voice is soft, a wild juxtaposition from her clear, assertive singing voice.

"No. Just caught me off-guard." I'm confused about why she's suddenly touching me. She gently tugs the sling's strap, indicating that she wants me to pull it over my head. I oblige and allow her to take it off.

Now, her voice is in my ear, low and soft. "Let me know if I'm going too hard."

What?

Before I fully understand what is happening, I feel a slender, feminine hand sliding over my uninjured shoulder near the base of my neck. I feel a delicate thumb kneading with a pressure that makes me groan aloud.

Jesus Christ, that feels incredible.

I can't remember the last time a woman gave me a massage. It's been years… at least. Rob's prodded me to book a masseuse, but, as he stated so brashly at lunch, I don't step out of my comfort zone often enough.

I feel her digits undulate against the tense muscles of my neck and shoulders, careful to avoid the shoulder I had surgery on.

I melt beneath her touch.

Being this close to her, I can smell the gardenia perfume mixing with the scent of her skin. It's like walking by a fragrant botanical garden in full bloom.

I close my eyes and roll my head, feeling the bones in my neck crackle. She snickers. It's like such a wildly different reaction than Tawny ever had. Her hands would've instantly come off of me. Instead, Kira's hand digs deeper, prodding my muscles with her talented hands.

"You looked like you were in pain. That sling has got to be a nightmare."

Honestly, it is the least of my fucking problems today. I'll take this shitty sling for another couple of months over the bullshit served to me any day of the week.

I feel a stirring in my slacks at her touch, her smell, and the way she's making me feel. This is the brightest point in my shit day, and I never want it to end.

…But the *beep-beep beep-beep* of her pocketed phone's alarm draws this heavenly interaction to an abrupt end.

Her hands slide off of me, and for a moment, I don't dare open my eyes for fear this is all a dream.

"Time for me to go get Miss Bella. I want to get there early so she doesn't have to wait."

I want to beg her to stay for two more minutes, to use those incredible hands on me again and massage away all of the hatred I have for my ex-wife. But instead, I nod, grateful that she will leave before I have to try to stand with the erection growing between my legs.

"Thank you for this." I know she can sense the truly grateful tone of my voice.

She smiles, and it's beautiful. "Anytime."

And just like that, she's got her shoes on and wafts out the room like a pleasant, dissipated dream upon waking.

I glance down at the throbbing bulge between my legs, face hot and flustered.

Fuck…

26

Kira

Why did I do that? He's going to think I'm kissing ass. It's just… he looked like he desperately *needed* it.

As I take the winding, maple tree-lined curves, I can't stop thinking about how he felt in my hands. I wasn't expecting him to be so muscular. His neck and shoulders felt like they were carved out of granite.

And that scent. Good Lord, what is that man shampooing with? It smelled like clean citrus and spice. The way it mixed with his cologne…

Kira, get a fucking hold of yourself. Of all the men in the world, the last one you should be daydreaming over is your fucking boss. There are billions of other fish in the sea.

People like *Jacques*. He's attainable. Cute. French. Knows how to cook… and, most importantly, is *not the gazillionaire who signs your checks*.

I pull into the parking lot and suck in a deep breath as I kill the whisper-quiet engine of the Tesla. I rub the dashboard lovingly. I'm growing fond of this sleek, electric masterpiece. The power steering works. It doesn't need a quart of oil every two days. It doesn't guzzle gas like a parched man in the desert. It doesn't rattle like it's falling apart the second I hit I-95. I will miss this baby when the job is over, that's for sure.

I head inside the building and take a seat in the waiting room. It isn't long before Bella comes out, twitching beneath her therapist's shoulder grasp.

"Hey, Mouse!" I am overjoyed to see her even though it's only been two hours. She looks exhausted but smiles warmly when she sees me.

"Bella did great during her therapy tonight." The therapist assures me before looking down. Her hair is pulled back in a loose bun with chopsticks speared through the middle. "Didn't you?"

Bella nods up at the aging woman.

I wave Bella over to me and take her tiny hand in mine before asking the woman, "Do I need to relay any information to Mr. Salko, or is she good to go?"

"Nope, she's all set. I'll call Eric and Tawny tomorrow and give them a progress report as usual."

"Alright, Squirt!" I say, looking down at the nine-year-old whose muscle tics feel suddenly very noticeable and consistent. "Let's go home so you can hang out with Sernik and your papa. I have a feeling your dad could use a big ol' cub hug from his favorite person."

Bella smiles, unaware of how right I am. My nosy ass saw the injunction her missing-in-action mother filed featuring words like "seeks

sole custody" when I was rubbing Eric's...
incredible... shoulders.

My mind keeps replaying the name *Tawny* on a loop. Part of me knows that her drama is absolutely none of my business. But the other part of me is curious as to why that woman deserves any sort of progress report after abandoning her daughter.

No, after abandoning them *both*.

27

Eric

"Wow, is it six o'clock already?" *Jesus, today feels like a nauseating blur.*

"Yep," Kira says as she adjusts her jacket and then grabs her tattered leather satchel. It needs to be tossed. I don't even think it could be donated to charity at this point. The fact that she can get it to hold anything frankly *astounds* me.

"Would you care to stay for dinner? Jacques always makes plenty."

I want her to say yes. I don't know why, but I *don't* want her to leave. I don't want to be alone right now with just Bella. I need a distraction. I am afraid if I look at my daughter for too long, that dark thoughts of Tawny tearing my child away from me will win. I don't want to cry in front of Bella. That's not what she needs. That's not what *anyone* needs.

I have to be strong, but Tawny has *always* known the ways to cut me to the quick. She seeks an Achilles heel and stores it in her memory to abuse later. I saw her do it to her friends and family over the years.

It's just the way she's wired.

I know she doesn't even want our daughter. She just wants to *hurt me*. To hurt us *both*. To collect another *asset* she can use to her advantage and brag about on social media.

"I don't think I should," she answers, and I realize I have been swept up in this momentary trance, buried in my thoughts and worry so long that I forgot a question had even been asked.

"*Pleeeeeease*, Ree-Ree?" Bella's holding her hand. Seeing it makes me smile. Her tics have been more pronounced since therapy, something that's always concerned me. I feel like the supposed treatment just exacerbates her twitches.

"No, Squirt, as much as I'd love to, I think I should be going so you can get the weekend started with your dad."

"Get home safe, okay," I say with reluctance, "Whereabouts do you live again?"

"Right off Housatonic in Bridgeport."

I fight the urge to wince. Every time I've been in that area, I've been accosted by a transient or prostitute or some crazed old man literally screaming about God. I hate the thought of someone like her having to live and sleep in such a sketchy place.

"Twenty-minute drive? That's not too bad." I finally say. I've never been stellar at small talk.

"Closer to thirty with as slow as I have to drive with my beast." She points toward the back door and puts her jean jacket on. "She's no model-S, that's for sure. Everything's ludicrous on it *except* the speed."

That makes me laugh out loud. It feels like the first time I've smiled since before that sneaky bastard sidled up next to me at lunch.

"Well, get home safe." I open the door for her. As she exits through it, I feel sorrow the second she crosses the threshold. A moment later, I'm left with nothing but the ghostly wisp of her flowery perfume. It lingers in the air like a fond memory.

"Go wash up for dinner, honey," I finally say to my daughter, whose face echoes a kindred expression, one as lost as my own.

I look down to see Bella standing at the back door with me, watching Kira pull out of the drive like we are two dogs, ready to howl in protest.

"If you eat all of your dinner, we can watch whatever you want in the theater."

She gasps with excitement. "Can we wa—"

"*Yessssss,*" I groan, knowing exactly what she wants to watch. It's what she *always* wants to watch. And if by some small chance in Hell, Tawny *does* take her from me... I know I'll *wish* I would've watched it with her every single chance I got.

28

Kira

I toss the oil-streaked cardboard in through the back door, throw my satchel in the passenger seat, and settle into the groaning bucket behind the wheel. I say my silent prayer that this piece of shit will start yet again and turn the key. It sputters and eventually roars to life. Although, there is a new sound now as I make my way out of the gated estate. A *knocking* noise. I feel sick to my stomach. This car is on its last legs. I have to move out of the apartment in less than two weeks, and I'm about to have to spend my first paycheck on car repairs.

And if it's in the shop too long, it will probably be my *final* paycheck, too.

***

Instead of going home, I tempt fate and limp my pile to the bar near my house. I don't have the money for drinks. I can only hope that someone might buy me one if I play my cards right. Plus, the company would be welcome. I don't want to be alone tonight.

This day has been a doozy, and I can't get the bittersweet image of my father singing old folk rock out of my head. I want to cry every single time it replays. They say time heals all

162

wounds, but I don't subscribe to that notion. The loss I feel is like ice-cold, rushing water carving its path through lumps of rock, cutting a deep, unbridgeable crevasse into me every day.

The day he died, I basically became an orphan, left alone to struggle in every way in this world. It seems like such a dramatic term to use since the woman who birthed me is still alive, but since I've barely seen her since, I feel like...

What's that saying?

A man without an island.

I'm floating, never belonging anywhere. Never smart enough, or clever enough, or obedient enough to fit in. Since that day, the concept of family was shattered. Emotionally, I'm a wandering vagabond, flitting from job to job, from one lousy one-night stand to eventually another. There is no place in this world that I belong.

***

It's about fifteen minutes of sitting like a pathetic sap before a man is finally kind enough to buy me a drink.

His name is Larry. Or Harry... or was it *Barry?*

Shit, I should've paid more attention.

He buys me a dark chocolate milk stout, which I greedily down. He wants to buy me another, but I decline due to its astonishingly high ABV. *The last thing I need is a friggin' DUI on top of all of my other problems.*

The whole time he talks, telling me the details of his job. But my mind rudely drifts away to thoughts of Eric and how devastated he looked in his music room, buried in the back like some piece of hidden memorabilia. I don't know why, but I truly wanted to comfort him. I wanted to lay his head on my lap, stroke his hair, and tell him everything would work out with Bella. I wanted to tell him that no sane civil judge would ever pry her from a loving, wealthy father only to hand her back to the woman who just up and left for…

I have no idea why she left, actually. Or where she went, for that matter. I can't even fathom a scenario where that makes sense. Bella and Eric are amazing. I've never had a man treat me as respectfully as Eric, and I've never known a child as caring as Bella.

Tawny's *nuts* to have abandoned them.

…But then again, I know first-hand better than anyone that crazy mothers exist. Sanity isn't guaranteed simply because you have a husband and children.

I thank the man profusely for the stout, and I head out to my vehicle despite his eager attempts to get me to come home with him.

But the word itself sounds so bizarre to me.
Home.

I haven't been to a place that felt like a home in *so* many years. The concept of it doesn't even make *sense* to me some days. And the allure of the word when he says it, it's almost

164

enough to make me fold, to make me follow him...

Just in case he's right. Just in case I can get a *faint taste* of what it's like to be... *home.*

Once I'm alone in my vehicle, I stare up at the word BAR in neon. My slight buzz mixes with feelings about my tumultuous childhood, ending up altogether in one horrendous mash. I think of *Bella.* Of Tawny. Of my own mother and my late father. And finally, of Eric, a man I know well enough from a week and a half to know he doesn't deserve what's happening with Tawny.

My body shudders, and my eyes flood with stinging tears. I sit in the silence of a vehicle as damaged and battered as I am.

I'm comforted by the blur of soft neons cutting through watery darkness. The only sound is my hitching breath and the hiss of the cry stuck in my throat. I wipe my face on the sleeve of my jacket, but it's useless. I press my head to the steering wheel and feel the whole SUV shimmy softly with my juddering.

This world is so ugly sometimes.

29

Kira

I awaken to the sound of my phone chiming, which means I must have slept past the *Do Not Disturb* timer. I hear a series of three texts coming in back-to-back. I grab my phone, unlock the shattered but functional screen, and scroll carefully so as not to cut my fingers on the glass.

I smile when I see who they are from.

> **ERIC: Sorry to bother you on your day off, but Bella wants to go feed Howard this morning.**
>
> **ERIC: She doesn't remember the name of the park.**
>
> **ERIC: And she said you feed him peas???**

I laugh through the grogginess and text back, running a hand through my messy hair.

> **KIRA: Babcock Preserve. 10 mins from ur house.**

**KIRA: Right next to
Rockwood Lake.**

**ERIC: Okay. I will GPS it.
Can we just feed him bread? I
don't think Jacques keeps
frozen peas here.**

**KIRA: No bread. It's bad for
birds.**

There's a long pause, and I see three
bubbles pop up and disappear.

Then, they pop up and disappear again.

As this starts to happen a *third* time, I laugh
and shuffle off to the bathroom to brush my teeth.
I have to do something with this crazy lion's
mane. I look like I just discovered a new
scientific theory and am about to run through the
halls of an Ivy League university screaming
about my findings.

Finally, after the dots disappear for a full
minute, a new text pops up.

ERIC: Care to join us?

My stomach does a flip when he asks. I feel
giddy.

But why *would* he ask? It's a *Saturday.*
Most people would be busy doing fun stuff on a
weekend.

I mean, *I'm* not, but that's beside the point.

Another prolonged bubble with three dots, and then:

> **ERIC: If you're busy... no worries. It's the weekend, after all, and I totally get it if you need a break from us.**

I chuckle because I'm already sifting through jeans to go meet them. My body bolted at the opportunity long before my mind made a conscious decision.

Not only am I *not* tired of seeing them... I'm excited to see what Eric is like when he's not in work mode.

> **KIRA: Omw in ten. Meet you at ur house. We can ride together. I'll show u the way.**

> **ERIC: :)**

> **ERIC: 894023**

I stare at the gate code on my phone momentarily and then look around my room. Everything is in disarray. Half my belongings are already in the boxes Cassandra not-so-subtly left in the corner.

I shake my head. I'm supposed to spend the day apartment shopping, but I'm about to put those plans on pause to go feed a duck.

As I dig through a box to find my cute little top with the plunging neckline that makes my assets look *unreal*, I laugh at how ridiculous it is that I'm getting dolled up to throw frozen veggies at waterfowl.

My thoughts turn to Eric. I could never date someone like him in a million years. I could never even understand what it's like to live a life of opulence and familial warmth, being the parentless kid from the trailer park that I am.

Still, I can't help thinking about how attractive he is despite our wildly different statuses in life. If we were stripped of all our money and earthly material possessions, he wouldn't be so unattainable then. And I would, frankly, rock his world.

Stop thinking like that! You need *this job, Kira. Without it, everything falls apart.*

I tug on a pair of tight, clean jeans and dig out a stylish pair of obnoxiously bright neon-blue tennis shoes. They might be inappropriate for work, but today I'm off the clock, and these are some of the only shoes I have that don't have soles flopping open like some puppet's mouth.

My head is trying to be sensible, growling thoughts like:

Kira, call it off. Stay and find an apartment. Don't risk it. You're running out of time. February will be over before you know it. And what then?

But my heart is a *fool*. It says:

Relax! Go have some fun. You only live once.

On my way out the door, I raid the freezer for another bag of Cassandra's frozen peas and leave two of the last five rumpled dollars from my purse in its place.

30

Eric

As Kira exits her vehicle, the midday sun lights her like an angel, kissing her long blonde hair with its beams. Her dark sunglasses glint and I feel a pulse of adrenaline at the sight of the bit of cleavage making its way over the lacy hem of her cerulean shirt. It's so *goddamned* sexy.

"You're not cold?" I ask, pointing to her acid-washed jacket.

She shakes her head. "I'm fine. I—"

"—Run hot, yes, that's right. I forgot."

She smiles at me. "You look very stylish."

I smile and adjust the edges of the gray wool Eurocoat I have on, which covers me all the way down to my knees. I figured it would be the safest choice in outerwear in case I get any unwanted... *er*... *movement*... down there.

Bella rushes outside in a fur-lined pink parka with a rolling suitcase in tow being dragged across the concrete behind her. She races up to Kira, wrapping her arms around her with a loud squeal, and my heart feels warm watching how excited my daughter is to see her.

"Miss Kira!"

"What up, *Mouse?*" Kira asks it in a silly way, dragging out the '*ow*' noise in a way that makes Bella giggle.

"*Huh-huh-huh,* are you working today?"

"No, sweetheart," I interject. "I asked Miss Kira if she wanted to feed Howard with us at the park before I take you to Babcia's."

"Yay!" Bella twitches through her outward celebration, joy twinkling in her eyes. She stares up at Kira like she's a deity.

I can't say I blame her. With the way the morning sun is hitting her right now, I feel like Kira is the kind of person the Greeks would've labeled a Goddess and written stories about for centuries.

***

The preserve is packed, and I'm not sure why I'm surprised. It's the weekend and an unseasonably warm one at that. We walk down the trail toward Rockwood Lake, waving politely to hikers returning from their morning jogs. Sprays of bright forsythia bushes mark the nearing power of spring as their vibrant branches bloom like bright, yellow explosions throughout the woods. Scrawny dogwood trees are budding, and tiny, striped rodents scurry through the detritus and crunchy leaf litter.

"Awwwwww! *Huh-huh,* a chipmunk!" Bella's voice rings out over the squat waterfall we're nearing.

"Hey, Squirt, catch!" Kira hollers.

Bella looks just in time to catch the small bag of frozen peas mid-air. She pulls one of her mittens off with her teeth and uses her bare hand to rip the bag open while walking toward the water's edge.

"What do we say, Bella?" I ask sternly.

"*Huh-huh*, thank you!" Bella sings, loading up a handful of round, green ammo. She gasps. "There he *is*, dad! *Mon canard blanc!*"

She points to a white duck, and I laugh, shaking my head at how similar he is to the one from her favorite movie. Bella is nothing if not predictable. I can't fault her. She likes what she likes.

She certainly gets that trait from me.

"Wow, I can't believe you remembered that, Bella. I'm so proud of you!" Kira turns to me with a look of surprise in her eyes. "She said 'my white duck' in French."

"She learns *fast,*" I say with a nod. I wish I could pick up a new language that easily.

I walk up to the edge to get a better view. Bella sprays a big handful of peas out onto the water, and they all hit like fat, little raindrops. The geese and swans rush over to us to gobble them all up. Bella giggles like crazy.

Suddenly, I smell a waft of blooming jasmine and feel a nudge at my waist. It's Kira, sunglasses atop her head. She pulls my hand to her. I can feel the warmth radiating from her palms. She floods mine with cold pellets, but it's hard to concentrate on the peas because I'm arrested by her fern-colored eyes. I've never seen them *this* close before. They're absolutely striking.

I swear that her smile stops my heart just for a moment.

"Some for you," she says innocently. But I am lost, tumbling like a spaceman through a cosmos of green, enveloped by the intoxicating scent of her jasmine perfume as it fills my senses.

She is springtime incarnate, in all of its blooming glory, brightening such a long, dark winter.

Kira turns to the water, and finally, her spell over me is broken. I feel breathless. My heart races in my chest, and a blazing warmth washes over me like I've just run a summer marathon in ten sweaters.

She has an effortless intensity that draws me to her like nothing I've ever felt.

I suck in the cold air of the woods, feeling the blood in my body slink south below my belt. It's been less than half an hour, and I'm already grateful for the length of this coat.

I throw my handful of peas over to the white duck, and the whole squawking flock chases them like their lives depend on it. But my mind is elsewhere, floating down this rushing river, savoring the electric buzz coursing through me and clinging to the fading scent of her sweet floral perfume.

31

Kira

I dip my fries two at a time into a pool of ketchup and devour them. I haven't had a *proper* meal in almost a month. Everything I've eaten has been microwaved from a frozen state, with the exception of my vast array of dried soups. Fortunately, I found an Asian Market in Orange that carries a bevy of flavors that the chain stores don't, so it keeps me from getting bored with the same ol' dull flavors. You can't go wrong with a pack of noodles and powder for a dollar twenty-nine. Although, I shudder to think about my sodium levels. Thank God I can't afford health insurance right now, or else I'd probably have to face some harsh dietary facts about myself.

"This is Bella's favorite place to go out to eat," Eric says.

Every time I look at him, I feel his golden-brown gaze on me in a way that makes every cell of my body feel *alive*.

There is so much about him that excites me. He's the whole package, from his thick, effortless-looking waves to his intense stare, to his muscular build and those manly hands…

Oh God, I've pictured those hands on every inch of my body. Touching me. Pleasing me.

I find myself lost in a momentary fantasy every time I look in his direction, however short.

"This place is *deeeeee-lish. Huh-huh-huh,* I love all the burgers here, but this one is my favorite," Bella points down to the mess on her plate.

"Thank you for inviting me to lunch," I say to both of them.

"What do you say to that, Ella-Bella?" But Eric's eyes never stray from mine. I feel my face bloom with a slow, simmering heat as I blush.

"It's our pleasure." Bella smiles at me.

"Wow, I am stuffed," I mutter, dabbing my mouth with the cloth napkin before laying it beside my empty basket.

"Yay! You're done! Ree-Ree, do the hand thing with me!" Bella is abuzz with renewed energy.

"No, this is too nice of a restaurant for that."

Eric snorts as if the concept is ridiculous. I realize that what I consider classy is 'slumming it' to him.

"What's the *hand thing?*" he asks.

"*Pleeeeease,* Miss Kira!" Behind her, expensive yachts bob in the undulating waters of the Long Island Sound as a cold, late-winter wind whips at the marina.

I sigh. "*Fine.*" I pretend that she's won, but secretly I fucking *love* this game. It brings out my competitive side.

"You're top," Bella says.

"I'm always top. If I were bottom, that means I'd have to smack you, and I don't think you could handle the bit from these twenty-four-inch pythons," I joke and flex my arms comically like Hogan.

Eric and Bella giggle almost in unison.

I hold both hands flat in the air, side-by-side, palms down. Her tiny hands are beneath mine, hovering two inches away, palms up. I stare into her little eye.

"Do your *worst*, Squirt," I taunt.

I can feel Eric's searing gaze out of the corners of my eyes. Bella studies my face, staring as if all of the answers she could ever need will be projected on my face.

But they won't. I have no tell.

Her hands jerk out from under mine, swing over, and attempt to wallop the backs of my hands.

I pull away just in time. Never once looking down, using only my periphery. My unblinking eyes are locked on her precious, giggling face.

"Dang it!" she exclaims, and I see Eric's chest bob with amused laughter. "*Huh-huh,* okay, your turn."

"No." I shake my head. "I can't strike a child, Bella. You have no idea what kind of *power* these guns are capable of."

"Fine. *Huh-huh-huh,* I want to see you play dad, then."

"What?" Eric and I ask in unison.

"Your dad couldn't handle my speed."

"Whoa, shots fired!" Eric snickers.

"Plus, he's got a handicap right now. I could hurt him." I can see the smile fade from his lips for a brief moment before returning.

"*One-handed,*" he growls playfully. "Right now. Let's go."

"Pfffft, that's not the game!" A group of people at the next table look over at us, and I offer an apologetic smile.

"Sure it is. Put one hand behind your back, and the playing field's even," Eric mutters confidently.

"Yeah!" Bella squeals with delight.

"You're both making a mockery of this game." I laugh.

Eric turns toward the open seat next to him and motions to it with his free hand. Suddenly, I feel another flash of heat rip across my face.

"Naw, I can't strike my boss." I wave him away.

Bella makes a chicken sound and flaps her bent arms like wings, calling me out.

"It's Saturday. You work for me Monday through Friday. You're not on the clock. I must insist you put your money where your mouth is and accept the duel." His right hand extends, and he has a smug look of satisfaction beneath his finely groomed beard.

"What are you a gunslinger now? Is this high noon?"

Bella laughs, and I'm positive she has no clue what we are talking about, but she's deriving joy from it nonetheless. "Alright, if you *insist*." I scooch out of my seat and shift to the seat next to him.

I can smell his cologne from where I'm sitting. My folded knee accidentally touches his as I settle into the chair, and his eyes flash at me like a bolt of lightning the moment our extremities make contact. His gaze pierces me before returning to his daughter.

"Care to make a wager on who will be the victor, young lady?" He asks Bella from across a cold, empty plate with nothing but an untouched slice of tomato and a balled-up napkin.

"Yes, *huh-huh-huh.*" She twitches as she contemplates. "The loser has to pay me, *huh-huh-huh-huh,* ten dollars to go play the claw game."

I laugh. "Hey! That's not fair, I don't have two *nickels* to rub together, and your dad has, like, a *quadrillion* bucks."

She judders with laughter until she hiccups. "There's no such thing as a *quadrillion bucks.*"

She suddenly reminds me of Cassandra for a moment, and I can feel a broad smile spread across my face.

"You seein' this?" I look at Eric and point to Bella. "This is like a mafia shake-down or something. I feel like I'm on *The Sopranos* right now. I'm gonna start calling her Tony."

He tries to fight another bout of laughter at his daughter's silly chuckle. "Sounds like someone's afraid she might *lose*."

I gasp theatrically. "Alright, game on!" I extend my left hand, palm facing up. "This isn't even fair. We're both righties, but now I gotta play *leftie*."

"Excuses, excuses. I'm sorry I didn't need surgery on my other arm." Even though he's teasing, Eric has a softness to him when he's around Bella. It's sort of heartwarming.

"I feel like I am about to play *Miss Suzie,*" I joke.

"Oh my God! *Miss Suzie!*" He shakes his head, and his waves of coffee-brown hair bounce with it.

"What's *Miss Suzie?*" Bella cocks her little head to the side like a cocker spaniel.

Without another word, Eric claps his hand into his lap and then against mine in some painfully awkward, single-handed rendition of the children's game. In unison, we chant:

"Miss Suzie had a steamboat, the steamboat had a bell. Miss Suzie went to heaven, the steamboat went to hell-o operator, please give me number nine, and if you disconnect me, I'll kick you from behind... the 'frigerator, there sat a piece of glass, Miss Suzie sat upon it, and cut her little ask...me no more questions—"

We can't continue anymore because Bella is giggling so hard that her face has gone beet red. She looks like she's about to have a coronary.

I whip my hand away. "Enough distractions! Let me *school you* so you can pay your daughter."

180

"Will you," Bella laughs until she chokes a little, "teach me that song?" She's laid sideways across the chairs, face swollen and dark from all the laughter. Another violent hiccup attacks her.

"That's up to your *dad*. I don't want to be responsible for corrupting your young mind."

Eric's face softens with his genuine smile, but his eyes, on mine, don't seem to blink. They have a brilliant sheen, like foil, twinkling in the light of the stylish overhead fixture full of bulbs.

"Ready?" he asks.

For a moment, I forget what he's even asking about, though the answer would be a resounding *yes* to anything he could ask me right now.

I have no clue how this gorgeous man is still single.

His flattened hand fills the space between us. I hold out my palm again, tucking my right arm behind my back. I study his hands for a moment, hands I imagined roaming my body several nights this week as I wore down my last pack of AA batteries.

His eyes are too distracting, so I stare at his lips instead. Still, when the hint of a smile creeps upon them, I feel another surge of warmth rip through my body like a tornado, leaving hot gooseflesh in its wake.

Like the crack of a whip, my fingers slap the back of his hand, and I look up at him apologetically, surprised that he didn't even flinch.

181

He pulls his hand away and shakes it. "Yowza!"

"Dad, you're terrible at this! You're supposed to pull away!" She giggles to herself, rolling on her back in the seat of two side-by-side chairs.

"Sorry, I was distracted," he says, but the low volume of it and the unflinching gaze tells me that the comment wasn't meant for Bella. It was meant for me. My pulse throbs, and my heart drums hard in my chest.

Bella's giggles fill the restaurant with the innocent sounds of pure elation that only a child can make. She slides from the chairs onto the floor.

"Best two out of three?" he asks quietly.

I shake my head and feel heat touch every inch of me like ink poured into water.

"Well, fair's fair, I suppose. Time for me to pay up," Eric smiles.

Bella pops up beside him like a curious gopher, and he feigns surprise at her sudden presence. She holds her hand out. "Money, please." The politeness of the demand is adorable. Then, she says, "When will you learn, Dad? The house always wins!"

We erupt into laughter. Eric hands her a crisp bill, shaking his head all the while. As she races off to the claw game with the cash in her hand, he leans in toward me. "I don't think she knows what that means."

I feel myself blushing at the closeness of our bodies as his eyes meet mine again.

After an electrified moment of silence, Eric finally speaks again. "What are you doing for the rest of the day?"

I'm taken aback by the question. *"Apartment shopping,"* I say with reluctance.

I hate apartment shopping with a passion. The places I want are always just out of my price range, and what I can *afford* feels like it would be a perfect set for an indie horror movie.

On Thursday, after I left Eric's house, I had my Realtor acquaintance show me a place in downtown Bridgeport. I opened a dishwasher in a second-story unit only to watch a horde of German cockroaches scatter in the light. I took a 45-minute piping-hot shower afterward and had nightmares of insects crawling on me.

Hard pass.

"You're moving?"

I nod solemnly. "Have to. My roommate is getting married next week."

"Oh, you didn't request any time off."

"I'm not going. Destination wedding. They didn't even ask. She knew I couldn't afford the ticket. But I have to be out soon. Hubby's moving in with her after the honeymoon, and they don't want a third wheel."

"Oh. Sorry to hear that." His face has gone very serious. "Are you staying in *Connecticut?*"

I feel his gaze fall to my bent leg, the one that has been touching his knee since I sat down.

183

The one I haven't had the balls to move for fear of drawing more attention to it.

"Oh yeah," it occurs to me that his expression might be one of fear that I might be *leaving*, "although I may not be able to stay in Bridgeport. Rent is getting *outrageous* there."

"Property taxes are the highest in the state there, I hear. It's double most of the other counties."

"Why?! Who wants to live in *Bridgeport*? I don't even want to live in Bridgeport."

He laughs. "Indeed. That *is* the baffling question."

After a pause, he straightens his posture, glances at Bella as she drops another stuffie from the claw and grimaces, and then looks back at me. "You should blow it off and come spend the afternoon with me." He traces the textured jean seam on my calf with a rugged finger.

I know it's an innocent touch, but I feel like I almost can't *breathe*. The excitement has me seized. Finally, I take a deep breath and say, "And do *what*, exactly?"

I can't believe I'm entertaining this idea. I really need to look for a place. And the longer I'm around him, the more I just want to tackle him and shred his clothes like a wolverine.

Fuck. Don't do it, Kira. You cannot lose this job.

My inner voice is right. I have no parental home to grovel back to. I have no living siblings to fall back on. I have no savings to speak of,

184

and my vehicle is knocking like an unwanted house guest.

If I fuck this up, I could be *wishing* for the Ramen noodle life. I could be waiting in line to eat my fucking noodles out of the goddamned Bridgeport *soup kitchen* like that crazed vagrant who wears a fake preacher costume and screams bible verses like they're obscenities.

"Well, Bella spends every Saturday night with her *Babcia*. Mom says it's because she wants me to have time to get out and go 'do adult things.'" He smiles and removes his hand, bolting up straight with an apologetic look in his eyes for touching my jeans. "Sorry."

I want to tell him it's fine, that I want him touching me, but I'm blushing, and it all comes out as a messy 'no worries' wave.

"I was thinking, instead of sitting around at home like I usually do, maybe we could go do something... *fun*."

"Like what?" I'm intrigued.

"Well, I have an *idea*, but I'd rather keep you on your toes. It's something I haven't done for a long time. But it's a bit of a drive."

There is a long silence between us.

Finally, he says, "*Come on.* You can still look for apartments tomorrow. This'd be so much more fun if I didn't have to go alone."

I smile at him, heavily debating whether to be mature and deal with my responsibilities head-on or whether I should throw caution to the wind and go on an adventure...

185

I'm not known for caution and foresight.

"I still have to pack." I protest quietly.

"I'll tell you what. If you go out with me tonight, I'll pay for a professional mover service for you."

My eyes widen. I think for a moment. "Is this excursion... *expensive?* Because, if so — "

He leans in near my ear. I can smell his cologne and feel the brush of his soft, trimmed facial hair against my smoldering cheek, stoking the coals beneath the surface until they burn hot again.

His voice is a mix between a pleading whisper and an order. "*Say yes.*"

I'm thankful that I have this chair to hold me up. The soft force of his demand has me melting like ice cream in the summer sun.

The throbbing pressure between my legs intensifies to an almost painful level.

"Say... *yes.*" He whispers again, quieter yet with even more dominance.

I can barely find my voice.

"*Yes.*"

32

Kira

Good lord, his mother's home is massive, too, though not *quite* as grandiose as Eric's. I doubt this place has a humidor and basketball court, but it feels equally impressive as we drive up to her gate. Eric punches in the gate code, and the gate swings open on its automatic motor, allowing us to roll up the driveway.

It isn't until I help Bella out of her car seat that it finally dawns on me that the Tesla we are in is maroon with a metallic sheen.

"Did you get the car painted?"

Eric laughs. "No. This is just the purple one."

I'm stunned by the admission. "How many of these do you *have?*"

Suddenly, Bella wraps her arms around me like a little monkey.

"Three." He pulls her scuffed suitcase out of the back seat and extends the handle. "Three Teslas and a Rolls."

"And the Rivian," Bella adds. "Dad says I can have the Rivian when I'm old enough."

I want to faint. I'm unable to comprehend what it must be like to have even *one* properly working vehicle.

"You know, when *I* was sixteen, my uncle bought me a gutted Taurus from the junkyard for six hundred bucks and made me put a new transmission in it before I could drive it."

"You're probably a lot handier than I am beneath the hood, then," Eric says. He seems impressed.

"That was ten years ago. Plus, fat-lotta good it does me *these* days." I feel a flush of embarrassment overwhelm me. For twenty-six, I should really have *my shit together* more than I do.

"*Halo!*" an older woman shouts from the doorway in a coordinated pink and white outfit, arms open wide. Her Eastern European accent is thick.

"*Babcia!*" Bella screams as she peels away from me. She snatches up Sernik's tiny travel carrier from my hand, the one shaped like an adorable little school bus with a tiny water bottle, and races toward the tiny, older woman.

"*Halo, my baby, Bellaaaaaa,*" her chipper voice is like a song. She hugs her granddaughter with vigor and smiles wide and genuine. She smooths down her short white hair and looks at Eric.

"Hi, Mom." He bends down to kiss her on the top of her head. She's an adorably short woman. Probably a hundred pounds soaking wet. She comes up to Eric's pecs. Surely, he must have gotten his height from his father.

"And who ees *this?* Beautiful!" Her voice is like a cheery songbird warbling.

"Mom, this is my assistant, Kira." He motions to me.

"*Ohhhh*," she says with the flirtatious bob of her white eyebrows.

"*Mom.*" He rolls his eyes like a teenager. "Kira, this is my mother, Zuzanna."

Looking at how put-together this woman is up close, I now feel completely out of place in my jeans, tank top, and blue jean jacket.

"Nice to meet you. This whole time, I thought your name was *Babcia.*" I chuckle nervously.

"*Babcia* mean *grandmother* in Polish," Zuzanna says brightly.

"*Ohhhhhh.*" *Duh.*

"Kira," Zuzanna says my name like *Keeeeeeeee-dah*, "ees so nice to meet you. Are you not freezing?" Her soft hands take mine. She rubs the skin on them lovingly.

"No, ma'am. The cold doesn't bother me."

"You lucky." She laughs.

"Babcia, look! This is Sernik!" Bella shoves her travel carrier right in her grandmother's face, too close to see. "What ees 'dat?" She fights the sudden urge to wince in horror at the rodent.

"*Huh-huh-huh,* he's my new best friend!"

"*Ohhhh*, dat ees nice." Eric's mother flashes her son a glance that says, *why have you brought a pest into this house? Are you nuts?*

Eric makes a tense, apologetic face, and all is quickly forgiven.

"Alright, I take Bella. *Iść.*" She waves Eric back toward the car. "*Go.* I see you tomorrow night for *kolacja.* I make kielbasa with the homemade, uh, *sau-er-kraut.*" She pronounces every syllable precisely and then looks at me. "You welcome to come, too!"

"Oh, thank you so much for the invite, but unfortunately I can't."

She looks at us in slight disappointment, and then a cheery look flashes back across her face. She claps her hands together. "Okay, you go now, because, uh, it is *za zimno.* It ees too *cold.*" With that, she rubs her bare arms and whisks Bella and Sernik inside.

***

We've been in the car for what feels like an hour now, and Eric still won't tell me where we are going. Although I must say, I can't even *remember* the last time I took a long, leisurely drive for *fun.* With my SUV in such disrepair, I don't usually go a single mile further than I have to because I know doing so tempts fate.

The drive has been anything but boring, though. Eric answered a million prying questions I had about his mom.

I was shocked when he told me he bought the mansion for her as a present after he made his millions… sorry, *billions*, with a *B* on a few bold all-ins on the stock market.

He tells me that she loves to clean and refused the maid staff he tried to hire after his father died. She claimed that all of the scrubbing and dusting gave her something to do between her hours toiling away in her home gym and the volunteering she does at the local theater company she's involved in. She strikes me as the theatrical type, even just from our brief interaction.

Half an hour ago, Eric let me sync up my phone to play some music, and I spent the next stretch of eastbound I-95 curating a playlist of all the best songs by Lobo, James Taylor, Olivia Newton-John, and, of course, my favorite, John Denver.

Soon, our path strays from the interstate into a long stretch of wooded, winding roads, the ones that Connecticut is well-known for. They'd be the perfect roads to take in the autumn on a color tour of the foliage.

"Where are we going?" I ask again, hoping this time he'll tell me.

But just like all the other times I've asked, he just says, "You'll see."

And soon enough, I *do* see.

A stunning glass complex comes into view with repeated signs alerting us that we are on tribal territory, and I know *exactly* where we are despite only having been here once.

"A *casino?*" I gasp. Partly out of excitement and the thrill of the afternoon adventure and partly out of absolute *terror.* The peas for the birds this morning wiped out all but three rumpled singles that now sit, wadded in my purse. If I don't gamble, I can use it to give a waitress a dollar tip on a couple of free alcoholic drinks and consider this day a huge win.

"I haven't been here in a while." He stares up at the building, and the light hits his dreamy eyes in a way that makes them dazzling.

"Same," I say, swallowing hard.

"I usually do my gambling on the NASDAQ." He finds amusement in his reference, but I have no clue what that is, frankly. "I'm going to use the valet. Too hard getting in and out of those tight spots with this... *sling*."

He says the word like he's disgusted with the taste of it.

I nod, taking in the moody February sky, casting its steely gray stare down over New England.

Eric pulls the car up to the valet, hands off the keys, and holds his uninjured arm out like a gentleman, waiting for me to take it.

As I slip my hand through the crook, my senses seem to come alive.

I *hear* the coos of the pigeons nearby and the sound of my jacket rustling against his long, woolen coat.

Beneath a layer of gray padding, I can still *feel* the flex of his hardened biceps.

I *see* the skin on his neck, red and irritated from where his arm sling is pulling.

The *aroma* of a fine cigar wafts from nearby like a cooling pie in a cartoon window, mingling with the heavenly scent of his aftershave.

But there is *one sense* that feels wholly neglected. And as I watch him in the ascending elevator, I find myself wondering exactly how his lips might *taste*…

33

Eric

I can't get over the stunned look in Kira's moss-green eyes every time I lay a couple of measly five-hundred-dollar chips down on the blackjack table. They bulge and stare with a look of utter shock.

I flip my cards over and smile.

"Twenty-one." The dealer stares deadpan as he pushes back my initial chips along with another thousand.

"Somehow, I just knew you were going to be my good luck charm," I look at Kira.

There is a smoldering intensity when she looks back, offering an expression of what looks like lust and intrigue. Gone is Bella's silly tutor, the fledgling errand-runner, the retail flunkey.

What is in her eyes now seems serious... *impure*. Her look is as wild as a joker and has my ace standing high.

"Think you can do it again?" She bites her lip and then stirs her drink with its tiny straw, never taking her eyes off of me. The look of her inviting mouth makes it hard to focus.

There hasn't been a night in the last two weeks that I've known her that I haven't gone to sleep without touching myself to the thought of that pretty little mouth.

Or to the rest of her…

I've imagined fucking her in nearly every room, in just about every position I could contort that stunning body in.

Jesus, I'd shove over this entire stack of chips right now just to be inside of her.

To *taste* her on my lips.

To feel her *writhe* in my grasp.

To make her *scream my name.*

She is the type of woman you go to war over.

Kira glances down at the newly dealt cards and rests the straw against her pink tongue for a moment. I swear to God, with everything in me, I want to take her right now on this fucking felt-lined blackjack table in front of everyone.

I wave the flitting waitress behind her down. I need another drink before I do something stupid. "Excuse me, ma'am. Scotch and soda, please."

"And for you?" She sounds as tired as she looks.

"I'll have another one of these, please." Kira waggles her empty cup, clinking the ice around.

The waitress scribbles something on a tiny notepad on her black tray and walks her sequined body out of sight.

"You look nice today, by the way." The way Kira says it out of nowhere stuns me. "You look great in a suit. I don't think I've seen you in one before, except in pictures, like, around your house."

"Thank you." I smile.

If she only knew how long it took me to get into this thing with my shoulder, she'd laugh. I had to have Conchita help me get the jacket on. It was fucking embarrassing.

"You look lovely as well."

That's a hell of an understatement. Sexy as hell would be a far more accurate choice of words…

I place a $500 chip on the table in front of Kira and one in front of myself and smile up at the dealer.

Kira gasps and whispers in my ear. "Oh God, no, Eric, I can't."

Her flowery scent sends another message straight to my dick, arousing it further.

I lean in to whisper back to her, but all I want to do is leave a trail of frenzied kisses down her delicate neck…

"*Relax,*" I finally coo after snapping out of my blissful fantasy.

I swipe a tendril of blonde hair away from the side of her face. She shivers, and I am aroused by the fact that my touch affects her in such a way.

She pushes the coin forward into the designated spot on the felt for bets. I follow suit along with the others at the table, whose faces have long since disappeared into the chaotic background like whispers in the wind.

Kira stares down at her cards like she's studying for her SATs. My thigh brushes against hers beneath the table. Her eyes settle on my face, but I'm too busy watching goosebumps flash across her exposed skin.

She breathes out, slow and deliberate, and raps a closed fist on the table. The dealer deals her another card.

"Twenty," the dealer says, looking at her cards. She signals to stand.

I stand right away.

The dealer busts.

Kira exhales deeply like she's been holding her breath. The dealer shoves over our winnings. She slides the cool grand in chips over to me, and I reject them.

"*Double it,*" I say firmly.

"Excuse me?"

"Double the bet on this round. If you win, you can keep it all."

"What if I *lose*? That's a *thousand* dollars."

"Then you aren't out anything." I smile at her. I could swear her eyes are glassy as if she's fighting off tears.

She looks down at the chips for what feels like forever.

Finally, she slides them into place on the table, and I see her hand tremble.

I double mine, too.

The bored Native American man in the cheap vest deals our cards again. He has fourteen showing. We look at our cards.

After a moment of deliberation, Kira signals to stand with a three showing.

I shake my head. There are so many more cards that could get her to twenty-one than ones that would bust her, but it's her decision.

I hold on my eighteen.

The dealer hits. It's a jack. *Dealer busts.*

The man sighs and shoves our doubled winnings over.

Tears stream from Kira's eyes as she erupts into an emotional mess over the outcome of the hand.

She's reacting as if she lost everything. I'm confused, unsure if I need to explain the rules of the game to her, though her knowledge of the hand signals tells me she understands the game rules just fine.

But.. *why* then?

"*Are you okay?*" I whisper discretely into her ear.

But the tears keep coming.

She acts like relief just swallowed her up. Like she had ten million dollars riding on that hand.

Suddenly, instead of being excited over our respective wins, I feel *horrible* that I've somehow managed to take part in upsetting her. My heart thuds. I don't know why, but all I want to do is scoop her up and hold her until she isn't sad anymore.

"Kira?" I gently tilt her face toward me with my hand and sweep away the wet blonde hair from the sides of her face, wishing I had both arms readily available to comfort her right now. I stroke her cheek softly with my thumb.

"What's wrong?"

"That's just… *so much money.*" As soon as the words come across the threshold of her beautiful, pouting lips, another deep sob escapes her.

I pull her to my chest, feeling her hot tears seep through my Dior shirt. A moment later, the waitress returns with our drinks, setting them on the wood panel in front of us. The woman stares at me expectantly.

I reach into my wallet and fish out a fifty, hand it to her, and mouth *keep it*. Her expression brightens and she trots off.

I tip Kira's chin up with a bent finger and gaze into her mascara-muddled eyes.

I have never wanted to kiss a woman so much in my goddamned *life*.

I'm trying *so hard* to behave, to not get caught up in some complicated, regrettable web of feelings…

But she just looks so fucking beautiful. I'm drawn like a man in a rowboat to a beckoning siren.

"Hey, let's go take a walk, yeah?" I say, allowing the angel on my shoulder to win. The devil on the other is having a shit-fit.

She pulls away, and I feel like my heart is vacating my chest, along with her dissipating warmth. She wipes the smudged makeup from her eyes and nods.

"I am so sorry," she says apologetically before grabbing her drink and shoving all of her chips over to me. "And... I don't deserve these. This isn't my money."

Without another word of argument, I collect her winnings and deliberately place the acrylic circles in her trembling palm. I smile and toast to her with my drink, but I almost feel too lost in her tear-filled eyes to take a sip.

34

Eric

We shuffle slowly through the connective mall between the two main casinos. It's a spacious two-story area with haughty retail shops along the ground level. In the middle of the breezeway sits a monumental two-story glass sculpture, as fragile as it is bizarre with its many vibrant squiggles and curves. If Dr. Seuss could blow glass, I'm sure his creations would look something like this eyesore.

Escalators lead up to a second floor that looks like it's carved out of faux rock walls. From where we are standing, I can see three separate indoor waterfalls, each substantially bigger than the real one at the duck pond we were at this morning.

The upper tier of the mall is dotted with steakhouses and sushi restaurants, and there is a gap between them leading to the concierge desk of the high-end, attached hotel.

The thought of the hotel being so near to us sends a wave of warmth through my torso, down to my groin. I want to be in one of the rooms with Kira right now, feeling her stunning curves against my fingertips. Hearing her moan my name in a quiet room, save for the breathy affirmations and growled expletives uttered in ecstasy. I want to taste her. I want to take her breath away and leave her grasping at the covers like it is her only tether to this earthly plane. I want to be inside of her, watching the color of her face flush with her arousal as she settles down over my cock.

I want to make her orgasm and shudder...

And dive back in for more until I drown in her...

Until she begs me for *mercy*.

Even though we are here in this breezeway, staring at this atrocious glass monstrosity that people seem to be photographing like *art*, I feel so good in her presence. It's peaceful. I'm not certain why, but I feel like she never *expects* anything from me. She doesn't seem interested in my money even though she has less than anyone I know.

She reminds me of how things used to be with women long ago before I gambled wild and made a literal fortune in a hyper-volatile stock market bubble.

That time and those decisions changed the course of my life forever. They put me on Forbes lists and shot me into a wild world of fundraising causes, gourmet restaurants, private jets, and stuffy business luncheons with celebrities and thousand-dollar bottles of wine.

Yet, I had more fun eating dive bar burgers and feeding friggin' *ducks* with her today than I have with *any* of those things.

"Can I ask you a question?" Staring up at the glass sculpture, she licks at the chocolate-cherry-loaded cone in her hand. I swear I've never wanted to be something inanimate so bad in my *life*.

"Sure. Shoot." I swirl the last ice cube around in my glass that once held scotch and soda, fidgeting with it to keep from staring as that talented tongue of hers makes quick work of the frozen milk and sugar.

"What was your ex-wife like? Tawny? That's Bella's mom, right?"

"Yes, she is, unfortunately." The question takes me a little off-guard.

I nod and motion for her to follow me. All the people gathering on this bridge to see the sculpture make me feel antsy. I stroll toward a giant rock wall with a forty-foot-wide fountain of water cascading down the face of it from two stories up. I hope that its volume will mask how hard my heart is drumming in my chest when I'm watching her savor the dripping cream. I feel like a savage animal, ready to tear her clothes off at the first hint of a green light.

No. No damn green lights, Eric. You do not need that kind of drama right now! You have enough going on. The last thing you need is some sexual harassment suit to wipe you out or fuck up your chances at the custody hearing. One

203

word breathed to the wrong lawyer, and she's rich from your money. Think about it. If she claimed you took advantage, it'd be your word against hers.

But looking at her in front of me and thinking back through the days she spent with Bella and me, I can't *fathom* a world in which this woman would be able to do something so heinous.

"Hey-o, earth to Eric." She's waving at me with a bright smile gracing her lovely face. Maybe it's the way she's looking at me. Maybe it's the booze mixed with the lack of food. Maybe it's that I haven't talked about it with anyone. But for a moment, I'm softened, pliable enough to talk about Tawny.

"We met a little over a decade ago. We were both right around twenty and in college. She was nice enough. She seemed interesting. Smart. Driven. It wasn't long after we started dating before she gave me the news that Bella was on the way."

I lower my voice. "It was an accident, but I'd *never,* ever tell Bella that. As far as she knows, we planned her." I lean back against the railing, feeling an aerosolized spray of water moistening my skin from the waterfall behind me.

"A few months after Bella came along, she became very distant. Cold, even. Said she never really wanted to be a mom."

I laugh at the irony, but there is pain behind it. I think about the fucking custody paperwork she just had me served with and grind my teeth.

"The years went by, and she all but disappeared from our lives. I feel like she was *weaning* us. *Preparing* us for what was to come."

I hear the crunch of waffle cone and look over to see those green eyes staring at me, enthralled.

I want to freeze time at this moment. She's not like anyone I've ever met before. She's fun. Layered. She's tough as nails but cries when she wins at blackjack…

"Don't leave me hanging!" She looks like her favorite show just blinked to black during a power surge, at the best part.

"Alright, well, one day, I came back from a meeting with Rob. We usually meet up in New Rochelle for lunch to talk about clients and stuff once a week or so. I get back, and… she's nowhere to be found." I point with a flattened hand at nothing. "But her cell phone's there. So, at first, I'm just going around the house and property looking for her. I thought maybe she'd gone for a walk or fallen asleep in the pool house or something. Hours go by, I bring Bella home, and we both scour this time. *Nothing*."

I wish I could fold my arms angrily. God *damn* this stupid sling.

"That night, I called the police. Now, we were expecting, like, foul play or something. I

205

was really fucking terrified. Especially because right around that same time, there was that whole Jennifer Dulos thing…"

Riveted, she nods, wiping the crumbs off of her hands.

"Cops come. They look around. They file a report… and that's it. For *weeks,* I was going around putting up posters. We organized a fucking search party."

My cheeks are enflamed from my embarrassment recanting this. I can feel them burning.

"I went on a local *TV show* looking for her." I exhale long and hard through my nose, greatly annoyed by the memory. "Turns out, she just… ran away."

"She *what?* Like a *teenager?*"

"Thank you! That's what I said! Yes, exactly like a fucking bratty little teenager." I nod. "She ran off to fucking *Tampa,* of all places. Someone finally found her in a literal *tent*, camped out on the sidewalk outside a Best Buy."

"What? Why?!"

"She said something about how it was the only place she could find to charge her phone." I shake my head. My legs restlessly bobble with nervous energy. "Her *new* phone."

The appalled expression slathered on Kira's face makes me feel settled. *Validated.* Like she truly can somehow fathom the level of stress and embarrassment Tawny caused us. Even through it all, there isn't a single hint of judgment in her eyes. I adore that she is so… *understanding.*

She *listens.*

She *cares.*

I *never* had that with Tawny, not even in the beginning. Hell, as time goes on, I can't remember what actually drew me to that woman in the first place.

"I just don't get how anyone with a kid could do that," she says, voice dripping with compassion.

"I don't either. She said she wanted to start a new life. To, quote-unquote, *find herself.* She didn't leave a note. I found out she was still alive when one of my clients was in Tampa for work. He texted me. Happened to be in the right place at the right time and recognized her from a charity fundraiser we'd been a part of a while back. For, like, two months, I thought she was kidnapped or dead. I lost about thirty-five pounds. I wasn't eating. I barely slept. We'd combed the fields around the estate…"

"What? God, Eric, that's horrible!" She shakes her head. "What'd you do when you found out she was camping out down there?"

"I dropped Bella off with my mom and had the private jet fly me down immediately. Begged her to come home. I felt like a fucking *jackass* when she refused. She said she couldn't go back. Not to being a wife, or a mother, or to the cold. She said it all made her feel dead inside, which, a marriage and home is one thing, but… how do you even *think* that about your own child?"

I fill my eyes well with tears, but I grind my teeth hard to keep them at bay.

"Pfft, Bella's mom could almost give *mine* a run for her money in the crazy department." Kira leans up against the railing to my right. It's strange, but the fact that I can feel the heat radiating from her in such a vast space brings me comfort.

"So what happened with all of that?" She asks.

I can feel her eyes peering up at me. Still, the impending tears threatening to fall from my own keep them darting around the mammoth space between the tee-pee-inspired tented ceiling and that god-awful glass sculpture.

"Well, she was Baker-Acted. They put her through a 72-hour hold and a psych evaluation, the whole nine. They recommended medication and let her walk right on out after a couple of days. She stayed down there for months. Met some asshole who owns one of those new-age crystal shops with the damn sage and tarot cards and all that. I thought it was some sort of weird phase she might snap out of one day, but later, she served me with divorce papers, and, to be honest, I couldn't sign them fast enough."

This raw, open wound still stings, even to this day. I think about the newest packet of pain she recently served me with, and it makes me *furious*.

My errant gaze finally steadies on the buffed polish of the floor tiles. "This week, she filed for sole custody. She wants to move Bella down to Florida."

"What?! *Why?*"

"I don't know. It doesn't make any sense. She fled to get *away* from that kind of responsibility. Now she wants it again?"

Goddammit, I just want to break *something.*

I take a deep breath and hold it for what feels like forever before finally exhaling.

"Maybe she's just doing it to hurt me. Or maybe she's actually had a change of heart. I don't fucking know."

I swallow hard.

Do not cry.

Do you hear me? Do NOT fucking cry!

After a moment of reverent silence, I feel Kira's warm hand slide into my palm, fingers clasping around mine. Her other hand wraps around my bicep. She lays her head against my shoulder.

Even though the gesture is simple, her wordlessly hugging my arm while holding my hand…

It's the most comforting thing I've ever felt in my entire life.

35

Kira

"Go twenty-three, go twenty-three, go twenty-three!" I chant, rising up from my seat at the video roulette table.

Beside me, Eric laughs. "It's a *cold* number, Kira."

"So what? It's my *lucky* number." I roll my shoulders back and stare at the spinning wheel on the screen. "And, okay, sure, whatever. It's a *cold number.* That means, I think, *statistically*, it's likely to come up again *sooner* than the others." I look at him and smile. "Although, I never took a course in statistics, so…" I shrug and make a fart noise with my mouth.

Eric laughs, shaking his head as the screen flashes the number fifteen, and takes my money.

I groan and put yet another $3 minimum bet on number twenty-three. "C'mon, baby. This time, you got it." I caress my kiosk.

Eric waves down another waitress. They've been on us like flies on dung for the last hour after Eric chummed the waters with a rather obscene tip with one. I suck down the last of my bloody Mary just as Eric mouths to her, *'Another round, please.'*

210

She nods, U-turns, and diligently swishes toward the bar, anxious for the prize awaiting her upon her return.

"Go twenty-three, go twenty-three." I rise again from my seat out of the sheer intensity. The payout, if it hits, would mean groceries for a *month*.

Eric is amused by watching me as he plays through several rounds of video blackjack at his kiosk for the maximum five hundred dollars per hand.

I see the word BUST spread across the middle of his screen, and cool-as-a-cucumber, he maxes his bet again.

The red number seven splays across the large video screen in front of the gaggle of us degenerate gamblers.

I sigh. It bleeds into a whiny groan. "Right color, wrong number."

I hesitate over the $1 button again, debating whether or not I should bet again. I'm almost down a *hundred dollars* from the money Eric insisted on me keeping from the blackjack table in the other casino.

I lean back in my seat and look around, desperate for another drink to take my mind off the stinging loss.

"You're not going to bet again?" Eric places a hand on the back of my chair, rubbing my spine with his thumb. I am suddenly only aware of his touch despite the carnival of lights and barrage of noises around us.

"Nope." I shake my head and noisily suck the last of the liquid from the bottom of my glass with the tiny straw until there is no more to be had. "You're right. Twenty-three is ice cold. I'm just wasting money on it."

"But you *believe* in it, right? You believe it will hit?"

"*Eventually,*" I shrug, still thinking about his gentle touch on my back. I fight the urge to lean into his hand, eyes shut like a purring kitten, which is all I want to do right now. It reminds me how much I always long to be touched, especially lovingly.

"You're not gonna bet?"

I shake my head and fold my arms, subtly leaning back into his hand. "Sittin' this round out."

No more bets flashes across the screen, and that little white ball flies around the checkered ring, bouncing in and out of spots until it finally settles...

In...

Twenty-three.

What in the ever-loving f —

I spent *one hundred dollars* chasing that elusive little slot, all to have it *hit* the very first time that I didn't bet.

I jump out of my chair and hold my head. "Are you shitting me?"

Eric laughs and then attempts to disguise his smile with a more serious expression.

"Is this real life?! What the HELL?" My eyes are wide with horror, mouth agape.

Eric chuckles again, and his face is pink from trying to hold it back. "I swear I'm not laughing at you. Just… the situation."

His screen flashes, 'Dealer has 21,' and I watch another five hundred dollars disappear from his balance. He doesn't care one bit that he just lost a hand worth half my rent.

The waitress arrives with our drinks, and I'm sad when Eric's hand slinks away from me. I take my drink with a smile, sucking down half in one big sip out of frustration.

Eric tips her with a twenty from his breast pocket.

"Good luck," she says before scuttling off.

I growl quietly as she walks away. "Yeah, where was that '*good luck*' five minutes ago?" I'm fuming.

Just then, Eric starts feeding crisp hundred-dollar bills into my machine.

Three of them, to be exact.

"Eric! What're you *doing?!*" I try to stop him, but he brushes my hand away gently. In a flash, he switches the chip denomination to one hundred, then pounds his finger down on the number twenty-three several times.

No more bets flashes across the screen again.

"*Are you insane?*" I whisper as loud as I can, settling back down into my seat. Seeing three hundred dollars riding on *one* number that *just* hit makes me think I might actually vomit.

213

"Do you believe in twenty-three," he asks.

I nod with reluctance. "…But it's not going to hit again twice in a row!"

"*Do you believe in twenty-three?*" He repeats.

"Yes."

"Good. You believed in twenty-three, so you bet on it." He smiles. The golden rings in his irises refract the display of shimmering LEDs all around us. "Now I'm bettin' on *you.*"

The way he says it makes me smile. His words are like warm honey, coursing through me. The ball makes its dizzying odyssey around the spinning wheel and tumbles into the grooves, bouncing through reds, blacks, and greens until finally landing in…

"*Red, twenty-three.*"

I can't breathe. The animated icon on my screen pops up, and the winnings beneath it spin as the number inflates.

It finally stops…

At $10,500.

I really think I might be sick right now.

"I knew you were a good luck charm," he says, slapping his free hand on the kiosk with excitement, but I can't hear anything over the sounds of my joyous internal scream.

Is this real freaking life?

Eric cashes out the voucher and waggles it between two fingers at me. "Please, don't quit now that you're flush with cash. I still very much need you."

Quit? Is he serious right now? I don't know what to say. I can *not* accept it. I didn't *earn* it.

"I can't take that," I say, swallowing hard to keep the bloody Mary down. "I can't."

I can't, but my God, that is an insane amount of money. Why is he being so nice to me?

"Of course you can." He stuffs the rectangle of white paper into my palm. "...But dinner's on *you* tonight."

I laugh. My vision's flooded with tears again. I feel lightheaded. I can't tell if it's from the vodka, the voucher in my hand, or the way Eric's eyes are lingering on mine.

He stands, pressing the button to cash out the remainder on his own machine, which is surprisingly close to his starting balance.

"*Mmmm.* I could *really* go for something to eat right now," he mutters. His leisurely gaze trails up my body, and suddenly, I'm not so sure he's talking about dinner...

36

Eric

The waitress sets the check in between platters with leftover ginger and wasabi from the rolls of sushi Kira annihilated. I watched with intense fascination, savoring my single spicy tuna roll and two pieces of sashimi.

Despite it being one of my favorite foods, I couldn't bring myself to eat much. Although I seem calm, *inside,* my nerves are a jangled mess.

All I've wanted to do all day is kiss the hell out of her.

There are a million reasons that I *shouldn't.* Besides the fact that she's proved to be a surprisingly decent assistant and is phenomenal with Bella, I don't want her to think that she is somehow *indebted* to me between work and today's outing.

I don't want her to want me out of *fear.*

But God damn, I *do* want her to *want* me.

This woman brought laughter back into my sphere. She brought *life* into my quiet home, resuscitating it from its damn near flatline state. She's brought my daughter out of her shell in a way that's meant the world to me.

And my God, she is fucking stunning.

Her casual, goofy personality is the *yin* to my stolid *yang*. I am absolutely dreading the moment that she says she wants me to take her home.

I don't want this day to end.

Kira reaches for the check, and I scoff, gently swatting her hand away. I pluck it off the table.

Her shoulders slump. "What the heck? You said I was buying dinner!"

"Kira, that was a *joke*."

The bill is a pittance, less than a hundred bucks. I place three fifties atop the receipt and struggle to get my wallet back in my pocket with this stupid sling in the way. Once I do, I stand and hold out a bent arm for her to take.

"Thank you for dinner," she says, taking it.

"Of *course*."

"I was so excited you suggested it. I haven't had sushi in *forever*. I was just surprised when you picked this place. People are always so love-hate about it."

"It's an acquired taste," I say, locking my gaze on her elegant face.

She gives me a strange look for a moment as if she is surprised by the comment. She shakes it away and moans, "Mmmmm, that hit the spot."

Dear God, I want to make her moan again...

Just like that.

Blush radiates across her porcelain-smooth cheeks as if she can hear my thoughts. I whisk her through the path between the cramped tables, and we make our way out to the second-story balcony rail.

I lean against it, soaking in the view before us. Vivid indigo lights are splashed across the rock wall where I bared my baggage to Kira earlier. The whoosh of the dueling waterfalls on either side of us calms my racing heart. Something about her touch makes it feel like it is about to beat out of my chest.

Kira turns to me, dangerously close. I'm in awe, drinking in her natural beauty. The gentle indigo-kissed waves of her wheat-colored tresses frame her face like something out of an oil painting, one I'd pay a million dollars to hang in my bedroom. I'd love for that to be the last image I see before drifting off to sweet slumbers.

Her green eyes stare up at me. She starts to speak and then stops herself.

"What?" The word is paired with the most nervous laugh I've ever emitted in my life. I try to ignore the fact that my body feels like it's vibrating from standing so close to her.

She finally speaks.

"This is the best day I've had… in *such* a long time."

She means it. The way she says it removes any possibility of doubt in my mind.

There's a zen-like calmness about her right now. Like she is Gaia, and I'm a raging storm, thundering with nervous energy. The wild juxtaposition right now in our temperaments is ridiculous.

I feel myself inching toward her like I'm being sucked into her orbit without a choice.

My head says I should stop now. It screams that it's not too late to go home to fully salvage our professional relationship. It yells that it's time to call it a night so loud that it echoes back in my own head.

But something within me is hitting the override button on all logic. Something that urgently insists that if I don't kiss her, I'll regret it 'til the day I die.

I don't know who to listen to.

I feel her lean in toward me, too.

I watch my hand as it touches her. As if it's no longer responding to my commands. It's as if it has direct orders from someone higher up.

A swath of red blooms across the skin of her chest, and my cock throbs at the thought of her body being so affected by me.

She stares wordlessly as my thumb caresses her luscious, pink lips.

Lips I just *have* to taste...

I catch the smallest glimpse of her glistening tongue through the darkness, and I can't take it anymore. As I press my mouth to hers, all of my senses come *alive* at once, as if I can feel all of my synapses firing simultaneously.

This is *reckless*.

This is *impulsive*.

This is what Heaven must feel like.

A rush of oxytocin floods my veins like a drug I could blissfully overdose on, and the scent of jasmine is absolutely driving me *wild*.

I feel her press back against me, eager mouth parting. Her tongue is fantastic and bears the faintest taste of the fruit-filled sangria we enjoyed with dinner.

It's just as I feared…

I want *more* of her.

I want all of her.

I trace a finger down her neck to her sternum. I can feel her heart thudding like the bass beat at a nightclub beneath skin and bone. Her flesh is like a furnace, burning beneath my touch.

Kira's hands brush against my beard, wrap around my head, and pull me close. I want to collapse into her arms.

I feel my heart vacate my chest as her lips tear away from mine. I'm breathless, struggling to stand upright. The spinning vortex I'm in spits me out, and I am left with the sobering reality before me.

What the fuck have you just done, Eric?!

At this moment, I feel lost and spiraling. I want all of her. The need is worse than ever. Every cell in my body is suddenly longing for her touch.

But, to my surprise, she hasn't pulled away completely. The smile on her face could bring a man to his knees.

She speaks a single sentence quietly, her voice like the pianissimo overture for the most moving symphony the human ear could ever hear...

"*Didn't you say this casino has a hotel attached?*"

37

Kira

The seven minutes we spend waiting for a room card at the decked-out concierge station feel like an absolute eternity. My cheeks feel like they are beet-red, and I feel like I could climb the fucking walls waiting for that thin piece of plastic.

Finally, with the room key in tow, we journey down a long, snaking corridor toward a bank of tower elevators that ascend to the suites.

On one side of the corridor is a wall of windows displaying miles of hilly forest bathed in moonlight. The other side of the wide hall is all wall, pulsing with ceiling-mounted canister lights every four feet. They throb in a new, vibrant color before dimming once again to a pleasant, dusky ambient level.

In the middle of our trek down the carpeted path, the lights brighten again, this time in a moody shade of glacier blue.

Eric turns and presses me against the illuminated wall. He stares at me like a sculpture at the Louvre, drinking me in, studying the rhythm of my breath and the flush of desire on my face. The way he is looking at me makes me feel like nothing else around us exists.

His desire at this moment feels like kerosene on my already-raging flame, and I want more of him. *All* of him.

I know that all of this is impulsive and foolish, but my body buzzes at the thought of being ravaged by him. At the thought of being *devoured.*

Every nerve ending in my body is *alive.* This fevered yearning is like nothing I've ever felt before.

"*Are you...*" he can barely get the whisper out, pinning me like a lion would his prey, "*Sure you want to do this?*" He traces the line of my jaw softly with a finger, lips hovering mere inches from mine.

My head finally offers a single nod, eyes wide. It's all I can manage beyond a breathy "*Yes.*"

His lips near my ear, and he says lowly, "*I want you.*" Without another word, his mouth crashes into my neck and presses me into the wall with a force that makes me feel like I am going to faint.

I run my fingers up through his silky waves of hair, and my eyes roll back with pleasure as he kisses my neck.

My breath hitches, and he pulls away with an almost devious half-smile that leaves me without words.

A moment later, I'm dragging him through the thrumming lights down the remainder of the corridor, savoring the rush of cool air on my hot skin.

We show our card to the uniformed tower gatekeeper and then swipe the card at the elevator. Much to our chagrin, when it opens, it already has several occupants, all headed up. The silent moments in the elevator make me swallow hard. I can feel the other men leering, no doubt wondering why I'm pink and panting like I just finished a marathon.

The ding of our floor excites me, and now it's *his* turn to pull me excitedly through the hall. He struggles with our door, and for a moment, I'm panicked, wondering if we will have to get another key. Wondering if this is a sign that we shouldn't be doing this.

On the third try, it buzzes. The lock clicks open. I offer a sigh of giddy relief.

The door hasn't even clicked shut before he's against me, entwining his delectable tongue with mine.

I gasp as his mouth moves to my neck and trails down to my chest. I breathe deep, taking in the intoxicating scent of his cologne.

He wraps an arm around the small of my back, swings me around, and walks me backward until I can feel the comforter brush against the back of my thighs. The feel of it sends an almost violent shiver through me.

"Are you okay?" He holds me close, pressing his forehead to mine. His strong jaw is lit by a kiss of moonlight seeping from our massive picture window, one that overlooks acres of skeletal trees, each beginning to bud with the promise of new life.

"*Just excited*," I whisper with a nod.

I stare up into his eyes. They're sparkling brightly in the luminance of the waning moon, and I swear, in this moment, I've never seen a more attractive man.

I suddenly feel luckier than I have all day, despite the pile of cash we walked away from the casino with.

His knee slips between my legs, and I *instantly* know that I am not the *only* one excited. I can feel his cock, bone-hard, through the fabric of his slacks against my upper thigh.

I stifle a soft whimper at the thought of so much man being inside of me.

He starts to take the strap of his sling over his head, and my hands rise to help him.

"I'll be gentle, I promise." My gaze is serious.

"I won't." His words are a promise that sends a woof of fire rushing through every inch of me.

The moment his arm has shed its mesh confinement, both of his hands are on my face, sweeping hair from my eyes... touching my skin.

I help him out of his blazer, tossing it on the lounger chair in the corner that looks like a threatening black mass. I unbutton his shirt and lay kisses on his bare, chiseled chest where each button was. His hands play softly with my hair, pulling it away from my face in a fisted ponytail. I trail downward, sitting on the bed to undo the final button. I caress the trail of dark hair on his chest, leading down like an arrow to what I desperately crave.

I stare up as Eric takes his shirt off.

He is a God among men. His physique is toned, even more than I'd pictured it in my nightly fantasies. I leave a trail of breadcrumb kisses down the center of his abdomen, though I have no intention of finding my way back.

I drag my tongue through the cut muscular grooves where his torso meets his thighs as I unbuckle his belt. My hands slither inside to caress the hard-on trying to burst through his slacks, but he grabs my wrists firmly.

He shakes his head with a mischievous smile and lowers to me, like an apex predator going in for the kill.

"Not until I fucking *devour* you." The words sound like a threat, and the look on his moon-splashed face is gravely serious.

My breath hitches again.

The way my heart is beating right now, it feels like it's about to thud right out of my torso.

His mouth presses to my ear again, voice gravelly. "And then… I'm going to fuck you until you can't take any more."

I nod almost imperceptibly, feeling the almost painful throb between my thighs. I nibble the lobe of his ear and whisper back after a soft moan, "*Challenge accepted.*"

38

Eric

I pry her jean jacket off and toss it on the growing mound of discarded clothes. I kiss her again.

Hard.

With *feeling*.

I softly bite her shoulder as I peel down the straps of her camisole like I'm unwrapping the most anticipated present one could ever receive.

I want to make her feel every *ounce* of pleasure that she's capable of. I want to *shatter* her expectations in the best possible way.

I want to fuck her like she's never been fucked in her life.

I try to settle the tremble rattling through my hands, but I can't help it. Her body excites me in a way I've never felt before.

When I touch her, I feel like I'm *molding fire*, touching malleable, wispy, red-hot flames, harnessing her power in my palms.

Her bra is silky and soft. I catch a hint of pale red in the moonlight, though it almost looks black in the darkness. The material is so thin that her hardened nipples jut through the material spectacularly, crying out to be fondled and shown the loving adoration they so deserve.

I caress them with my mouth, one at a time, drawing them out through the almost non-existent fabric. I drag my teeth gently across and they tighten beneath my hot breath.

She gasps, pulling me in, as if her muscles are begging me not to *ever* stop.

Her hands sift through my hair, nimble fingers sliding through like silk, continuing down over the scar on my shoulder with tenderness.

I inhale and lick, exciting the peaks of her perfect breasts, dampened by my roaming tongue.

Her knee slides against my cock through the fabric, and I groan into her, vibrating her nipple with my voice.

She emits a half-pant-half-giggle from the sensation. "*Oh my God*," she whispers like it's a tawdry secret.

I unbutton her jeans and tug them down her curves, grateful that they are stretchier than they look. She covers her face, mortified.

"What?" I panic instantly, fearful she's having second thoughts that she doesn't want to continue. My heart races. While it would shatter me inside, I'd obviously respect her wish.

"I *swore* to myself I wouldn't do this. As a deterrent, I made sure my underwear didn't match today." She giggles, and my heart releases from its stranglehold.

A wave of relief washes over me, and, for a moment, I can only stare at her smiling face, absorbing how lovely she is.

How *alive* and *intoxicated* she makes me feel.

I want her to be *mine*.

I want to leave the same indelible mark on her life that she's already left on mine.

I could care less if her underwear is a matched set. Part of me wants to shred it off of her body, ruining it for good so that she will be panty-free on the drive home.

I lower my face between her legs, leaving a trail of kisses up her thighs. I slide a hand up the center of her stomach beneath the impossibly thin material of her bra, caressing her areola with my fingers and cupping her perfect breasts in my palm.

I nip playfully at the lacy, white fabric of her panties, teasing her through the material. She sucks in heaving lungfuls of air. Her body writhes. I drag them down around her deliciously thick hips and stare up from between her knees, basking in the glorious moonlit paradise before me. There's nowhere I would rather be in this world at this moment than worshiping at this altar.

She leans back on her elbows, watching like a hawk, squeezing her eyes closed with every squeeze of her nipple. I hear the ghostly hint of words making their way through hot breaths.

"Hmm?" I mumble, buried between her milky thighs.

"*I want you to fuck me,*" she breathes. "*Please.*"

The sound of her *begging me* to be inside of her sends the last of my brain's blood supply straight to my dick like a bullet train south. My cock is engorged right now, throbbing and painful. But I shake my head.

"No. *Ladies first.*"

I feel like I want to cry as his tongue slips into my soaked pussy. He dives deep, plunging, lapping me up like I'm ice water, and he's a man wandering a scorched desert.

I bite my lip to keep from screaming at how fucking good it feels.

He's meticulous and takes his time, languidly sucking, licking, seeking out spots that make my body tremble.

My cheeks simmer like coals on a fire, radiating heat. His tongue dives deep, making me squirm with satisfaction. A throaty moan escapes me into the quiet darkness.

His luscious lips make their way up, teasing and sucking, enveloping my clit with a suction that makes me want to scream with pleasure. But as I try to find the voice buried deep beneath my pounding heart, I find I can only whisper expletives and iterations of his name over and over.

"Fuck, Eric."

The hand massaging my tits retreats ever-so-slowly south, and my eyes roll back when I feel one of those talented fingers slip between my parting legs and slide inside my pussy.

I suck in a deep lungful of air as a second soon joins it, fucking me with languid waves of pleasurable pressure as he makes a meal out of every inch of me. I run a hand through his hair again to affirm that everything he is doing is *fucking perfect.*

His fingers slide deep inside of me again, and this time, they hook upward in tandem, putting glorious force on my G-spot. My back arches, and I groan into the darkness. It's almost like he's holding my whole body up with those two talented fingers.

It feels fucking incredible.

He feels fucking incredible.

Watching him through my nearly-closed lids, I shiver at the intensity of his stare from between my thighs.

His bicep ripples as he rocks his strong, curved fingers. Every muscle in my body relaxes and tenses again.

An orgasm rips through me like a fucking storm, leaving nothing but a flood in its wake. My body shudders, and I cry out like I'm in mourning, like my body knows it will never be the same after him.

My vision darkens, and all I'm left with is the undulating waves rippling outward through every muscle, flooding me with a rush of chemicals like I'm mainlining a narcotic; *only Eric is ten times more addictive.*

After the quaking subsides, I feel his torso glide up the sheets next to mine, gently leaning

232

against my side to alleviate pressure from his still-healing shoulder, but still, the fingers of his other hand are inside of me, massaging the spot inside of me that makes my body go berserk.

I bury my face in his chest and clutch with both hands, savoring the flexing muscles of his taut back beneath my fingertips. I pant into the thatch of hair on his chest as he sends another shock wave rippling through my thighs with the simple, skilled pulse of his hand.

He kisses me with a passion, unlike anything I've ever felt before. Like he wants to fuse and become one with my body.

Like he can't get enough.

That feeling warms me like a roaring furnace in this chilled, moonlit space where he and I might as well be the only two people in existence.

He gently slips his wet fingers out of me, and my body bucks again. I sense his smile through the blur of tears welled in my eyes. It is hard to catch my breath. I feel like the occupants of the next room can hear my heart knocking like something out of an Edgar Allen Poe story.

My body erupts in goosebumps as he slides on top of me, spreading my legs wide with the force of his knees. He showers the side of my neck with hot kisses.

I feel so vulnerable, naked, and splayed beneath the fabric of his clothes.

My hands slide into the narrow chasm between us, and I finish undoing his belt, button, and zipper.

He grinds against me, savoring my dewy skin with his tongue. With a quiet click, he unclasps the front of my bra, unveiling my excited breasts, firm and ultra-responsive to his gentle caresses. His glinting eyes flash like lightning before his insatiable mouth is on them, hot and ravenous.

My feet squirm, tugging his tailored pants down to his calves. I feel him reach back into their pocket and lob something weighty on the bed.

As he kicks them to the floor, I slide my hand into his boxer briefs and wrap my fingers around his girthy cock. My eyes widen at the feel of it, and I instantly feel a rush of anxiety.

"*Ohhhhh my God,*" he moans quietly into my neck with his eyes pinched tight, enjoying the way I stroke him.

"*Oh my God,*" I echo it, but for a completely different reason.

He snickers shyly and looks up at me.

"Oh, wow. *Um...*" I mutter, so nervous I could almost choke on the sound of my own words.

He can sense the apprehension in my voice.

I massage his cock firm and slow, naked body still writhing against him. "*So, uh...*"

I feel patches of red blossom across my cheeks like spreading red ink.

"This is… a little embarrassing."

"What?" he pants softly, planting a kiss on my ear and then another on my mouth.

I smile, fearful that my voice might crack while I'm explaining.

"It's been a *while* for me, and I wasn't exactly expecting, Jesus… *alllll* of this." I exhale a nervous breath. "That's… wow…"

I don't know what to say. His face morphs into a proud, beaming smile full of straight teeth at my apprehension.

"*I promise… to go very,*" he takes one of my aroused nipples into his mouth, and my eyes flutter closed, "*very…*" he sucks the other, gently kissing the areola, "*…slow.*"

His words are a promise that I know he will keep, if for no reason other than to savor the act. I feel his cock grow harder in my hand as if it's carved out of an ivory tusk.

"*Okay?*" he asks, running his fingers along the side of my face in an act of adoration.

Words evade me. I can only nod.

His lips press to mine. I can taste myself on his tongue, and my body trembles, crying out silently, wanting *more* of him.

Wanting every… intimidating… inch.

40

Eric

I rise from the warmth of her body and feel the instant chill of the frigid air in this room. I'm astounded by the heat she radiates. Without a word, I strip out of my underwear and pull the condom from my wallet.

A sudden anxiety washes over me.

Jesus, I have no idea how old this fucking thing is.

She props herself onto her elbows, and the way the light from the window hits her, the image is forever burned into my mind, capturing every intimate detail like it's the most incredible photograph ever taken.

I walk over to the armless chair in the corner by the window and launch our clothes off of it with the swipe of my hand.

I take a seat on it, settling into it like it's my throne. I tear into the gold foil magnum wrapper with my teeth and roll the condom down my throbbing cock as the discarded casing flutters to the ground like a dead autumn leaf.

I smile, taking in the sight of her for a moment, allowing my nerves to unwind. My eyes travel from her lustrous blonde hair to her perky tits to the mysterious circular tattoo on her side that I'm only just now seeing.

My smile falls, and I beckon her over with a finger.

There's no trace of a smile on her face as she obediently approaches, looking like her heart is in her throat.

I entwine my fingers with hers and kiss the inside of her wrist before pulling her toward me. I grasp her tapered waist, sliding them down to her curvy hips, and a rush of excitement zings through me all over again at the thought of soon being buried inside of her.

I pull her close and pat the tops of my thighs, silently ordering her to sit on them. Timidly, she does. I wrap my arms around her lower back and tug her close until her pelvis is pressed against my engorged cock.

I stroke her hair and kiss her, pulling away only to stare right into her eyes for a moment.

I slide a hand up the back of her head and gently pull her toward me with a fistful of hair until my mouth is against her ear.

"It's okay," I whisper, rubbing my other thumb across her bottom lip. "You're in control here." I release her hair and nibble her neck until her body relaxes in my arms.

She moans.

My hands relax by my sides for a moment, and I coo, "You don't have to do anything you don't want to."

There is a moment of silence between Kira and me, one where she is clearly deciding what she wants to do. She has the power to devastate me, and I swallow hard, waiting for her next move.

She leans forward, grinding tighter against my body with her own. The way she kisses me, grasping my face in her hands, eases my worried mind.

I feel her rise on her feet and shift closer until the head of my cock is resting beneath her slick folds, poised.

I nearly forget to breathe as she crosses her wrists behind my head. I brush my fingertips up and down the China-smooth skin of her sides, and she starts to sink down onto me.

I groan, and my hands slide to her perfect ass. She moans softly, perspiring forehead pressed to mine.

"*Slow,*" I order in a whisper, brushing the hair from her ears.

"*It's okay.*" I softly bite her bottom lip and feel her slide down.

My cock slips deeper. She feels like Heaven around me, taking me all inside of her.

Kira takes another deep breath, and I feel a light sheen of sweat moistening her curvaceous body. She's a shaking inferno in my arms.

"*Mmmm, you're doing so good, Kira,*" I whisper. She groans, trembling in my arms, legs wobbling, trying her very best to take *all of me.*

I press my face into her breasts, and she sinks down, taking another inch of me.

And then another.

She's so fucking tight that I feel lightheaded. Every pint of my blood is in my lower half right now, and it's everything I can do not to buck my hips and drive my dick inside of Kira.

"*Oh, fuck*," she whispers, throwing her head back, using my neck to stabilize herself.

"Are you okay?"

She nods, biting her lip, and presses down the last inch, burying my dick inside of her warm, wet pussy all the way to the hilt.

"*Fuuuuuuck,*" I growl.

Her breath hitches again, eyes watery, face as serious as a heart attack as she looks at me.

I hold her hips absolutely still on my lap, allowing her a moment to catch her breath and relax. I pull her close and whisper into her ear, "*That's a good girl.*"

41

Eric

Over the next ten minutes, Kira fucks me, slow and leisurely, in the armless throne through two more of her own leg-shaking orgasms. I love the way she shudders and shakes and the way the moon bathes her bare breasts.

After her third, I order her onto her knees on the bed, where I press myself into her from behind, burying myself fully into her depths.

She feels even more amazing in this position, warmed up, soaking wet, and taking my whole pulsing cock with ease now. It doesn't take long in this position until I come so hard that I nearly crack a molar from the intensity with which I smash my teeth together to keep from howling out.

We curl up together, panting and slick with sweat in a rumpled mess of covers. I caress her in the silence of the night, and it isn't long before she's asleep in my arms.

For hours, I hold her, tired but flooded with thoughts and vigor, studying the curves of her face, breathing in the intoxicating scent of her perfume mingling with our sweat.

As the glow of dawn oozes into the room, I find myself counting her eyelashes like some kind of love-sick teenager. I wish I had another condom so I could make her moan again when she finally awakens.

***

My eyes peel open to the bright morning sun, and Kira is staring at me.

I smile. I can't *help* it. It's like a veil of euphoria has fallen over me. "Good morning, beautiful," I muster through a yawn and bleary eyes, suddenly nervous about my dragon breath.

She doesn't reply with words. Instead, she caresses my face with her feather-soft touch.

I love this. *Waking up next to her.*

I wish this was our life and not some fleeting crescendo of our palpable sexual chemistry.

A man could get so addicted to waking up like this. This sort of touch is something I've never felt before, not from any woman I've ever been with, though that tiny pool *is* rather limited.

I tug the covers down the side of her body, and she giggles as I shower her naked breasts with kisses. She pulls me close, running her fingers through my hair, which I'm sure looks absolutely crazy right now.

I lovingly circle my index finger over the curious tattoo on her side, one that I could barely make out in the darkness last night. It looks like two circles composed of cursive words connected to a spot in the center by what looks

241

like spokes. From further back, the whole thing looks like a Ferris wheel.

I read the words aloud. "*If I had a wish that I could wish for you, I'd make a wish for sunshine all the while.*"

I recognize it immediately from the John Denver song she played me just a few days prior, which feels like a lifetime ago already.

"You really *are* a Denver fan, aren't you?"

But when I look, her expression isn't one I expect. It's solemn, with *gravity*. It's a look that carries the weight of the world in it.

"It's for my father," she finally says.

I look at her, hoping she will explain.

"...It's from my last really good memory with him," she mumbles numbly beneath her breath, almost unintelligibly.

"I'd like to hear it." I fold my good arm across her stomach and peer up into her eyes, giving her my undivided attention. "*If* you want to tell me."

She takes a deep breath and caresses my injured shoulder with a feathery touch. "My dad, he used to take me to all of these cool carnivals. From the moment he took me on my first one, I couldn't get enough of the Ferris wheel. It's always been my favorite ride. I just *love* the views from the top. Some are just... breathtaking."

She swallows hard and tries her best to smile through the melancholy. "He took me to Compounce, Coney Island, The Big E., you

242

name it. But my all-time favorite is the one at Steel Pier in Atlantic City. Every year for my birthday, he'd take me there."

She takes a deep breath. "The week before he died, he took me there again. At the top, we looked out. The beach was all sunny and beautiful from up there, and it… it actually moved him to tears. He quoted that part of the song, and we just sat there together, just the two of us, taking in this… *view*."

Her green eyes well up. "That's the last memory I have of him before the murder." She wipes her lash line to catch a tear that is threatening to fall.

Oh, Jesus, did she just say… murder?

I want to ask so many things, but I don't want to pry. It's obvious that she's hurting.

Instead, I wriggle up beside her, pull her tight to my chest, and lay a soft kiss on the top of her head. I can feel tears leak into the groove where our bodies are joined.

After a long silence, she pulls away and sniffles. "We should get dressed. It's almost ten. We have to check out of here soon. I still have to apartment-shop today."

I shake my head and lift the covers. "No, ma'am." I slide beneath the sheets, kissing her abdomen as I disappear into the darkened depths of this white fabric world I want to live in… *just a little bit longer.*

"I hear this place has an *incredible* continental breakfast, and…" My voice is muffled by the covers. I spread her legs slowly.

She giggles, and her whole body tenses at my touch. I see her fists ball up excitedly beside me, grasping onto the fabric like she's holding on for dear life. I dive in, teasing her clit with my lips and the very tip of my tongue.

Before I devour the hot, delicious little dish in front of me like a man starving, I growl, "I'm not going anywhere until I'm *sated*."

The last twenty-four hours of my life feel like a dream, but I know from the soreness in the muscles of my thighs and the tenderness of everything between them that everything at the casino hotel was real.

I want to faint when I think back to some of the things Eric said and did to me in that room.

I'm lost in my recollection of him whispering dirty little things in my ear…

How he felt *inside* me…

All the fucking *orgasms*…

That's why I have no damn clue what the lady in front of me is yammering about.

"Don't you just love the space?" the Realtor chirps, and I'm snapped backward from my filthy memories like a sprung rubber band.

"Hmmmm?" I raise my brows.

The Realtor's face sours a little. "*Well*, what do we *think?*"

"I think… it is basically on top of the train station."

"Yep. It's a close walk. And with a $20 ticket, boom, you're in Grand Central."

I didn't say close. I said on top of. There is a difference. My yard would basically be train tracks.

"Does this looney screaming bible verses on the sidewalk come with the place? Or is he extra?" I point to the old man outside waving a Gideon and yelling at someone who isn't there.

"Look, you'll be hard-pressed to find something better than this in your price range, Ms. Blumquist."

The way she's telling me to settle reminds me of Cassandra right now. Always the logical pragmatist.

For a full minute, I pretend to look around the apartment. In reality, I am blankly staring at these grubby walls, reminiscing about this morning just before check-out when I was on my knees, attempting the nearly impossible task of trying to take all of Eric deep into my mouth. I wished that I could unhinge my jaw like a snake. I choked, and he pulled me back. I stared up at him and massaged it firm and slow, slick with my saliva, all the while staring up through watery eyes as he slowly licked his bottom lip.

"*Mmm. That's a good girl,*" he hummed before encouraging me to try again.

If I hadn't already been on the ground, the sound of his naughty voice saying those words would have buckled my legs and put me there anyway.

"*Ahem. Well?*" She's annoyed.

246

And now *I'm* annoyed because she interrupted my train of thought.

"What else have you got?" Just as I ask, a real train screams through the neighborhood, and I watch it barrel through Bridgeport through the window behind her. "This one's not for me."

43

Eric

I set a cappuccino in front of Kira and then place my own near my keyboard. I take a seat at my computer and struggle to hide the big, dumb grin that keeps trying to spread across my face.

Keep it professional, Eric. You've muddied the waters enough…

Seeing her on the other side of this desk after what we did is surreal. I thought being with her would finally break her body's spell over me these past couple of weeks, but it did the exact opposite. The pull to be near her is ten times as strong as it was before.

Sitting in front of her now, I feel mesmerized by her beauty. She's just quietly sipping coffee in front of me, and all I want to do is wipe everything off my desk and fuck her right here on the glass.

I spent hours yesterday on the couch in my music room while Bella watched cartoons, just picking at my acoustic strings, trying to forget her. Within minutes, I found myself googling tabs to *Lobo songs.*

I thought about her tattoo and the fact that while I feel like I know her, there is so much yet to explore.

"So," I clear my throat, praying that the hard-on I feel forming in my pants subsides before I eventually have to stand, "how did apartment shopping go yesterday?"

She scoffs as she sips, nearly blowing the foam clean out of the cup. "Total bust." With a bent finger, she scoops the fluffy froth back into the cup and winces apologetically. "I found one that might work. It's like a shoebox, but it's an okay part of town, so that's something."

"Well, I was thinking," I lean back in my chair, and suddenly, I have a flashback of myself doing the same in our room, beckoning her to me. It takes me twenty seconds or so to join her back in reality. "I don't want the timing of this to seem weird because of…"

I make a weird motion with my hands, but I don't know how to finish that sentence.

Because of us.

Because of what we *did*.

Because of what I'm fucking *dying to do again* in every room of this goddamn house…

"...the casino."

That's what you finally settled on?

I continue, "I know the timing of this is not the best. I was actually going to offer it on Friday."

"Well, color me intrigued."

"The pool house. It's a one-bedroom studio with a full kitchen and a full bath. My mom and dad lived there for a bit while I was having their house built. Now, it's just… sitting there. I've

249

been using it as storage for some of the crap Tawny left behind when she skipped out, but otherwise, it's just… vacant."

"Oh, I couldn't."

Her cheeks blush, and I'm transported back to how they bloomed red with my touch in the long hall near the hotel concierge.

"Please, just consider it." I clear my throat and rejoin her in reality. "And here's why."

She chuckles and rubs the muscles on the sides of her face near her ear. I don't think she knows she's doing it, but my cock grows hard as steel, as I vividly recall the reason her jaw is sore.

She's on her knees, a ponytail of her hair in my fist just before checkout…

"I'm listening."

Jesus, Eric. Snap out of it.

"Okay," I suddenly find myself excited that she's even *entertaining* the idea. The thought of having her close to me… *and to Bella*… fills me with a strange comfort.

"First of all, it's free, so you could save up toward a better car or a down payment on a house or something with the money you'd save."

She sits back in her chair, sets the cup on the desk, and fidgets with it, gaze distant.

"You'd have full access to all the amenities of the main house. Indoor pool, chef, movie room. Plus, privacy. I wouldn't come out there unless it was some kind of emergency."

"What if I asked you to?" A smile creeps up onto her lips, and with her face still tipped down, her lime-green eyes lock on mine.

I rub my neck and exhale deeply. "Well, if you asked to borrow a cup of sugar... what kind of neighbor would I be if I didn't give you exactly what you need?"

Her eyes dart back to her drink at the double entendre.

"Oh, and that *commute*." I motion the chef's kiss.

She laughs. "Well, according to Rob, this job ends in about two weeks, so I don't know how much *that* part would help me."

"Oh no. You're not getting off *that* easy."

My own cheeks blush now at my accidental wording, and I feel another pulse of blood rush down to my crotch. She actually does get off quite easily.

Pervert. It's like you're twelve again.

"That came out wrong." I suddenly feel like I'm burning up, melting beneath my suit. My eyes land on hers. "Stay. You've done a great job with the ledgers and making spreadsheets. Plus, I just got an email from Rob, who said that the Steinmans loved the new client welcome packet you created. He said they thought it was a really nice touch. Plus," I motion to the door, "Bella loves you. You're like her best friend. What kind of a dad would I be if I let you go?"

She smiles like a ray of sunshine through a curtain of blonde hair and neon green wayfarers

251

that match the camisole taunting me beneath her half-buttoned black-and-gray flannel. "Are you offering me a full-time position? Am I hearing this right?"

"You are."

"Is this... because of..."

"No," I assure her quickly with a violent shake of my head. I sit back in my chair and adjust the strap of my sling. "It doesn't have anything to do with that."

After a moment, she smiles bashfully. "I *would* like to stay on as your assistant. I don't know if living right there would be a good idea. You and Bella have a good thing going. I wouldn't want to meddle in that."

"You wouldn't be *meddling*." I fidget with my Cartier pen. My nerves have me feeling like a flailing live wire, squirrelly and electric. "You'd be saving money to better your situation and cutting down on mileage. It's just a practical solution."

"Thank you," she says quietly. "I'll consider it."

"I hope you do. Offer's on the table." I anxiously rub a smudge off the surface of my desk.

After a moment of silence, she takes a huge sip of her coffee and licks the foam off her luscious lips. "So, boss-man, what sort of job do you have for me today?"

I grow silent, staring at her like a moose in high beams.

Fuck. I've only had one kind of *job* for her on my mind, and it's one she already proved to be *sublime* at.

On her knees…

Just before checkout yesterday.

44

Kira

"You're sure about this?" I ask, eyeing the inviting interior of the pool house. Decorated in warm shades of terracotta, tan, and white, it's nearly the size of the apartment I split with Cassandra and Gandalf, only not covered in cat hair and George's dirty clothes.

"Yes. Positive," Eric says lowly from behind me near the doorway. The sound of his voice near my ear excites me. My body is abuzz, wondering if it will ever see a repeat of the dirty things we did at the hotel-casino.

Or should I say, *hoping*?

"It's a little small," he says.

"There is nothing about you that I could possibly associate with the word small." *I cannot believe I just said that out loud.*

I cover my mouth with a slightly trembling hand, and he snickers bashfully.

I clear my throat and lower my hand.

Act like a fucking adult, Kira.

"This place, wow, it's huge."

Now it's *his* turn to laugh. I suppose, in comparison to the rest of the estate, this place is probably the size of his *suit closet*, but this little guest house offers more square footage than any place I've ever lived.

"I love the decor."

"Yeah?"

"Mmm-hmm."

"I asked the decorator for 'Tuscan *villa*,' and he gave me this." I sense some disappointment in his voice.

"I've never been to Tuscany, but this does look like I would have pictured."

"Tuscany is *incredible*." He says the word with wonderment and reverence, that I find myself gravitating toward him. There is something so sexy about a passionate man.

"You've been?"

"Of course." He nods. "*Couple* of times. Although, I spent far more time in Rome and Ostia than in Tuscany."

"What's it like?"

"Oh, it's unbelievable. You hit it at the right part of the year, and the weather is warm, the people are inviting, and the architecture is spectacular. Some of it just blows your mind. Rome is so rich with history and folklore." He snaps back into the moment and looks at me. "I love it there. I go every year."

"So, you speak Italian?" I look at some ceramic plates in brass holders on shelves. They are ornate and look hand-painted.

"No, not really. Just enough to get by."

"So let me get this straight," I sit on the boho chic comforter. It looks hand-stitched and expensive. "You go to Italy yearly, but you've never once been to *Paris*?"

He lingers near the bed, still standing, touching its strings like he's playing with fire.

"Yeah, Rob gave me hell over the same thing the other day. He says I like what I like and never try new things."

My grin says far more than my words ever could.

He tries to fight a titillating smile. "So, what do you think?"

What do I think?

I think you're wearing entirely too many clothes right now. Covering one inch of that body ought to be illegal.

"I think… I love it," I say, looking around.

"So you'll take it?"

I nod.

"Fantastic. Call the movers. Charge it to the Amex, not the business account."

I smile. "I don't know how to thank you."

"Well, before you get any ideas, I didn't offer it as *quid pro quo*. I just wanted to help you. I didn't have any ulterior motives. Please don't think I offered so you'd feel indebted or think you need to be some sort of..."

"*Concubine?*" I rise to my feet and step toward him.

He's speechless. He looks like he wants to say something but has no idea where to start.

"We didn't actually talk about whether what happened this weekend was a one-off or…"

"Or…" he says, standing dangerously close, looking down with those bourbon-colored eyes of his. "I didn't want to *presume* anything, but I'm not big on one-offs. I don't know how you feel—"

My hand slips beneath the bottom of his buttoned suit jacket and clasps his belt and buckle. "I feel like we should *celebrate*."

"*Oh?*"

"I was thinking something like a private housewarming party."

I stare up with eyes wicked and unblinking as I unfasten his buckle.

"Something… *intimate*."

He caresses my jaw softly with his fingers, pleased at my verdict. "Oh yeah? *When?*"

I tilt his arm and glance at his Rolex. "I have forty minutes before I need to pick Bella up from school."

"Forty minutes?"

"*Tick-tock*—"

Like a frenzied ocean wave, his mouth crashes into mine with all the force of a raging tempest. I'm quickly lost in it, set adrift in the waters of euphoria.

45

Eric

A bead of sweat rolls down my forehead and stings my eyes. "Fifteen… sixteen…"

I hiss as I exhale between the lifting and lowering of each dumbbell.

"Seventeen…"

Each repetition is more painful than the last.

"Eighteen…"

I roar, and my groan echoes throughout the gym.

"*Mmmmmm.*" I hear Kira's flirtatious hum voice behind me.

"Nineteen…" *Jesus Christ, I'm dying.* I fight the violent shake, making its way through my arm. I hiss again. "Twenty."

I can't lower this fucking weight fast enough. I place it on the ground and rise from my bench, catching a glimpse of Kira in the mirrored wall in front of me.

"Good morning, Mr. Salko." The words themselves sound polite, but her smoldering, narrowed eyes look lustful."Has anyone ever told you you're a work of art when you're sweaty?"

The way she says it, I can't help but smile. I towel myself off with a rag and start toward the array of colorful runner weights. I select the ten-pound one and sit back down.

"How can I help you?" I start slow, deliberate reps with the small weight with my injured arm.

"Well, I just wanted to let you know that I found some more information on the new electric SUV that Rivian rolled out yesterday that you might find interesting."

"Yeah?"

"Yeah, it rolled out less than ten grand under what people were predicting, and I think it's better looking than people expected, so the outlook seems optimistic."

I'm amazed at what this woman has been able to pick up in only a month of working for me.

"I went ahead and emailed you a link along with a few bearish projections about the stock price within the next few months."

"Great. Thank you." I raise and lower the weight again, grimacing at the sharp pain that comes at the edge of every extension. "Did you find out why the pot stocks took a nosedive yesterday?"

"Nothing concrete. A few sites rumored that a few more states were planning on trying to legalize, but I think the bills got squashed. I'm still looking into that."

"Thank you." I wipe the sweat dripping down my nose and put the weight down. I hook my knees onto the foam rolls, cross my arms, and start my sit-ups.

"Anything… else?" I grunt. *One… two…*

"Yeah, wow." She snaps out of whatever haze she's in, staring at me. "Um, I just buzzed Doctor Udoka through the gates. He's here for your checkup."

"Oh fuck…is that today?" *Nine… ten…*

"Yes."

"Okay, yeah, send him on back once he's inside."

"Once *who is* inside?" James pops his head over Kira's shoulder in the doorway and beams a mouthful of pearl-white teeth that sparkle against his espresso complexion.

***

"You been doing your PT?" James asks, examining my healing incision site.

"Every Monday and Thursday, the therapist comes to do the passive stretches and all that with me. Last week, he moved me up to "active-assisted" and said as long as I was careful and only used the *tiny* weights, I could do some initial strengthening exercises as long as I don't over-exert or tear anything."

"Oh, that's phenomenal news then." James peels his gloves off and stuffs them into the pocket of his corduroy jacket. He squats on the bench in front of me, straddling it like a small horse.

"Well?" I feel my head jut forward, eyebrows high.

260

"Well…" He claps his hands together. "If you promise to take it easy, you can ditch the sling."

I feel a wave of cold rip through me. "Yes!"

"I know that's what you've been dying to hear."

"It is." I run my hands through my wet hair and stare at the vaulted ceiling. As my sight settles back on James, I smile. "This actually comes at the perfect time."

46

Kira

I mill around this pool house, nosing through storage boxes full of abandoned stuffies and neatly folded baby clothes Bella outgrew years ago.

Curiosity piqued, I sift through a stack of photos, all of which tell a rich tale through their faded images, moments in time seized perpetually on film. Seeing these remnants of Eric's former life makes me doubt there is really a place for me in his present one.

He deserves someone amazing, like an heiress with her own fortune, or a celebrity, or a jaw-dropping lingerie model...

I'm realistic. This isn't a fairy-tale. I'm not Cinderella. I drive a pile of scrap metal and grew up watching Jeopardy through the window of my neighbor's trailer on my tip-toes.

There is a common theme in this stack of pictures in my hands as I shuffle through a decade from dating to destruction.

In every photo with the two of them, Eric looks adoring, doting, and genuine. Tawny looks bored or irritated, usually with a lackluster expression across her youthful face. It's as if she can't be bothered to smile or laugh or find any joy in the day.

There are pictures of them near gondolas, along with snapshots of Italian food and architecture. There are photos of Tawny on the beach in a one-piece, waving the camera away. Shots of the two of them exploring what appears to be a Tuscan vineyard. The displeasure is there in every picture, stuffed beneath Tawny's skin like a brooding disease.

She's pretty, but honestly, not what I'd call *stunning,* even on my drunkest community college night. Her short crop of blond hair, hard features, and stern expression remind me of my mother.

The image of my own mom sends a convulsive shiver through my body as a wave of dread slips languidly through me.

Seeing this stack of photos makes me feel more connected to Bella, in a way, because I, too, had a mother who could never find happiness. She always managed to successfully evade joy's grasp.

At the bottom of the box, I scrounge through other items, curiosity piqued. My hand settles on a small camcorder. I fish out the little power cable wrapped next to it, under a plush raccoon, and plug the device into the wall.

I power it up and play the first video.

It's Christmas morning. Several years ago, I'm guessing from the age of Bella as she unwraps her mountain of presents in front of a gargantuan, tinsel-strewn tree that rivals the one at Rockafeller Center.

Eric hands Bella a huge box with a giant bow atop it. Bella shreds it like a tiny wolverine and squeals with childlike wonder at the new table-and-tea set printed on the outside of the box.

Suddenly, Tawny groans from behind the camera, and Eric's smile falls flat.

"What?" His tone is innocent, non-combative.

"I told you not to fucking *get that* for her, Eric!"

Eric looks confused, unsure what the problem is.

"We talked about this whole gender-related fuckin' toy thing." She's flustered. "God… dammit, Eric. We agreed *on only* gender-neutral toys. Craft supplies, bikes, books—"

"It's fine, Tawny. Men drink tea, too."

"From *pink goddamned cups?* I don't *think* so."

"Tawn, watch your language, *please*," he points to Bella.

The low battery light flashes in the corner of the screen. I pause the clip, scroll through the thumbnails, and see that there have got to be at least thirty short videos on here.

I set the device on the dresser, power it off, and put it on charge so that I can watch the rest another time.

I stare out the window at the empty outdoor pool just beyond the window. It's flanked by orchards of leafing cherry trees and even has a charming little hammock strung up between two of them. This property looks magical at night. Stars are sprinkled through the black velvet night like coarse salt, and I have a clear view from the lack of light pollution.

I look at my watch. Ten thirty-five. Bella is certainly asleep by now, but the light in Eric's bedroom is illuminated.

I grab my phone and text.

KIRA: U up?

Moments later, I grow excited at the sight of the three dots in the bubble on my screen.

ERIC: Yes.

ERIC: You should send me a duck pic.

ERIC: You know you want to.

I laugh aloud and see the darkened shadow of his form enter the window facing the pool house.

I wave.

He waves back. I feel like I can almost see his smile from way over here, even though he is nothing but a shadow against the amber light.

KIRA: Just unpacked my swimsuit. Fancy joining me for a dip?

ERIC: You know there's no water in that pool, right?

I laugh again.

Smart-ass.

My eyes drift to the drained outdoor pool in front of me.

KIRA: I meant in the INDOOR pool.

KIRA: You know, that giant decoration you pay a team to chlorinate?

ERIC: Ohhhhhhhhh. That one.

KIRA: I know. There are so many.

Then, his silhouette disappears. A moment later, another three bubbles.

And then…

ERIC: Meet you there in five.

47

Eric

"Oh… my… sweet… *Jesus*." The words tumble from my mouth like a slow rain of hail. I can't help it. She's wearing a red bikini, and she looks even better in it than she did in my fantasies.

"You like?" she asks coyly, though her body language is confident as if she's somehow aware of the hold her form has over me.

"I *love*," I growl like an animal and dunk half of my face beneath the water's surface. As I tread, the exercise feels equal parts painful and amazing on my shoulder.

"Are you okay to swim after your surgery?"

"As long as I take it easy," I smile. She stands at the water's edge, framed by a jungle of tropical plants with misters intermittently spraying down on them. She looks like the human embodiment of a typhoon, a stormy icon sheathed in crimson. "Dare you to cannonball."

A mischievous smile forms on her face. "*Challenge accepted*," she says, racing to the water's edge.

She jumps and grabs her knees, splashing into the placid waters like a petite explosion.

"9-0." I clap as she surfaces, whooshing her wet mop of blonde hair back.

"Ooooooh, it feels great in here," she says, pleased.

I press forward, taking a slow lap from edge to edge, trying my best to stretch my slightly atrophied biceps and forearms with every stroke.

Kira swims to the shallow end and dives under for a moment. Two stunning legs burst out of the surface, toes pointed skyward. She holds the underwater handstand for a long time, shifting toward deeper waters before finally flipping. She surfaces again, smiling like an otter.

"Holy crap, I can still do it!"

I chuckle.

Sometimes, Kira reminds me of a child full of youthful wonderment, taking pleasure in the simpler things life has to offer. It reminds me of when I derived joy from normal activities, too, back before the accountants, the lawyers, the million-dollar portfolio management, and the stress of an earnings call. Back before I had to wonder about people's ulterior motives and knew who my friends were.

"How was the rest of your night?" she asks.

"It was really nice." I bob in place ten feet from her. "Bella and I did paper mache tonight."

"Ooooh, fancy!"

"Yeah, we finished her science fair project. It was funny; I was playing some Duran Duran, and afterward, she was wigging out, running around the living room, singing *Hungry Like the Wolf* into the remote. Got floury muck all over everything. She thinks her name is *Rio* now."

Kira giggles, and it sounds so pleasant, echoing off the glass walls and the surface of the water around us.

"I'm just glad you're giving her a good education."

"Well, yeah, with all that mess, she better know how a volcano works backward and forward now."

"Oh no, I was talking about her *musical* education. If you think she likes Duran Duran, you should see her with the Rolling Stones. She does the little Mick Jagger face now and everything."

"And where, pray tell, did she learn any *Rolling Stones?*" I raise a brow.

"She *mayyyyy* have been listening to some on the rides back home from school." Kira tries to hide her smile. "…And she *may* know how to do some of his old stage moves."

I can't help but laugh when I picture my nine-year-old, mouth contorted, hands in her armpits, flapping her elbows like chicken wings as she dances to *Start Me Up*.

Kira swishes past me, taking long breaststrokes until she is on the other end of the pool.

"What about you? How was your evening?"

She sprays a mouthful of chlorinated water out and wipes her eyes, choking a little. "Oh jeez, I took on water." She shakes her head like a hound dog and grins at me. "What was that?"

"I asked how was your night?"

269

"Oh, it was great! After dinner, I finished my book and unpacked a bit more of my stuff, and then I *may*," she continues sheepishly, "have snooped a little through some of your storage boxes."

"Yeah?" My eyebrows raise. I could care less about what's in those boxes. It's mostly old clothes and Tawny's crap. I wanted to bin it after she left anyway. *Goddamned lawyers...* "Find anything interesting?"

"I found a stack of old photos." She smiles. "I think some were of your parents. I'm assuming, anyway. The guy next to your mom looked an awful lot like you."

My heart wallops for a moment in my chest. "Wait, were there any like graduation photos in there?"

"Yeah, graduation, vacations, pictures of them with Bella as a baby…"

I can't believe it. I thought those photos of my father had been lost for good. I feel like I'm shaking, dying to see them again.

She clears her throat and sinks down into the water a little. "…Your wedding."

A knot ties in my stomach, and I feel a bit of shame trickle through me.

"Sorry you had to see those." *I am.* "That was a long time ago. That's honestly a little embarrassing."

"Why? It's a part of what made you who you are. It happened." She shrugs.

"Yeah," I mumble.

270

"*Embarrassing* is coming back from running errands the other day and seeing you in the living room wearing that hot pink feather boa and drinking from tiny cups with Bella."

"First of all, I'll have you know I'm not embarrassed by that. That's *high-tea* that you walked in on. It's Bella's and my time to be *fancy* and for her to give me all the hot goss about the kids at school."

"The *hot goss?*"

"Gossip, Kira." I pretend to be overly serious. "God. School yourself on the lingo."

She holds her hands up. "Sorry!"

"Bella hosts a tea party every two weeks. It is, frankly, considered an *honor* to get an invite, so," I waggle a finger playfully at her, "don't take your jealousy out on me."

Her laugh echoes throughout the space again.

"Plus, if you want to talk embarrassing, how about when I found you passed out in her blanket fort last week?"

"She invited me in! It was cozy! What do you want me to do? Give her a rain check? That thing was friggin dope!"

"You were passed out and drooling." I splash her.

"So?!" She splashes me back.

"So? So, you were on the clock." I laugh. "Who do you work for? Me or Bella?"

"Sometimes I don't even know." She shakes her head and dips beneath the surface,

271

popping up nearer to me. "Hey, in all seriousness, I'm sorry I went through your stuff."

"It's fine. I'm actually glad you found those photos of my dad. Those are like," sadness rings through me suddenly like a plucked string, "all I have left of him, really."

"What was he like?" She circles me like a sea lion, listening intently.

"He was awesome. He's the reason I am who I am today. He believed in me. He took a chance on me. When I got my license and everything for day trading, Rob and I started our firm, and my dad took a second mortgage on his and mom's house, and he basically bet it all on me."

"Jesus, that's a lot of pressure."

I scoff. That's an understatement. "I told him about my gut feeling on a couple of stocks, showed him my research, and he basically…" I smile, "put it all on twenty-three."

She blushes at the mention of it.

I stretch my arm, waving slow circles through the air to work out the tense, injured muscles. "I nearly lost it all. The market was volatile. It all crashed. I thought I had lost all of their money. I was sick for days. I even lost some damn hair over it."

"Really?"

"Yeah, it just started coming out in the sink. I had a fucking ulcer over it, figuring out how to tell my dad I damn-near bankrupted him."

"What happened?" She swims behind me, and I feel her soft hands slink over my shoulders, massaging gently. It feels so good I want to sink into the water and drown right here in her grasp.

"I waited. Couple of months later, I doubled down. Put the last of my money in while prices were dirt cheap. Tawny threatened to leave me."

"Shoulda let her."

I laugh. "No shit. It would have saved me years of stress. Although, then, I wouldn't have Bella."

"So, then what?"

"Soon, the market swung again with a vengeance. I rode the high, pulled out at the perfect time, right at the peak."

She snickers, and I shake my head, unable to contain my grin.

"I reinvested it all into two more stocks, and soon they surged, too. And a month after pulling out of those, I invested in a penny stock that blew up. And… yeah. You get the picture. I bought this place and had my parents come to live with me while I had mom's house, the one you saw, built."

"Awww." The way she coos it near my ear makes me feel like I just shot a glass of whiskey, warm and relaxed. "So I take it he was proud of you?" She rubs a little harder, and my eyes pinch closed. Her hands feel amazing.

"He was so proud."

"When did he… pass?"

"About four years ago. Heart attack. He was working in his garden."

After a long silence filled with nothing but the gentle lap of waves against our bodies, she finally whispers, "I'm so sorry."

I shrug and spin to face her, wrapping my arms gently around her.

"He would have liked you."

"Yeah?" The expression on her face is strange. Like she didn't expect me to say it.

I nod and wipe a strand of blonde hair from her face. She stares at me, and I am lost in her eyes.

We are an island floating serenely in the middle of nowhere.

"What's it like to have your life together?" She asks. The question comes out of nowhere.

I laugh. "What do you mean?"

"I mean, you have a career, a boatload of money, a handful of cars, a house the size of a shopping mall... I'm guessing probably a yacht somewhere..."

"Pfffft, I'd hardly call it a *yacht*." That's a lie. I would most definitely call it a yacht. It's a 164-foot Belle Anna that sleeps up to sixteen people.

She laughs. I think she thinks I'm kidding. "...And you have Bella and your mom." The look in her eyes suddenly seems far away. "You have a family."

I don't know what to say to that.

She's *right*.

I *do.*

Although, I don't have someone to share my life with. The ups, the downs, the hard times, the celebrations...

Honestly, sometimes, it's real damned *lonely* at the top.

Never knowing who really enjoys your company or who really wants the best for you versus who just wants in your wallet or your social sphere so they can name-drop you as a *friend* at fundraisers, luncheons, and board meetings.

"Now it's time to ask you the hard-hitting questions." I pull her close.

"I'm sorry, but my client is not available for comment." She shields her smiling face, and I pull her close enough to almost rub our noses together.

"What do you want in life?"

"What do I want in life?" She scoffs. "I think it would be easier to say what I don't want in life."

"No, seriously."

"I don't know." She stares at my lips, and I have to fight the urge to kiss the hell out of her right now. "A working car…"

I laugh. "I mean, like… big picture. What do you want in life?"

A heavy silence falls over the massive space, and her eyes slink down to the waves.

"I want… to feel like I truly belong somewhere."

I wipe a bead of water from her brow, one that is threatening to fall into her eyes. "What do you mean?"

"I mean, ever since I was Bella's age, I have felt like a vagabond. After what happened to my brother and my dad, I had to go live with my uncle. But he wasn't around much. I was treated like garbage throughout school. I had this... *stigma* from my mother. After what she did, I never really had any family to speak of. I moved in with Cassandra the moment I was able to, but no place has ever really felt... like home. No one has ever felt like *family*."

Another silence. Then, her eyes meet mine, the color of emerald waters, deep and churning. "I think... I want that."

I'm not quite sure what to say to that.

She clears her throat and dips down through my arms, slipping from my grasp like a pleasant dream.

After a lap, she grabs the ladder and pulls herself out, dripping water from every curve. She plucks a rolled towel from the station between two long, slatted, wooden bench seats and starts drying herself off.

I swim to the edge of the pool nearest to her and lean up onto the cold stone edging. "You know, a few weeks ago, I had a fantasy about you in this *exact* outfit."

"Oh?" she mumbles, pleased, toweling her hair dry. "Care to make it a reality?"

I feel my dick harden instantly against the constrictive mesh of my trunks as she asks. I've never met a woman whose sexual appetite matched my own.

"Can't. It involves a hammock."

"Well, you're in luck. There just so happens to be a hammock outside my new place."

"Kira, it's like thirty-five degrees outside, and we're soaking wet." But I feel my heart thunder at the possibility of being inside of her again…

Of making her pant my name in moaning gusts the way that she does…

She pouts and looks down.

All of a sudden, a smile graces her lips. She takes a seat on the slatted bench and massages the wood strips on either side of her. "What would you say… to a *substitution*?"

48

Kira

Zuzanna's house is massive. You could park five of the single-wides I grew up in side-by-side in her living room and still have room to maneuver.

"Come, come!" She waves us in, wiping her age-spotted hands with a bleach-white tea towel. "Dinner ees a-ready." Her accent is charming and melodical. Even though her English is broken, her voice is a joyous song.

"Bella," Zuzanna looks down at her granddaughter's rodent travel carrier, grimacing, "Sernik no can come to dinner. He has to stay een living room, okay?"

"Okay." Bella doesn't fight her. She darts toward a low table, kneels beside Sernik, and has a one-on-one chat with him about how she won't be long and promises to bring him a piece of one of her pierogies to try.

"Best money ever spent," Eric whispers close to my ear. Even after several weeks, I feel my body's temperature rise at the sound of his voice.

The three of us are led by Zuzanna into a massive dining room to a long table that could easily seat twenty. A gold runner runs across the length of it, punctuated with three large flower arrangements with an assortment of gladiolas and lilies in a rainbow of rich colors.

As we breeze in and settle around the one end with place settings laid out for four, I see Eric kiss the pads of his fingers and press them to the face of a smiling man in a framed photo on the wall. He has some of Eric's features and looks vaguely familiar from the photos I found in the pool house a week ago.

"Come! Sit. Eat," Zuzanna orders as she takes a seat in front of ornate silver trays full of steaming pierogies, sizzling kielbasa, potato pancakes with sour cream, dill, and salmon on top, and a crystal bowl of cold sauerkraut. "Every-ting is-a homemade from scratch. For dessert, I make drunken plum cake and-a tiramisu, so… eat up!" She claps her hands together and gives us all a giant, genuine smile.

"Ms. Salko," I'm in awe, "this looks and smells delicious."

"Aw," she waves me away. "Please! Call me Zuzanna."

"*Huh-huh-huh,* I don't know what *you guys* are gonna eat," Bella stands and slides the huge tray of potato and cheese delicacies toward herself with outstretched arms like she's going to use it as her personal plate.

***

We gorge until we were all a bit too full. I stare at Eric with that regretful ate-too-much look in my eyes by the time Zuzanna carves up her spongy drunken plum cake, insisting we each eat at least one small piece while it's fresh.

It tastes like fruit and alcohol in the best possible way, and I groan. "This is delicious, Zuzanna."

Still, Zuzanna only watches all of us, barely partaking in the eating of her own food. If she weren't saccharine-sweet, I'd be suspicious that I was being drugged. But looking at her tiny frame, I can tell she watches what she eats.

Clink-clink-clink.

Eric's fork clinks against his brown bottle of Polish beer as he rises from his seat. "Excuse me, ladies."

All of our eyes are drawn to him, each with our own form of love and adoration.

Wait, did I just say love? I mean, out of respect *and adoration.*

"First of all, I just want to say that I'm so lucky to be here with all three of you right now. You are some of the most amazing women I have ever known."

I feel my cheeks pink up, and I try to hide my bashful smile with my hand as his eyes graze mine. Bella grins, fists pushing both sides of her face up as she rests her arms on the table in her food coma.

"Next week Miss Bella here turns the big one-zero."

I clap.

…And then I realize I am the *only one* clapping, so I stop.

"A decade has gone by since you came into my life. I plan to celebrate it in a way that seems fitting." He plucks three white envelopes and hands them to us. Each has our names on them.

I eye him suspiciously with a smirk. "What is this?"

"Well, Bella's birthday lands on her school's spring break, so I thought we would do her birthday right. Open them."

I shred my envelope.

"I think I know what this ees!" Zuzanna sings as she opens hers carefully.

Bella tears the side of her envelope open with her teeth like a rabid animal.

"Bella!" Eric's eyes go large.

"What?" She shrugs, white paper still between her molars. "I saw someone do it in a movie."

"What movie? *Cujo?*" I snicker. But my laughter doesn't last long as I see the contents of the envelope.

The first item is booking confirmation…

For a luxury apartment…

In *France*.

"What…?" I can't even get the words out. I read it twice more, just to be sure my eyes aren't betraying me.

"Aw, we no go to Rome again?" Zuzanna asks with a hint of disappointment in her voice.

"*Nie, matka*, I am taking you all to Paris. On the jet." Eric beams. He looks so handsome when he smiles like this that I want to *pounce*.

Down girl.

Know your surroundings…

"Oh, I love a-riding the jet," Zuzanna says, clapping her hand against the envelope excitedly.

"*Huh-huh-huh-huh*, this is awesome!" Bella hugs the ticket to her chest, twitching.

And me… I'm speechless. *I don't deserve this.*

"Also, Kira, you will be paid your regular salary while you're there, but your work duties will be different."

I offer him a stunned look, mouth agape. "Wh-what?" I'm flabbergasted. All of this… all of it is overwhelming in the best possible way.

"We will need a translator. You speak French." He smiles. "You may have to pull some double-duty as a tour guide, too."

"Sold," I say, but it's hard to see him through the tears welling in my eyes.

I haven't been to Paris in five years. And, frankly, with the state of my finances over the past half a decade, it was beginning to feel like I'd never see it again.

"You always speak so highly of it. I figured you could show us around, suggest activities and places to eat, and help us figure out what everyone is saying because I'm pretty sure Bella knows more French than I do at this point."

As the tears fall from my eyes, I mouth *thank you* to keep from full-on blubbering.

While Bella and Zuzanna's heads are down, looking through the rest of the envelope, Eric subtly blows a kiss in my direction, and I melt.

This man is made of straight sugar.

I shuffle through the rest of the papers in the envelope and wipe my face before the others have a chance to notice how hard I'm crying.

I know this is a gift for Bella, but it is most definitely a gift for me as well.

There are more printed papers that show off the features and amenities of our palatial lodging. And to top it all off, the building is located right at the edge of the *Champ-de-Mars* park that stretches its long rectangle all the way up to the Eiffel Tower.

I want to faint.

This can't be real.

This place is opulent. I'm sure it cost more euros for a couple-day stay than my job at the Sweater Barn paid in *months*.

Zuzanna and Bella joyously chatter beside me about all of the things they want to do and see, and I can't make out a word of it. I'm too focused on how much I want to shower Eric's handsome face with kisses of gratitude.

Eric looks at his daughter and mother. "I figure we can also do a day of shopping on the *Champs-Élysées* and get you something cool for your birthday, Bella."

"*Oh, Champs-Élysées...*" Bella sings joyfully. I laugh, surprised that she remembers the tune. I only played it for her once on the way home from her therapy. That was *weeks* ago.

There's something else in my envelope that the others don't seem to have: a folded sheet with tickets to *Le Moulin Rouge* in Montmartre.

I touch my fingers to my mouth, and my face grows hot.

But it's the handwritten note at the bottom that makes the tears fall like rain. It says:

I was wondering if you would accompany me on a date?

I look at Eric and nod yes, trying to swipe the wet streaks from my cheeks.

"*Bardzo dziękuję,*" Zuzanna sings, reaching over to hug him.

Bella is next in line for a squeeze. "*Huh-huh,* thank you, Dad!" Her arms squeeze his neck in a loving choke-hold.

I know he is worried about losing her. I know he will be inconsolable if Tawny succeeds in her selfish quest.

The love he shows for Bella makes me feel a surge of buried-deep longing for a similar embrace from my late father. As I watch Eric hold his daughter, I realize with certainty that I want a family like this one day.

"Wow, we are going to be so fancy. I'll bet they have golden teacups for their high tea." Bella sifts through the pictures of the apartment, licking kielbasa grease off her face with her giraffe-like tongue.

"Better pack your *boa*," I mumble to him, laughing through the tears.

He flashes me a *hey, watch it* look and then kisses Bella on the side of the head. "Happy early Birthday, Ella-Bella."

A moment later, I feel his comforting hand caress my knee beneath the table.

49

Eric

The flight on the private jet isn't quite the *mile-high club* adventure that I hoped. Bella called dibs on the seat next to me the moment we boarded. Across from me, Kira and Mom sat side-by-side, facing Bella and me, talking like old friends from the second they sat down.

While I can't hear every word, I get bits and phrases. I hear Mom telling her about my father, his passion for gardening, and all the vegetables he used to grow. She tells Kira about Poland and the town of Sanok, where she grew up. I hear little clips about her and my father's escape from communist clutches, all familiar stories I've heard at least a dozen times throughout my life. I could probably recite many of them verbatim from memory.

As the hours pass, and the sun has long tucked itself away for the night, Bella passes out cold, portable DVD player in hand, playing that God-forsaken duck movie while using my left arm as her personal neck pillow.

Their conversation in the dim light of the cabin changes from being about my mother to Kira's hometown in Florida, the origins behind

286

her nickname, and all about her eventual move to New England to live with her uncle.

Eventually, I put my book away for the evening and recline my chair to sleep. As my eyelids start to close, I can still hear them talking like giddy best friends. Their conversation has evolved into discussions of passionate pastimes, music, and movies. They talk about world travel and all of the places both women have been to and still want to go.

It makes me happy to see them getting along so well. Mom was always pretty open about her disdain for Tawny, especially during those last two or three years of our marriage when Tawny mentally checked out.

The odd thing is, the more I hear Kira talk about all of the places she's yet to travel — mostly due to *budgetary* constraints — the more I feel this *desire* inside of me growing.

This… need.

The need to show her the world, one city at a time.

The need to step outside of my comfort zone.

The need… to call her *mine*.

It feels so good to stretch my legs after the nine-hour flight and the fifty-minute limousine ride to the doorstep of our new Parisian apartment for the next few days. This whole adventure feels like a lucid dream I wouldn't dare to wake from.

Seeing the top of the tower peeking above the ten-story buildings throughout the 15th Arrondissement of Paris makes my stomach flutter with giddiness. I'm buzzing at the familiar sights and scents of this incredible city.

The limo parks on the tight one-way in front of a row of massive interconnected buildings, and Eric helps us exit the vehicle gracefully. The driver promptly retrieves our luggage from the trunk and carefully brings it into the lobby.

Eric holds Bella's hand and points to the top story of the building. "We're all the way up there on the top floor."

Bella squeals, "*C'est Magnifique!*"

Holy crap, that kid picks up new vocabulary quick.

***

As we pile out of an elevator that feels tighter than a coffin, we follow the narrow hallway to our room door, and Eric scans the card.

CLICK.

As he opens the door, we are suddenly basking in the glow of natural sunlight pouring in through a long, narrow foyer with seating around a real living tree in a massive pot in the middle. Beyond it, the panoramic wall of glass overlooking the park is aglow with the light of this perfect day.

I gasp. My heart feels like it skips three whole beats as the stunning view of the tapered metal tower oozes into my field of view.

Paris looks like a postcard from here.

Our apartment is a warm, cream-colored masterpiece, bright and inviting. It looks like something out of an interior decorating magazine.

None of this feels real.

Pinch me.

At this moment, I don't feel worthy of being here… of being in such a breathtaking city, rich with history. I don't feel like I deserve to set foot in this stunning penthouse with this amazing man and his loving family…

Deep down, I'm just a broke kid with no parents, living in my uncle's trailer park, eating microwaveable boxed mac and cheese twice a day because it's all I can afford.

Eric breezes through the massive main room full of cozy tufted furniture punctuated by a white grand piano. A modernist, circular chandelier dangles like a giant shell wind-chime over a dining table.

He continues into the stunning open kitchen made for gourmet cooking. A giant welcome basket sits on a gray-and-white island made of thick marble. The wicker container is chock-full of wheels of cheese, jams, baguettes, and bottles of burgundy and cabernet.

"Alright, so this place has three bedrooms. Ma, I know you and Bella like to stay together, so you will be in the big suite."

Eric motions to a gigantic room with a king bed, a wooden day bed, and a spacious en suite bathroom.

"Yay!" Bella celebrates, rushing past her father, nearly bowling him over to get inside. She jumps up on the bed, clutching her stuffed animal and twitching her head to the side compulsively. She spins around, carefree, and stares out the window at the view of Paris from over a sea of gray rooftops.

"*Huh-huh,* this place is *bonkers!*"

The adults all laugh in unison, and Eric's smiling eyes catch mine for an intimate, secret moment that only lasts a second. In it, it feels like we are the only two people on earth.

"Oh, you no have to do dat. You take big room." Zuzanna waves him away and heads into the kitchen.

"No, Ma, you and Bella get the master." Eric shakes his head and stares at the ceiling.

There is no response from Zuzanna. Just the soft clink of wine glasses followed by a variety of kitchen drawers opening and shutting as she presumably searches for a bottle opener.

"Miss Kira, your room is down here." He waves for me to follow him further down the hall. He subtly holds his hands behind his back and wiggles his fingers. I understand exactly what he's implying, and I slide my hand in his, our bodies obscuring our secretly public display of affection.

At the end of the hall, two doors sit side-by-side, each with a modest queen-sized bed and little else beyond a dresser and wall of windows with massive floor-to-ceiling curtains.

As I enter the first room and walk around, I feel Eric slide his arms around me from behind, resting his chin on my shoulder. "This one's mine. Yours is next door. And… there are two reasons I chose it for you."

"Yeah?" I fight the urge to beam brightly.

He presses us toward a door joining the two rooms. Releasing me, he slips his arms up the jamb. "This *door* is one of them."

I smile, feeling heat radiate from my blushing cheeks. I mumble quietly, "Ah, *easy access.*"

"Mmmm-hmmm. And this," he walks us in, "is your room."

My hands fly up to my face to hide the tears filling my eyes, each threatening to fall right onto the plush, pristine shag rug beneath our feet.

The view of the Eiffel Tower from my room is *breathtaking*. I have a completely unobscured vista sprawled before me. I nestle against him and stare up into his eyes. He strokes my exposed shoulders and wet cheeks with a feather-light touch and then finally kisses me.

The second we hear tiny feet galloping down the hall, we pull apart, *leaving enough room for Christ between us*, as my uncle used to say.

"Dad, I'm hungry," Bella whines, popping her flaxen head in the door to my new suite. Then she gasps loudly. "Hooooooly crap! *Huh-huh*, look at that view!"

We burst into laughter, but Eric manages to reel himself in. "*Hey*, language, missy."

"What? I just said *crap*." She pouts a little, trying to hide her mischievous smile.

"Well, Miss Kira," Eric says to me, "what place would you recommend for lunch?"

I grin.

"What?" He's confused.

"Nothing, it's just funny, is all."

"What's funny?"

"Well, when I met you, you were so organized that I thought for sure you'd be the kind of guy that would have like a minute-by-minute itinerary for a vacation."

"Well, I have no itinerary. And I'm glad I subverted your expectations of me being some type of uptight, obsessive, type-A planner."

"Yeah, I'm glad about that, too. It's gonna make this trip a lot more fun." I take a deep breath and pat my thighs. "For lunch, I've actually got just the place in mind. It's a short metro ride from here."

Eric looks pensive at the sound of the word subway. "No. No subways. Let's take the limo."

"No. I'm afraid I must insist. Chartered private *jet?* Great. Love it. *Limo* from the airport? Amazing. But I'm afraid you have to ride the rails on this trip. I gotta draw a line in the sand on this one."

"We aren't riding the subway, Kira. Bella's nine."

"*Huh-huh*, almost *ten*," she corrects.

"The limo is great, but you should experience the city and walk the streets. If you take a car, you miss out on all of the buskers, dancers, mimes… and just the *journey*."

"What's a metro?" Bella chimes in.

"It's what they call the subway here," I say.

"*Huh-huh*, what's a subway?"

"It's like an underground train that takes you anywhere you want to go in the city. And it's full of talented people who perform for you…"

"Dad, I wanna go on the metro."

Eric's lips press into a tense line as he stares at me.

I try to squelch the chuckle brewing in me. "I'm sorry, Eric, but it looks like the birthday girl has spoken."

"It's not her birthday *yet*," he grumbles.

"Dad, I think we should go, too. I'm afraid I have to draw a line in the sand on this one."

I laugh again. There she goes again, mimicking me.

"She's like a *macaw*." Eric pinches his temples between his fingers.

"C'mon! There's nowhere we can't get to from the metro here. Let your driver go and come slum it in the streets a little. It'll be so fun!"

Eric huffs and shakes his head. "*Fine.*"

Bella cheers and dances out of the room. From the hall, she yells, "*Babcia*, help me get a subway dress on!"

"*Subway dress?*" he asks, confused.

I shrug and lean in. I touch the tip of my nose to Eric's, allowing my lips to hover dangerously close to his.

"Thank you."

"You owe me one." His fingers rest on my shoulder for a moment before sliding inward and south, brushing the fabric over my left breast.

"I know. I do. But don't worry, I *always* repay my debts." My hand slides down the firm crease of the outside of his zipper, feeling the hard girth hidden behind. His eyes flutter closed.

"I'm going to go change and freshen up," he says before nibbling my earlobe in a way that makes my knees buckle.

"Me too. I'm not about to let Bella's subway dress show up my own."

He laughs. "Don't be long. I'm starving." He starts through the adjoining door to his suite. Then he adds, "Lotta pressure on you to pick a decent spot for lunch. Don't let us down."

"I won't. There's a Nicoise near *Place de la Bastille* that will change the way you feel about salads forever."

51

Eric

Kira wasn't kidding about the Nicoise. The unique combination of flavors is something I won't soon forget. I have to make a note to myself to have Jacques start making those at home.

Standing here on this rattling subway, leaning against a chrome pole to steady myself, I watch the three women I adore converse over the sounds of a rather talented busker playing her ukulele and singing a haunting rendition of *La Vie En Rose* for euros at the other end of the car.

Kira stayed true to her word about wearing a *subway dress* so that Bella wouldn't feel out of place. She looks ravishing in the long, floral summer dress as the dappled sun stipples inward through the metro windows.

Springtime in Paris looks so damned good on her.

She seems to be explaining something to Mom and Bella about the French Revolution and Bastille Saint-Antoine, whooshing her animated hands as she talks.

The musician's pure melody is like a new soundtrack played over this moment, tuning out all of the rattle and hum of the grinding metro, the talking, and the sound of people sifting through the car in preparation for their next stop.

I watch Kira explain things to them with a level of detail and fascination that makes me fully aware of her intelligence. Despite not having a private school education or her choice of colleges... she's smart. I imagine she gathers knowledge about life and culture through things like genuine curiosity and stubborn persistence over traditional schooling.

My mother and daughter are entranced by Kira's stories as she romanticizes the City of Lights like some ultra-passionate tour guide.

We have four more stops left before we get out, so I make my way over to the ukulele player as she finishes her song. I lean in close so that she can hear me over the grind and roar of the car.

"Excuse me, do you, by chance, happen to speak English?"

The woman nods. I lean in again.

"Do you happen to know any John Denver?"

She thinks for a moment and then looks down at my hand, which has a folded bill in it. Fifty euros.

"Do you know *Sunshine on my Shoulders?*"

She shakes her head. "No." Then she smiles. "*Take Me Home, Country Road?*"

"Good enough." I hand her the fifty and head back to Bella, Zuzanna, and Kira.

I smile, grabbing onto the chrome pole again. Zuzanna says something to Bella about her dress that I can't make out, and they begin to chat about her birthday plans.

As the busker plays the opening notes and begins her soft rendition of the song, Kira grins at me. She points to me and mouths, '*you?*'

I nod almost imperceptibly.

She lays her head back against the glass and beams as the music plays, shoulders relaxed, cheeks rosy, eyes bright.

As I watch her mouth along to the lyrics and hear the stringy tune, a knot forms in my stomach. I'm not fully sure *how* or *when* this happened, but I realize something that I'd pay any amount of money to not have to admit…

I'm falling for this woman.

52

Eric

Bella looks adorable, blushing in the middle of the sidewalk. The *Arc de Triomphe* peeks through the rainy mid-morning haze in the background. The squared monument stands proudly and steadfast at the end of the lengthy avenue behind her.

" — *Happy birthday, dear Bellaaaaaa… Happy birthday to youuuuuu*," the three of us finish singing in near-unison. I stop the video recording on my phone and quickly glance at the stock updates while Mom and Kira give Bella her round of applause. Out of the corner of my eye, I see Bella curtsy, and I snicker, slipping my phone back into the pocket of my suit.

"Ten years old," Zuzanna sings, hugging her granddaughter joyfully. "*Wow*."

The *Champs-Élysées* bustles with life, glistening with runoff. More rain threatens to fall, darkening the skies with a blanket of foamy charcoal-gray. This place is like Fifth Avenue and Rodeo Drive, all rolled into one long stretch of high-end shops.

Massive chandeliers glitter through the windows as we walk past the high-end stores. I watch a gaggle of children that can't be more than Bella's age dressed in earth tones, smoking cigarettes at the top of a set of stone stairs leading down to the metro, flirting with the grown women ascending from the terminal below. I can't help but laugh at the bizarre scene.

My mother laughs at something Kira says to her beneath the large, black umbrella they're sharing like long-lost sisters. Mom tucks under an awning and waves for me to join them in the doorway of a high-end jewelry store.

"Come! Come!" she barks, grinning. "I want to a-look at de' jewelry." She struggles with the last word, trying to cram in some sort of extra syllable.

The lot of us dart inside, shaking off our coats, umbrellas, and footwear. Mom is like a kid in a candy store. Within seconds of being inside, she starts pointing to things, aiming Bella's attention toward anything sparkly. She keeps pressing her fingers to the glass like she's in an aquarium and *not* one of the world's most expensive & premiere jewelers.

Kira follows a different row of glass cabinets, hovering from well over a foot away, hands clasped behind her back. She views the contents with reverence but looks like she doesn't deserve the right to approach for a closer view.

My phone chimes and I lean against the entryway wall to check my text.

**ROB: TSLA is crashing.
President dropped a bomb**

My heart leaps into my chest at the thought of what sort of sudden turmoil is taking place politically back in America.

I've been gone for two-and-a-half days, and the president has dropped a goddamned *BOMB?* In what country? What the fuck did I miss?!

**ROB: Shell in his address
today.**

**ROB: Sorry. Almost dropped
my phone in the fucking fish
tank while I was feeding the
clownfish.**

ROB: Jesus. Close call.

I breathe a sigh of relief, even though I want to strangle him for scaring me like that.

ERIC: What's RIVN doing?

**ROB: It was down fucking 6.3
percent today at closing. 9%
for the week.**

ERIC: FUCK!

ERIC: REGN?

ROB: Wouldn't it be easier to just log on and look yourself?

ERIC: I just tried. My signal's weak. It's taking forever to update prices.

ROB: Point is, shit is hitting the fan. The Sterns and Mary Barnes want to pull out.

ERIC: Don't. Fucking. Let. Them. The numbers will come back.

ERIC: Mary Barnes is a whale, Rob.

ROB: Wow, I mean, she's gained a little weight, but whale is pretty harsh.

ERIC: Rob, you know what I fucking mean.

ROB: I know. I'm not an idiot.

I scan the room. All of the women are still preoccupied with looking at jewelry. I text him again.

ERIC: What happened?

ROB: Prez said inflation numbers were higher than expected, and interest rates and the jobs market are bleak.

ROB: Just wanted to update you.

ROB: How's the trip?

ERIC: It's been fun. Bella's B-day today.

ROB: Tell her bappy birthday

ROB: *Habby

ROB: *HAPPY! Fuck!

I see that Kira is interpreting Mom's broken English to the Parisian worker behind the counter. The woman pulls a bracelet out, and Mom turns it toward Bella, asking her a question.

Kira breaks away, and as I go to stuff my phone back into my suit pocket, I hear another chime.

ROB: That smoke show assistant give you a "thank you" blowie yet?

I won't dignify his question with an answer. As much as I'd like to shout it from a mountain while beating my chest, it's none of his goddamn business.

"See anything you like?" I whisper as I sneak up behind Kira.

She pops into the air like a scared animal with a quiet yip, clutching her chest. "Holy... you scared me."

I look down at the item that has seemingly caught her attention: a simple silver box chain with a colorful stone-encrusted pendant resembling a Ferris wheel. I smile.

Of course, she'd like this one.

"You need it," I say, catching a deep, intoxicating whiff of her perfume. It's a different flower this time... *roses*, I think.

"*Are you kidding me? In this place? This thing is probably like three years' salary. Minimum,*" she whispers.

"Yeah, you're right. Hmmm, if only you knew a filthy-rich guy..." I joke, looking around the room for an available clerk.

She snickers. "I'm not looking for a sugar daddy." A sudden wash of embarrassment overrides her smile as she sees me waving down one of the employees.

"No." She sounds firm now. "Eric, don't. *Please.* It's too expensive. I'd probably break it. Or-or-or *lose* it. All I own is, like, costume jewelry. Plastic and nickel garbage from the mall.

Most of what I-I own will turn your skin green if you shower in it." She's so flustered she's starting to stutter.

I peel away a tendril of damp, golden hair stuck to the side of her face. "That's *precisely* why you *should* have this."

"Please... don't." She pleads quietly with a level of seriousness I've rarely seen her display. "I didn't earn it. I can't afford it."

"You *deserve* it."

"No, Eric." Her voice quivers, but I adore the sound of my name being spoken lowly from her lips. It sparks something primal in me, reminding me of how she whispers it when my face is buried between her thighs.

Still, this situation saddens me. She acts like she's worth... *nothing*.

She deserves the *world*.

Even though she could beg for everything this world has got to give, she asks for nothing. *Expects* nothing. *Maneuvers* for nothing. She's caring but still charming. Casual, but still deep. Wounded but still giving.

She's fucking *incredible*. I really want to do this for her. I'm torn between trying to *treat* her and trying to *respect* her.

"Kira, I disagree. You deserve something a hundred times the cost of that."

I step back.

"But it's not my aim to make you uncomfortable."

"Thank you," she says quietly before allowing her eyes to finally drift away.

As I move away from the counter, I see her eyes zero back in on the necklace. I turn around and...

My mother is turned, staring at us with her arms folded. Disappointment is smeared on her normally jovial features. Her foot is even tapping.

Fuck.

53

Kira

Eric and his mother are discussing something in Polish at a speed that blows my mind. I know I'm the topic of discussion because his mother keeps motioning to me with her wild hand movements. She seems upset, raising her voice. Bella leans against her father, watching them bicker in another language like she's watching an overhead tennis match.

Zuzanna swats at his arm, irritated. She shouts something else. I wish I could speak Polish if only just to eavesdrop. If I had to wager a guess, I'd say Zuzanna saw him playing with my hair and figured it out. She's a smart woman. She's probably telling him he is a fucking idiot for *slumming it* with the help and that the jig is up.

She *knows* something is going on between us.

Eric runs his hand through his hair in frustration, growls, and turns, eyes piercing me from across the room.

Bella grabs the arm of his suit, which looks more blue than some of these sapphires beneath the glittering chandeliers.

"*Obiad, Papa! Obiad.*"

"Yes. Ugh, fine. *Obiad.*" He sighs.

Zuzanna is turned around, sighing deeply. Her gaze turns to me, serious as a heart attack, and suddenly, I want to dart out into the middle of the street and get squished by a taxi.

I'm fucking *mortified.*

I want to apologize to her for humiliating her *and* her son. He could have a Hollywood starlet on his arm. Or an heiress. Someone with a fat trust fund, acres of land, or social connections.

Eric collects our umbrellas at the door and sighs again. He rolls his neck, cracking it loudly, and forces a smile. "The birthday girl is hungry. Ready for lunch?"

"Famished," I lie.

His mother's reaction has churned my stomach, and it will take everything I have to even look at a menu without wanting to barf right now.

"We pass little bistro that look ama-sing a few doors down. The one-a with... the... *crepes* on the menu," Zuzanna's voice is once again sing-songy.

"Yay! Crepes!" Bella hops in place, singing. "*I love crepes, I love crepes.*"

Zuzanna chats with the woman at the counter for what feels like forever as the rest of us shuffle back out into the drizzly outdoors. Zuzanna joins us with a small bag and hands it to Bella.

"Your bracelet, okay? Don't lose!" Zuzanna places the bag in her hand. "Eet's very espensive. Daddy will put on for you at lunch, okay?"

Bella's nod is followed by two twitches and a big smile.

***

"I stuffed." Zuzanna pats the bottom of her bony rib cage with a grin and leans back in her chair.

"This was delicious," I say over the plate of what once was a savory salmon-and-dill crepe and is now nothing more than a faint smear of sour cream that I'd probably lick straight off the plate if I were alone right now.

Clearly, my appetite returned with a *vengeance*.

"I use restroom, and then we go, okay?"

Eric nods and wipes his mouth with his napkin.

"I'll go, too," Bella adds.

Eric takes the last swig of his cider, eyes darting everywhere but me.

Zuzanna looks pensive and grumbles, "Okay, but bring your coat. Ees cold." She tucks in her chair, puts on her wool jacket, grabs her purse, and shuffles off behind me with her burping granddaughter in tow.

Eric's eyes finally meet mine, and he stares at me for a moment. Even as Zuzanna and Bella leave my sight, I'm too nervous to ask about what happened earlier... about what was said in Polish about me.

About *us*.

"She knows, doesn't she?" I finally ask, nervous, dragging the tines of my fork slowly across my rumpled napkin.

He chuckles and sits for a moment before finally speaking. "She's known for *weeks*, Kira."

It is the last thing I expected him to say. My eyes bulge. I feel like I could be knocked over with a feather.

"What?" I stammer, "H-how?!"

"How? I *told* her. The night I told you all we were going to France. In the kitchen when you and Bella were trying to feed her rat a pierogi."

I don't know what to say right now. *What? How?*

He can tell by the stupefied look plastered on my face that I am absolutely flummoxed.

"You *told* her?"

"Of *course,* I told her. Why would I hide it? I'm a grown-ass adult. I can date who I want to date."

Date?

Did he just say date?

Are we… dating?

"What? I'm so confused! We've been sneaking around all this time—"

"For *Bella*." His hand spreads across the back of mine. "My daughter has loved you from the moment she *met* you. But with all the crap going on with Tawny and everything being so up in the air, I didn't think it was right to make it known until things settle down for a bit."

310

"So wait, your mom has known this entire trip that you and I are…"

"—*Seeing each other*, yes."

That's a nicer term than what I would've used. One that makes me pause and replay the words that he's just spoken.

I thought he was viewing me as a casual fling. A fun-while-it-lasts romp.

Seeing each other implies something ongoing.

I swallow hard. "I can't believe this. Wait, then what was she grumbling at you in the store about?"

"Because she's pissed *off* at me."

"Pissed over what?"

Silence.

I repeat the question, quieter this time. "Pissed over *what*, Eric?"

"She's pissed that I didn't buy you that necklace." His eyes lash to mine with rings around their center like gold coins eclipsed by black, and I'm lost for a moment in his electrifying gaze. "I told her what you said, that you didn't feel like you'd *earned* it or *deserved* it. She called me more than a few choice words, but I told her I wanted to respect your wishes and not make you uncomfortable. And *that's* what I did."

I lean back in my seat and fidget with the edge of my platter. "I can't believe she's *known this whole time.*"

"I mean, my Mom's no fool. People in my line of work don't *typically* need to take their assistants on an international vacation. She was going to know."

I snicker. "Fair point."

"She's going to have a picnic in the park with Bella tomorrow night for dinner while I take you for an actual, like, proper date."

Mmmm… Le Moulin Rouge.

I try to hide my smile at the thought of going out in public with him, showing him Montmartre, but I can't. I feel like I'm beaming wide enough that someone on the *moon* would be able to see it right now.

Zuzanna finally makes her way back to the table with Bella. She seems highly energized and ready to go, which seems typical for her bouncy self.

"To the toy store?" Bella asks.

"Yep." Eric smiles as he stands. "To the toy store!"

54

Eric

"Bella, please, I am *begging* you. That puppet is *hideous*. Please, sweetness, is there *anything* else in the store that you might want?" I ask in my most pleading tone.

I pray this girl changes her mind about the item that leaves with us. The godawful wooden foot-tall marionette she's infatuated with is a thing of nightmares. I assume it is some kind of witch, but it's hard to tell because there is so much ugly crap going on with this thing.

"I like her!" Bella whines. "*Huh-huh-huh,* she's cute."

"Bella, she is the absolute *antithesis* of cute," I protest.

Kira picks the ugly marionette up by the wooden crossbars and lifts it off the rack. With a flick of her wrist, she has the witch hobbling in a realistic fashion, walking along the narrow wooden countertop. She speaks in a wicked, old voice, "Who *dares* interrupt my slumbers?"

Bella giggles. "*Huh-huh,* how'd you do that?"

"It's easy. Plus, I used to make puppets like this out of stuff around my house. Fishing string,

Popsicle sticks, sponges, whatever we could get our hands on. Then, I'd put on a puppet show for my little brother."

"You have a brother?" Bella cocks an eyebrow.

"*Had,*" Kira says, trying to smile and frowning instead. "His name was Christopher. He died when he was your age, actually."

"*Huh-huh,* what'd he die of?"

"Bella, that's *rude,*" I mutter.

"No, it's fine." Kira looks at Bella. "He got very sick with something called *leukemia,* and we didn't have the money the doctors needed to make him get better." She clears her throat. "That's who gave me the nickname Ree-Ree actually."

Her words hit me like a brick to the face.

Jesus, I had no clue.

I can't imagine someone as young as Bella going through any of that, much less having *money* be the only deciding factor on whether she got treatment or died.

"*Oh.*" Bella looks at the floor and then back up at her. "I'm sorry. I wish I would have known you then. I'd have given you my allowance."

Kira smiles, but it's pained. "Oh, kid, I know you would have." She pulls my daughter close, hands her the puppet, and kisses Bella on the top of her head.

"Take her for a spin." Then, Kira looks at the woman behind the register. "*Puis-je?*"

The woman nods permissively. Kira gives my daughter a twenty-second tutorial on how to manipulate the doll, and I can't help but smile at the sight of her traipsing around the cramped store with it.

"Fee-fi-foe-fum," Bella seizes with her tic, but the doll keeps walking smoothly on its tiny wooden feet through the aisles. Then, for a moment, she stops and backs up, making the witch mimic her backward movement. "*Beep-beep-beep-beep.*"

I snort. Zuzanna laughs, sweet and high-pitched. But Kira is preoccupied at the register.

"*Excusez-moi, madame. Je voudrais acheter la poupée,*" she says to the woman behind the counter, pulling money from the pocket of her tattered satchel.

"*Oui.*" The woman nods and pulls out a box for the doll.

"Hey now," I interject, trying to brush Kira gently away while pulling one of my credit cards out.

"No," Kira pushes my wallet toward my chest. "I haven't gotten her a present yet. I'd really like to get her something from *me.*"

55

"*La pi-ed, huh-huh, du co…chon,*" Bella says, reading the words from the tented awning.

"Very good," I exclaim, high-fiving her tiny hand. "You're a natural. Now, what does it *mean?*"

Bella looks at her father.

"I'll bet none of you can guess what it means." I playfully point a finger around at all of them.

"The stomach… uhhhh, erm, happy," Zuzanna says, more as a statement than a question. "The… happy stomach." She laughs loud like she just heard a joke from a stand-up comedian.

Eric shifts his weight, bogged down by all of the paper bags he's clutching from our intense day of shopping. I hold my hands out to take the ones from his still-healing arm, and, with reluctance, he finally gives them over, mouthing *thank you* with a look of relief.

"It means *the foot of the pig*," I say.

Bella grimaces. "*What?!*"

I laugh at the way she says it.

"Everyone had better prepare to sleep with the windows open tonight because, girl," I poke Bella in the sternum lightly with an index finger, "this is the best bowl of French onion soup you're ever going to have in your *life*."

"Oh, sweet *Jesus*," Eric mutters, thinking about the forthcoming consequences.

"You're gonna love this place, Mouse. Everything is good here."

"I'll bet that's not true," Eric grumbles. "I'll bet they have steak tartare and all that gnarly stuff." He shivers, crinkling the paper bags as he does.

"First of all, steak tartare is *delicious*—"

"—It is an uncooked *abomination*. A slap in the face to any cow who has given his life for our sustenance." Eric's voice is firm, but he fights a smile. "This is how the French repay them for their ultimate sacrifice? They crack a raw egg on it and call it a day?"

I laugh at Eric's tirade over rare beef. "*Everything* on the menu here is delicious. Trust me on this. And to prove it, I'll let the birthday girl order for me."

"Sweet!" Bella squeaks as we make our way inside.

"*Table pour quatre, s'il vous plaît,*" I say to the well-dressed host at his stand.

"*Oui, m'dame.*" He nods and leads us to a linen-covered table in the center of the quiet restaurant, placing a thick book-style menu in front of each of us.

Our waiter arrives only a moment later, filling our glasses with his jingling pitcher of ice water. He's rail-thin beneath his suit and white gloves. His slick hair is greased back into something that looks like a duck's tail, and I can see Bella fighting the urge to laugh. But Eric's stony glare is enough to keep her snickering at bay.

"*Comment allez-vous?*" I ask him.

"*Bien. Et toi?*"

"*Fantastique.*" I kiss my fingertips. Then, I reach out and touch his wrist, "*Excusez-moi. Parles-tu anglais?*"

"Yes," he finally says quietly. I sense a slight hint of disdain at the question.

"*Excellent. Tres bien.*" I look at Bella. "He said he speaks English if you want to order for yourself this time."

Bella flops her menu onto the gold charger in front of her. "I already know what I want."

Eric rolls his eyes and looks up at the ceiling, probably begging God to spare us from a silent death in our sleep from the flatulence to come.

"Should we order?" I look around the table.

Everyone nods.

"A bowl of French onion soup, *s'il vous plaît*," Bella says, sealing our fates.

The waiter smiles. "Your French is… not bad."

"This bottle of Cabernet, please," Eric points to a line on his menu, and the waiter nods and scribbles something down on his pad. "And the Nicoise salad, please." He looks at me. "I'm *seriously* getting addicted to those."

"Our salad Nicoise is… *magnifique,*" the waiter assures him as he takes Eric's menu.

"I will have the… sal-mon." Zuzanna points to a spot on her menu, pronouncing the "L" very distinctly. "And hot tea."

He takes her menu, and I hand mine over to Bella. "What'll it be, Mouse?"

"Ummmmm," she doesn't open it. Instead, she hands it up to the waiter and twitches, "Bring her the weirdest thing on the menu."

Everyone at the table chuckles, including the waiter.

He looks at me as if to ask, *are you sure about this?*

I nod with confidence, and he traipses off with the menus and empty pitcher.

***

I don't know *why* I didn't expect it, seeing as though only half an hour ago, I was teaching Bella the English translation. But it isn't until the plate is lowered before me that I realize the mistake that I have *truly* made allowing Bella to choose my meal.

For one thing, I didn't know they made dishware this large. It almost feels like this had to be some custom-made joke, a gag gift for the kitchen staff.

But it's not a gag.

No, not a joke at all.

319

In front of me sits a massive pig's limb. Hoof, calf, and elbow… all roasted and dripping with sizzling fats. It's as if they just lopped the thing off at the armpit, removed the fur, and placed it in the oven covered in seasoning.

In fact, I'm positive that's *exactly* what this is.

Bella and Zuzanna can't stop giggling. Eric examines my plate with a look of utter horror, hesitant to place his own fork in his delicious-looking salad topped with tuna, boiled eggs, and cherry tomatoes.

Bella's soup smells heavenly, and Zuzanna's 'sal-mon' looks like something out of a magazine.

And here I am…

With *le pied du cochon*.

Literally.

I carve off a hunk of fat and try to take solace in the fact that this smells like a mountain of bacon. Though it may stop my heart, I am *nothing* if not true to my word. I grew up dirt poor. Pretty much all I ever *had* was my word.

As I ready myself to carve into the bony, fatty monstrosity before me, I laugh at how *literal* I can take the apt saying right now:

I've really put my foot in my mouth this time.

56

Kira

Back in the apartment's living room, Bella takes a seat at the beveled coffee table, shredding through her boxes and bags of goodies from our day of shopping. I'm sure Eric spent enough on her today to buy a brand-new car outright. "You have fun in that thing. Looks like a, *huh-huh*, death trap."

"*Death trap? Where does she even get this stuff?*" Eric whispers under his breath in my ear. Then, he addresses the rest of the room. "You guys going to be okay here?"

"*Oh, fine, yes, sure!*" Zuzanna says sarcastically, waving us out the door with a theatrical flourish. "Leave me here… with Miss *Onion-fart*."

Bella giggles like a chipmunk and finally finds the treasure she's been seeking in the bottom of one of the sacks.

It's the box with the marionette.

I smile.

"Eef I die from smell, I want you have my house back." Zuzanna laughs and tip-toes to try to kiss her son on the cheek. He stoops low so that she can reach him. It is a well-rehearsed motion.

Eric points to Bella. "Best behavior tonight, and if you're gonna *toot*, open a window. Your grandmother doesn't want to hot-box with your toxic methane."

"What does hot-box mean?" Bella asks, scrunching her nose.

"Oh, wow." He looks at me. "I answered my own question. Mystery solved."

I laugh.

"Byeeeeee." Eric's eyes bulge as he dodges Bella's question, stepping past the live tree to the door.

"Oh, Kira! Before-a you go," his Mom says my name like *Key-dah*, and I find it adorable. "I have some-sing for you in bedroom! Come! Come!"

I point to myself with a look of confusion and then look at Eric. He shrugs and flashes a knowing grin.

I follow Zuzanna into the room. She reaches into the pocket of her coat and fishes out a small paper bag. A bag that matches the design of the one Bella's bracelet came in from the jewelry store where she and Eric bickered.

I freeze in place as she tries to hand it to me.

"This for *you*," she says with a smile. "Eric, tell me that you like... the... the..." Zuzanna makes a big loop with her fingers, and I feel my face flush with heat like it's being fired in a ceramic kiln.

"Carnival wheel," she finally says.

I want to cry.

Or *throw up.*

I know what this is. And I can't *possibly* take it.

"Oh, no. No, Zuzanna, tell me you didn't." My breath hitches. I can barely see her through the wet blur forming in my eyes as she plucks out the velvet necklace box and places it in my hand.

She stands close and looks at me, serious. She says the words slow. "You make Eric... very happy. I see how he ees with you. His first wife... *no*." She makes a sour face and flutters her hand in the air. "She no good. She no make him... *happy*. He was..." she searches for the word, "*lonely*. He was *so* lonely, even when she *there*."

My voice is little more than a whisper. "I... *can't* take this."

I battle valiantly, but I can feel myself losing an epic war with my emotions.

She wipes a tear from my face, and suddenly I know where Eric got his compassion from.

"You are *beautiful* girl. With beautiful heart. You *deserve* nice tings."

She forces the box in my hand. "*Take.*"

I don't want to know what this cost, but she might as well be stuffing ten million dollars in my hands right now.

323

I open it, and more tears rain down when I see the glinting silver Ferris wheel. Its oblong buckets made of alternating sapphires, rubies, and peridots glimmer in the light of the room's chandelier.

I touch it, realizing now that it spins on its center pin, and sob harder at this new revelation.

I'm mesmerized by it, instantly flooded with thoughts of the last quality time I spent with my dad. I am overwhelmed by Zuzanna's words and this unbelievable act of kindness.

Finally, my leaking eyes meet hers, framed by whiskered smile wrinkles. Years of joy have been etched into her face, one line at a time.

"*Thank you.*" I'm not sure if I'm speaking the words or just mouthing them. Everything feels like it's spinning, like I'm riding the wheel in my hand.

"How did you…?"

She waves me away and laughs. "Twas easy." Her voice is like a contented meadowlark. "Bella and I pretend to go to bathroom, and I just… take her to store, and I buy."

"I… *I can't take this, Zuzanna.* This is so expensive."

"You are *worth.*" She smiles. It morphs into a frown a moment later, and she is suddenly choked up, too. "His wife, she… rip his heart out when she leave him and run off to Florida. *Please*," she begs, placing a soft hand atop mine, "don't… *hurt* him."

I nod and wrap my arms around her, clutching her tiny frame as if she might flap her wings and fly away.

Behind her, I see Eric leaning against the door jamb. I don't know how long he's been standing there, watching, but the genuine smile on his face tells me his heart is as full from this act as mine.

He holds out his hands. "Here, let me put it on."

My hands tremble as I hand off the jewelry box. He removes it, pinches the clasp, and latches it securely around my neck.

I feel as if I want to cry even harder the moment it touches my skin. I spin the wheel of it and hug Zuzanna tightly again.

"Now, go! Bella and I gon' to play the cards until she gets a-sleepy." She waves me away. "Go, go to the tower. Have fun time."

57

Eric

Watching Kira ride the merry-go-round on the edge of the Seine River is something I will never forget. The joy and excitement twinkling in her eyes as she watches the towering cultural icon whizz past makes my heart swell.

I love that, no matter how hard life has been for her, she hasn't let it rob her of her sense of wonder or ability to squeeze the joy out of every experience like a grapefruit in a vice. She has a zest for life that makes me want to travel the *rest of the world with her* just to be in the presence of such an enigma. She is someone I *want* Bella to emulate.

***

I love watching her stare out at the glittering City of Lights before her from the top of this mammoth wrought iron lattice beast. Even nine hundred feet in the air, atop the Eiffel Tower, she isn't afraid.

She's *exhilarated*. It's infectious.

I settle in beside her against the wire railing and wrap my arm around her.

"Can I just *stay?* I want to live here." She laughs. I know she's kidding, but Paris looks good on her. I can't blame her for the longing.

This city has a certain magical charm. Maybe it's something in the air here. In the rich flavors of the food. In the live music wafting through the streets. In the riverboats making their perpetual loops around Notre Dame. It's that certain something I can't put my finger on. In the monumental cemeteries. In the roar and rattle of the subway car, grumbling beneath the sound of festive accordion music.

The city is alive. A being of its own. Though she's silent now, I know that, if asked, Kira could gush a monologue about how she feels about this amazing place and barely scratch the surface of her thoughts.

I'd gladly listen all night long if she did.

Watching Kira gaze out at this city, I realize that this is a place where, for her, money never mattered. There are places in this world where what *does* matter is the magic that you feel when you walk the streets. When you feel the charge in the air there. When you savor the broth and wine or interact with a local.

She turns her head to look at me and smiles bashfully. "What? What're you looking at?"

I smile, refusing to answer. She knows *exactly* what I'm looking at. Right here, in this breathtaking place with one of the most objectively spectacular views in the entire world…

She is *all* I can see.

58

Kira

Zuzanna and Bella are asleep in the giant king bed by the time Eric and I get back. While he wanted to rent out one of the restaurants in the middle of the tower, I convinced him to join me for a picnic in the park instead. He obliged, and we snacked on cheese and crackers and drank red wine on a blanket in the park, one that stretches out like a lush green runner to the tower. We ate and laughed and drank, all the while watching the lights on the monument twinkle like excited fireflies.

The apartment is quiet when we burst giddily in through the door, save for Zuzanna's snoring and the drone of the city outside, alive and vibrant, even this close to midnight.

In the living room, Eric kisses me with wonton fervor. It's been days since we've made love, what with all of the packing and travel. It's the longest we've gone without tearing each other's clothes off since I took up residence in the pool house. Now, I suddenly find myself breathless in his arms.

He pulls away to toy with the preacher's collar of my leather jacket, pressing his forehead to mine. He dives into the hollow of my throat, kissing me, running his tongue through the deep groove in a way that makes my eyes flutter. He peels my jacket off gruffly as if I'm a stubborn orange, delightfully wet and ready to be devoured.

It is everything I can do not to gasp or moan, considering where we are. My face burns red-hot in the charged air between us.

Before I know it, I am being led down the hall into Eric's room. He shuts the door quietly behind us.

The moment the lock engages, he is against me, feverishly kissing my lips, our tongues entwining. Even this close, I still want more of him. I wish I could be one with him, morphing into a single erotic being for even just a moment.

He peels me out of my tight camisole, spins me, and presses me against the radiator beside the wide window overlooking Paris.

He unclasps my bra as if he's working against a timer, releasing my breasts into the cool night air, replacing the article of clothing with his warm, cupped palms, brushing his thumbs over my tightened nipples.

A sudden chill wafts over me. I feel a moment of embarrassment as if everyone in miles can somehow now see my half-nude body through the darkened pane.

I feel his hungry mouth planting feverish kisses and dragging his soft lips down my spine. He guides my hands up to the window lock above my head and tugs at the waistband of my skirt with frenzied movements, making my breasts graze the frigid glass. The sensation sends pleasant shivers through me.

He spins me, and I obey his silent demands, willing and pliable.

He kisses my breasts, enjoying every square inch of them, knowing full well how wild the soft licks and aggressive sucks drive me. He kneels, burying himself beneath my flowing skirt.

Masculine hands grip my soaked panties at the hips, and he yanks them off with force. He spreads my legs gruffly, and, again, I abide, face red and scorching.

I feel his nose against my skin as his tongue dives into me, swirling and tickling, sucking and dipping, relieving my days-long ache.

Over the next few minutes, I feel my orgasm whip into a frenzied crescendo until I shudder in his grasp, vibrating and juddering against his amazing tongue, squeezing around his slick, buried fingers.

I clutch his hair hard, feet clenched, toes curled, calves tensed, all from my perch on the radiator. He emerges from beneath my skirt with that charming smile, lips shiny, nose pink from

friction like he's been left out in the cold.

"*Did you…?*" he whispers, eyes twinkling with pride.

I mouth, "*Oh yes.*"

My nod is grateful, and my body trembles violently as he retracts his glistening fingers from my depths. I beckon him to me. As he rises, I unclasp the side button of my skirt and let it fall to the floor, leaving me completely naked before him, heart racing like I just jumped out of a plane.

He stands before me, taking off his suit and tossing each piece on the nearby dresser.

I love to watch him undress. There is something animal about the look in his eyes when he does it. Like a jaguar stalking prey, eyes focused with a simmering intensity.

He's about to attack.

He's about to leave me breathless again.

All I can do is brace myself for the primal sexual *force* that is Eric Salko.

He presses his forehead to mine and licks his lips, "You taste so *fucking* good."

I love when he says it.

I kiss him, sucking the traces of myself from his lips. Between our bodies, I feel his pants hit the floor, freeing his thick, excited cock from its tailored prison.

His lips are an inch from mine as he adjusts my hips and ass, settling me firmly on the radiator and pressing me against the glass again. I can feel the head of his throbbing dick poised for entry, but he hesitates. He slides his hand behind my neck. He stares at me so long that I'm almost concerned.

"Are you okay?" I whisper, running a hand up the back of his head through his thick hair. "What's wrong?"

With seriousness in every millimeter of his expression, he finally speaks. Only his words are not in whispers this time.

"I love you."

Every syllable pierces the silence.

I don't know what to say. I *want* to say it back, but I'm *afraid*.

…Afraid that it's the hormones talking.

…Afraid I might just be a lonely billionaire's passing fancy, to be discarded like worn shoes when something more appealing comes along.

But see…

I keep my shoes forever. They give up on *me* before I give up on *them*.

I'm like that with everything in my life.

Those three words aren't just strung syllables. They're serious. Meaningful. I don't take them lightly, nor have I ever said them to a man.

The way he utters it touches me, awakening some deep-buried part of myself, a part that has never felt this *alive*.

He sweeps a hunk of sweat-damp hair lovingly from my face, and I can't help but feel that he means it.

"Don't worry." He caresses my cheek with his thumb and smiles. "You don't need to say it back. I just had to say it. I had to make sure… that you *knew*."

A look of relief washes over him the way only sharing the burden of a million-pound secret can.

I press my mouth to his and pull his shoulders to me. He drives upward, burying himself deep inside me, so deep that I draw in a deep lungful of air as our open mouths graze each other's ever-so-softly.

59

Eric

"I don't know how you're not freezing in that dress," I say, feeling the bitter bite of cold spring air on my skin. My exposed hands ache.

"I told you it's—"

"It's true. You do run warm. You're like a little radiator." I smile.

She takes my chilled hand in hers. Her skin exudes comfort and warmth, thawing me in more ways than one.

"The day we met when I was giving you a tour of the house, didn't you say you like cigars?" I ask, hoping I heard her right.

"I do. They're just such a nice treat every once in a while. I just love the smell."

"Me too. It *clings*, but in a pleasant way." We make our way up a few more steep steps of the long stairway. "Favorite brand?"

"I'm quite partial to *Rocky Patel* and *Arturo Fuente,* but I haven't had either of them in a long time."

"Why not?" I ask, unable to take my eyes off how stunning she looks in her sequin gown. She shimmered all through the show at *Le Moulin Rouge*. So much so that I found her even

334

more entrancing than the topless women doing the can-can on the stage and wrestling anacondas in vats of water. It was a spectacle unlike anything I'd ever seen, but I struggled to take my eyes off Kira's frozen, excited smile for the entire show.

She makes a face like the answer's obvious. "Because they're friggin *expensive*. A good Churchill-sized cigar costs more than I spend on food for half a week. I like cocktails too, but you don't see me shelling out $20 for one of those puppies either."

I chuckle. The concept of a cigar being expensive seems *bizarre* to me now.

"You want to sit for a minute?" I motion to the bench at the top of the concrete platform, one framed by blossoming foliage and flowers.

She joins me. We peer out at the shimmering city before us, soaking in the grayed rooftops and streets punctuated by iconic monuments of every size and shape.

The massive, domed Sacre Coeur looms mere feet behind us making the area feel remarkable. Powerful with a form of reverent beauty.

I retrieve the cigar holder from my inner breast pocket. "I don't have any *Rocky Patel*, but I do have a *Perdomo Champagne,* a couple of *La Flors,* and a *Fuente Opus Lost City*."

She looks at my hands like I'm offering her a crisp hundred, eyes alight.

"Oooooh, I have always wanted to try a *Lost City*."

I pluck one out and hand it to her. She runs it under her nose, savoring the scent.

She moans, and my dick hardens like Pavlov's salivating dog at the sound of it.

I fish out my cigar cutter and shear off the end of both of our Gigante cigars. I pull out a box of matches and strike one, lighting her end. She sucks hard, staring at me with those green eyes as the cherry forms. Her lively face is framed by plumes of gray that soon replace the fog of our breath.

I light my own, snuff the match, and lean back into the bench. She snuggles against me, nestling into the crook of my arm, the one that, when broken, fatefully brought this woman into my life.

Thinking about that, I feel *grateful* for the injury. Without it, I wouldn't have met her.

We smoke in peace, basking in the brisk night air, sponging up the warmth of each other, the rich smells, and the unforgettable view.

I love this moment here, with Kira in my arms. And for a split second, I can see this being our lives together.

Suddenly, a sound I abhor rips through our quiet moment like an arrow. I pull out my phone to answer the generic ring, and my heart rate quickens.

It's Rob.

He wouldn't call without a damned good reason. He knows to only text.

I don't know why he's calling, but I instantly fear the worst.

"I'm sorry. I have to answer this," I say to Kira as I click the talk button.

She sits up, offering a nervous look from beside me.

Rob sounds manic. "Hey man, did I call too late? What time is it over there?"

"It's... fine, Rob. What's up?"

"Sorry, Eric, you know I wouldn't call if it wasn't important, but your lawyer just called. It's about the custody thing. He said to relay to you that Tawny's claiming your assistant is unfit to be around the kid because of some shit that happened with her parents or something. I don't know. It was hard to understand."

I sit up straighter. "Wait, *what?*"

"Yeah, Greg said that you shouldn't worry too much about it because Kira doesn't have any, like, *felonies* or any history of child abuse or neglect or anything."

"So, what is she *talking about?* And how does she have *any* right to tell me who I can and can't have around my child? She *left*."

"Eric, dude, try not to let it ruffle your feathers."

I realize now that Rob isn't out of breath because he's terrified. I hear the soft whir of his treadmill the moment he stops talking, and I realize he's running. However, this revelation doesn't bring me as much solace as I thought it would.

"I'm just tryin' to keep you in the loop in case you want to talk to Kira and find out what the fuck that cunt's even *referring* to. I mean, we ran a background. Plus, I googled her. All I could find was Kira's dad's obituary and an article about the, like, attempted murder-suicide."

Wait, what?!

"Nothing else after that," he continues. "Couldn't find any obit for her Mom or anything. I can put the P.I. on it if you want to dig a little more, but apparently, Tawny's lawyer is sayin' something about her being a potential threat on the grounds of, like, genetic *mental illness.* Again, the lawyer says it's bullshit. He thinks she's grasping at straws."

Suddenly, I feel strange as I look at Kira, wondering how well I *actually* know her.

I try not to pry, but now I feel like I *need* to know.

I take a long, deep drag of the cigar, smoke burning my eyes. I exhale deeply. "Okay, if you find anything out, email it to me, and I'll get with Greg about doing damage control as soon as I'm back in Connecticut on Monday."

"Yup. You got it, Salko. Later." With that, Rob hangs up, never much for pleasantries.

"What was that about? Sounds serious," Kira asks, rolling her Gigante nervously between two fingers like cricket legs rubbing.

"That was Rob. *Kira,*" I sigh. I don't want to ask this. I don't want to invade her privacy. But now that it's affecting my fight for Bella, I have to. "What happened… with your father?"

The look on her face changes immediately, her smile disappearing like a faint scent in high wind. Her emotions run the gamut from confused to offended to curious to apologetic, all in the space of two seconds.

"*What?* Why are you asking about that? What did Rob say?"

"He said Tawny's lawyers are trying to make the case that you're not fit to be around her because of something that happened with your parents. They something about some genetic mental illness."

She snuffs out the end of her cigar on the cement despite only having enjoyed a fraction of it. She lays it on the bench beside us, steps out to the balcony rail, and stares out in silence at the city, looking like she is going to be ill.

I wish she would say something.

Anything.

"Look…" I start. But *look what?* I don't know what to *say*. I don't know what to *ask*. But I am at war over Bella, and I need all of the information. *I can't lose my daughter.*

"Please, Kira," I beg. "Say *something.*"

The lights of Paris reflect in the tear streaks running down her face, and I feel hollow inside for bringing her to tears.

"Two weeks after my brother died, my father was murdered." She can barely get the words out. "If you must know the sordid *details*, he was shot in the face with a .38 at close range." She looks at me, arms folded across her shimmering gown. "Three times. The fourth shot was meant for me but missed. Five more inches to the right, and I would've died, too."

"*Jesus,*" I whisper.

She sits at the far edge of the bench. I try to take her hand, but she denies the contact.

"Did they ever catch the guy who did it? Like, did he go to prison?"

She looks at me with a level of seriousness I didn't know she was *capable* of. Her silly, casual nature is gone now, replaced by the look of a frightened child swathed in black sequins.

"Who said it was a *guy?*"

I look at her, puzzled, with my face tilted like a curious mutt. "Wait, it *wasn't?*"

"*No,*" she exclaims softly, almost offended. Then she looks out again over the city as tears wet her face. "It was my *mom.*"

60

Kira

Our return to the States was awkward and painful. I hate leaving Paris. I feel like I'm saying goodbye to my best friend as the jet's wheels lift off the ground.

I didn't tell Eric everything after the Moulin Rouge. It is for *me* to bear the brunt of those memories and events alone. I assured him that any allegations of mental illness are ridiculous. But, ever since my mother was diagnosed with various maladies, it *has* always been my worst fear that someday I could end up just like *her*. Hurting the ones I claim to love the most. Tucked away in a facility like some dirty little secret.

Out of sight.

Out of mind…

Until the wounds re-open.

I didn't tell Eric that my mother lives only minutes from his mansion in some gross little mirrorless place with a lovely-sounding name:

Pleasant Oaks.

What a fucking *joke*. It might as well be a penitentiary. That's what it feels like to be on those grounds.

I've never gone in. I can't *stomach* the thought of looking her in the eyes after destroying my life and ripping away everything I held dear. I could never face her after all she'd taken from me. She doesn't deserve my time. Or my energy. Or my emotions. I try not to even *think* about her.

What my mother did... it was unforgivable. Over the years, it's eaten me up inside like a metastatic cancer. But now, her very *existence* has put my ability to be around Bella and Eric in jeopardy.

Bella needs *stability*. She needs *love*. She needs people who will be *there* for her.

Hell, we *all* do.

I'm here in this pool house, shuffling around, doing anything I can to avoid unloading my suitcase from the trip. Unpacking means it's really over. It means that I'm back in Connecticut, back on this sprawling piece of property dotted with blooming cherry trees and big enough to probably play nine rounds of golf on.

The harsh reality remains... Here is nowhere near the spot in the park where Eric and I ate camembert and watched the triangular monument twinkle. It's nowhere near the subway car where Bella sang *Champs-Élysées* with an accordion-playing stranger while we all clapped. Nowhere near the bistro where we humored a giddy ten-year-old with her fanciest high tea. Nowhere near where Zuzanna brought me to tears with a necklace I refuse to take off except to swim.

Nowhere near the radiator where Eric told me he loved me.

Before my ugly past crashed down on me again like a dropped cinder block.

I open the bottle of cheap raspberry wine I brought back in my satchel from the bodega near our apartment and take a swig straight out of it. Gazing out my window, I focus on the light in Bella's room.

I check my watch.

Right about now, Eric is reading Bella her bedtime story. I settle into bed with my own book and catch a whiff of the intoxicating smell of its textured cream pages. I listen to the sound it makes as my fingertips rub against the page, hoping my body doesn't fight sleep.

My mind is still on Paris time.

61

Kira

The room is filled with the *click-click-click* of our computer keys clacking wildly.

Eric is working on emails reassuring established clients that yesterday's earnings report dip is normal and to be expected.

Meanwhile, I'm contacting his advertising firm about several ad spots we have in various magazines in New York next month.

Ring.

Eric's phone rings between us. I lunge for it, but being closer, he picks it up first.

"What is the point of having me if you're just going to answer your own phone."

Ring.

"You're my *assistant*, not my *secretary*."

"There's *not* a huge difference there.

Ring.

He looks at the caller ID, rolls his eyes, and groans.

"Who is it?"

After a pause, he says, "Tawny. I *don't* want to talk to her."

Ring.

I extend my hand. "Here, gimme." He slides the phone across his glass desk, and I answer it with a sugar-sweet pleasantness. "Salko & Sampson Finance, Kira speaking, how may I help you?"

"Why are you answering my husband's phone?"

"*Ex*," I correct.

"Is this Kira?"

My name, coming from her mouth, freezes my blood. "I'm his assistant, ma'am. Mr. Salko is not available right now. Can I take a message?"

Eric slides his legal pad and a pen over to me in case I need it, eyes on me like an eagle.

Her voice is venomous yet eerily calm. "You're the one with the schizo mom in the loony bin—"

I press the end call button without thinking. The corners of my vision blur black with a pulse of anger.

Eric's mouth drops open.

Shit. Shit. Shit.

What did I just do?

Did I just hang up on Eric's ex-wife?!

"She, uh," blood pulses through my temples. My hands are shaking so badly I nearly drop the phone. "She didn't want to leave a message."

Eric laughs. "Did you just hang up on her?"

I nod, horrified.

The phone rings again in my hand, scaring the bejeezus out of me. I fumble the phone and pick it up from my lap. My heart is racing.

It's Tawny again.

Without thinking, I press the button to forward the call to his voicemail.

"I'm sorry." My voice is small, panicked.

"I'm not," he says, and I can see the fire behind his gold-flecked eyes. Eric rises and approaches me. The sheer intensity has me frozen in place. He places his hands on the arms of my chair, gaze locked on me.

"The way she runs her mouth, I'm *sure* she deserved it. That was," he leans in and runs a hand up the back of my head, "fucking *hot*."

"Mmmmm," I purr, feeling his fist clench slowly, firmly around my blonde locks, sending a rush of arousal from my scalp straight to my vagina.

I whimper and bite my lip. He *knows* it drives me *wild* when he pulls my hair.

Eric yanks my head back and stares down like he's sizing me up, making me want him. Making me need him. And it's *working*.

He kisses me, slow and deep, controlling my motion so that he can use his tongue precisely the way that *he* desires. His hand slides between my thighs, massaging me through the material until I squirm.

He says only two words before releasing me.

"Bedroom. *Now*."

62

Eric

"Alright, a good *coq au vin* uses its ingredients to create a symphony of flavors," Jacques says the words so fluidly that, for a moment, I feel like I'm still back in France. "So, now that you've browned the chicken, you want to put it over there with the bacon. Now, the bacon really adds something special to the taste of it."

Jacques slaps a clean tea towel over the shoulder of his white chef's coat. He leans over the marble island to watch me work.

I feverishly arrange the pieces of chicken on a plate.

"You *sure* you don't want me to make this? I feel bad, you know. This is, like, the whole thing you pay me for."

"I think it'll mean more if she knows I made it. It's her favorite." I smile. "I appreciate you walking me through it like this, though."

"Ah, just this once, okay? Otherwise, I may teach myself out of a job."

That makes me laugh.

He continues, "When I get back on Monday, I'll make you all *pot au feu*. You will love it."

"Yes, I'd like that. And I'm going to need nicoise salads, seriously, like once a week. Indefinitely."

Jacques laughs at that. "France got its claws in you."

"That it did." I finish with the chicken and clasp my palms together. I glance at my watch. 3:46 p.m.

Plenty of time to get this finished before Kira gets home with Bella."Okay, chef, what's next?"

"Next," Jacques points to the cutting board loaded with fresh vegetables, "we chop our carrots, onions, and garlic…"

63

I resist the urge to nervously chew my pink fingernail polish. Bella gave me her version of a manicure on the flight home, and I don't have the heart to damage them further due to sheer sentimental attachment.

This kid is *really* growing on me.

I watch the last of the kids funnel through the doorway, scattering like roaches in the light to their assorted pickup spots.

No Bella yet.

Where the hell is she?

I tap my fingers nervously on the wheel.

My sworn enemy, Purple Jeep Lady, gets her kid and revs her engine. She speeds around past me, shooting daggers through the Tesla's tinted window with eyes that reek of piss-poor plastic surgery.

I roll my window down, flash a cheesy smile, and wave.

Yup. Hate you, too, ma'am.

The kids finished spilling out of the building fully. The last of the cars slither around me, leaving the pumpkin-orange car I'm in all alone in the school's pickup line.

I check the time on my phone, concerned. Bella's never been the last one out.

In fact, ever since I took her to the lake the first time, she's hot-footed it ever since.

I dial her cell, still astounded by how much nicer the ten-year-old's phone is than mine at twenty-six.

Straight to voicemail.

My stomach twists. My brain automatically jumps to the worst imaginable scenario. I start thinking about all the horror stories of Adam Walsh when I was a kid and buzz with nervous energy.

Before I freak out fully, I dial Eric.

On the second ring, he picks up. "Salko & Sampson Finance."

I laugh at the reference to earlier.

"Hey, don't you have some sort of assistant who's supposed to be answering your phone for you?" I jest, hoping that he can't hear the anxiety that I'm feeling about his daughter.

Eric chuckles. "She's not here right now."

"Oh man, she sounds unreliable. You should fire her." *Please don't, though.*

He chuckles. "What's up, beautiful."

I feel myself blush from the compliment, but nerves quickly overtake me again. "Have… you heard from Bella?"

There's no better way I can think to phrase it: *your only child isn't fucking here where she is supposed to be, Eric.*

"No, why? What's going on?" The anxiety spreads to him like a forest fire, compounding how scared I'm becoming.

"I'm just... sitting here in line, and everyone else is gone, and she hasn't come out yet. I tried calling her cell, but it's goin' straight to voicemail."

"Okay," there is a long pause. Then, he speaks again, "Stay there and wait to see if she comes out. I'm going to call my buddy, Derek. He works for Greenwich PD. I'll call him and see what he can do. Maybe he can put out some sort of Amber Alert or something."

"*Jesus.* Um, yeah. Okay." My hands are starting to tremble from the thought of Bella in the presence of someone malicious, possibly terrified.

I take a deep breath and try to calm myself.

It's only been a few minutes.

Maybe we're both jumping to *wild,* far-fetched conclusions, but hell, it's better to be safe than sorry.

"I'm going to get out and walk around, check inside, see if she's just, you know, running *late* or something."

"Okay."

"I've got my phone on me. If you hear anything, call, alright?"

"Of course," he says. "It's going to be okay."

I'm not sure if he said it for my benefit, or his, or both, but the way he utters it so matter-of-factly *is* comforting.

I nod as if he can somehow see me. "Bye."

I kill the call, stuff the phone in my purse, and hop out of the vehicle, wandering up to the school.

"Bella?!"

No answer.

I walk inside, whipping my head around like a hunter, looking for a blood trail. But the thought of a blood trail makes me *horrified,* and now my hands are patting my skirt wildly, fueled by my coursing adrenaline.

"Belllllla?" I shout again.

Silence.

A balding man in his late forties pops his head out of one of the doors like a prairie dog. "Can I help you?"

I sigh a breath of relief. "Yes, maybe you can. I'm here to pick up Bella Salko. She's usually out there right away. I just wanted to make sure that she didn't get like… I dunno, *detention* or something. She's not picking up her phone."

"Oh. Bella's class is right there." He points to a room a few doors down, and before I know it, I'm jogging toward it, waving with preoccupied gratitude.

But as I round the corner, my sense of dread doubles down.

The classroom is totally empty.

64

"What was she wearing today? The more descriptive you can be, the better our chances of finding her," Officer Derek Danvers says. His ginger buzz-cut is tight against his square, shiny head, and his paunch hangs out a little over his tactical belt. Surprisingly, he *is* taking the matter seriously.

Eric's fingers rub nervously up and down my spine as he stares at the policeman's notebook. "Um, she," his hand moves to the back of his neck. He rubs anxiously and looks at me, "Her parka is pink with brown fur around the edge, but I don't remember what she was wearing, do you?"

"Yeah," I nod. I remember commenting on it before I drove her there. "Navy-blue top like this." I point to my shirt. "And a, well, a blue skirt like this." I point lower and offer a sad smile. "I remember because I made a joke that we looked like twins. She said that she wore it because she wanted to dress like me."

"Anything else about her that might make her easy to identify?"

"Well, I can text you some of the photos we snapped at tea time yesterday," I rub Eric's arm and nearly laugh, "don't worry, I won't send any of the ones with you in the boa."

Eric's cheeks bloom pink as Danvers locks eyes with a look that says *I don't wanna know what sort of kinky stuff you're into.*

"Alright," Danvers scribbles in his pad and starts toward the front door. It seems so odd to me that he's using it. In seven weeks of being here almost daily, I've never seen a single person use it until tonight.

"We'll get an Amber Alert issued immediately." He hands Eric a business card from his breast pocket, and Eric takes it. "If anything changes, if she shows up, call me immediately."

"Yes, sir." Eric's face is solemn. Only then do I realize he isn't wearing a suit jacket, and the sleeves of his Italian Zegna button-down are rolled up to his elbows. I've never seen him look like this before.

"You called right away, which is crucial in cases like these." Danvers lets himself out even though it feels like he is in the middle of a thought.

"Thank you, Derek," Eric says just before the meaty door clicks shut with finality.

The minute it does, he turns to me. He's drained of all color. He approaches nervously and rests his forehead against mine.

I reach up and stroke the back of his neck and hair lovingly, wishing I could take all this fear away from him.

"It's gonna be okay, baby." I feel like I could swallow my own tongue.

Baby?

Did I actually just say that?

Before I get the chance to stutter and backpedal, he pulls me close in an embrace so comforting that it feels like our bodies have melded into one for a brief moment.

"I'm so glad you're here," he whispers into my ear, and I can feel the love in his tone... in the way that he holds me.

He sighs heavily and speaks again, "Where could she be?"

"I don't know." I look up at him and smell an intoxicating scent wafting through the air.

Something *delicious.*

Something *French.*

Something *familiar.*

But also…

"Is something *burning*?" I ask.

Eric's eyes expand into massive orbs in an instant.

"*Fuck, fuck, fuck!*" He chants, hustling to the kitchen.

I'm surprised.

Jacques seems far too attentive to burn something.

I follow Eric and see a huge, copper Mauviel stock pot bubbling over onto the stove, splattering dark liquid like brown fireworks, bursting in every direction.

It smells heavenly, *save for the char.*

"Where the heck is Jacques?" I look around.

Eric grabs gloves and pulls the stock pot off the heat and onto the three-inch slab marble island that must weigh a literal ton.

"I sent him home an hour ago. Gave him the rest of the day off." He blows into the steam, holding his body away from the spatter at an awkward angle.

"*Dammit,*" he groans, trying to cool the liquid with the rapid wave of his mitted hand. "I had him teach me his recipe for *coq au vin* so I could make you dinner tonight as a surprise. I'll bet everything on the bottom is scorched black now."

He's too busy looking at the splattered mess of chicken stock and wine all over the counter to see the huge smile plastered on my face. I can't remember the last time anyone made me something more complicated than microwaved pizza rolls... much less my favorite dish on the *planet*.

"I can't believe you *did* this," I coo.

"I can't believe I did this *either*," he says, scoffing, meaning the same thing in a completely different way. "I'm *sorry*."

I wrap my arms around him. "This is *so* sweet."

"This is all... such a mess."

I know he's not just talking about the *coq au vin.*

"Eric... we'll find her," I assure him.

Suddenly, we hear something. It's the sound of the front door opening followed by the patter of small shoes.

Eric and I bolt in tandem to the source of the noise.

My heart leaps with joy and relief as I hear the faint mumble of Bella's *huh-huh-huhs* emanating from the foyer.

But who the hell is she talking to?

And where the hell has she been?

We round the corner to see Bella kicking off her shoes while trying not to tip her tenuously-stacked double-scoop ice cream cone that is dripping down the back of her hand.

Behind her stands a blonde who I instantly recognize from her photos, despite the unkind years since and her new, longer hairstyle.

It's *Tawny*.

"What the...?" Eric's speechless.

I am, too. This whole thing feels like it's aged me ten years in one afternoon.

"*Eric.*" Tawny nods and smiles as if nothing's wrong.

"What the *hell*, Tawny?" Eric's fists are digging into his sides now, and his voice is tinged with fury.

"Well, I tried to call this afternoon to let you know I was in town and picked Bella up from school early to spend some quality time with her, but," she waves dismissively at me, "your little secretary hung up on me before she heard what I had to say."

357

Eric is livid. He rushes past Bella, enraged, and whisks Tawny back to the door by her arm.

"Get off of me," she shouts, wriggling free, but he corrals her with a muscular arm outside, shutting the door behind them. They burst into a heated argument on the other side of the frosted glass.

I wave Bella over to me and hug her tightly. "We were so scared, Bella. Are you okay?"

"*Huh-huh,* yeah, she took me to a movie, and we got ice cream." She stares at me with her hickory-colored eyes, full of confusion and innocence.

"Your Dad and I were worried sick. I showed up at the school to pick you up, but you weren't there. I thought something bad happened to you." I smooth her mussed, brass-colored hair.

"Sorry. Mom told me to turn off my phone so it didn't ring in the theater."

I try to smile. I want Bella's home to be a safe haven for her. I know what it's like to boil in a simmering vat of turmoil as a child. I feel the need to shield her from what is going on on the other side of that door.

Through it, I hear:

"She's my daughter, too, Eric! You can't just withhold my fucking child."

"You *abandoned* us. Don't you fucking get that? Why is that just not computing in your brain? You *left*. And the judge said—"

"That ruling is about to change. They *never* take kids away from their mothers unless they're totally unfit, and you fucking *know* that. I don't do drugs—"

"You were *arrested*, Tawny! For *vagrancy!* You were living on the sidewalk like a homeless person," he growls. "You had a *mansion* at home!"

"I don't want your little whore around my daughter. Her mother is in *Pleasant Oaks*, Eric."

"Is that supposed to mean something to me?" Eric asks.

"It's not a *retirement village*, Eric. It's a goddamned *mental institution*. Her mother is bat-shit crazy. And I'm sure that apple doesn't fall far from the tree. That stuff can be passed down through *genetics*, Eric. She could be a *ticking time bomb* for all you know."

"*Bullshit.*" He scoffs.

I've had all I can take of listening to them through the door. I leave the room with Bella in tow.

I feel like I'm going to puke.

65

Kira

There's a knock at the door to the pool house. I see two blobby figures outside the glass, both adult-sized.

"It's not locked," I mutter from the bed where I am trying to forget this day with my tawdry paperback. Eric enters, and just as I feared, Tawny follows him.

"So sorry to intrude, Kira," Eric says with his arms folded. "Tawny wants to collect a few of her things from storage." He glares at his ex-wife, furious and unblinking. I've never seen him so fired up before. Though, even now, he is showing her a level of respect that she doesn't deserve.

"I'll be quick. I'm just here to grab a couple of things." Her eyes are locked on me, sizing me up. I can't tell if it's jealousy or just disgust, but none of the daggers she's thrown have missed me.

I set my book on the nightstand and get up, pressing my back against the wall on the far side of the main living space, giving her total clearance to do as she pleases. She examines my book, picking it up in her hand and scoffing.

As she sets it down, Eric's eyes finally land on mine with a look of genuine apology.

Tawny shuffles around, and I feel anxious at the thought of her invading my personal space, my only sanctuary from all the world's familial drama. She's too close to my belongings, dragging her fingers across things she has no right to be touching. She makes her way to the side corner with some boxes stacked floor-to-chest-height.

As she's rifling through them, I look down at the box on the floor with the photos and video camera at my feet. I quietly slide it beneath the bed with my slippered foot.

"If you're looking for your jewelry box, it's in the top box in the pile closest to the kitchenette."

Tawny whips her head to glare at me with an accusatory look, and I laugh. *This whole thing is so ridiculous.* "I didn't take anything if that's what you're worried about. Your taste is hideous."

It was petty as hell to say, I know, but I blurted it before I engaged my brain. It didn't make me feel any better.

"Is that why you're moving in on my sloppy-seconds?" She points to Eric and looks at me. I feel rage simmer behind my eyes at the comment.

How dare she call him that.

"I'm surprised you didn't pawn this stuff." She cocks an eyebrow at me and flashes a smug smile.

"No, I didn't need to." My mouth is moving without my control, thoughts dangerously unfiltered. "See, I have a *new* plan for my life, and it doesn't require any money."

Tawny cackles.

I continue, "See, I'm just gonna throw caution to the wind and hitchhike on down to Florida and live off the land for a bit. And by land, I mean a dirty sidewalk. Just trying to narrow my choice down between the coasts. Daytona?" I weigh the air with one hand. "Or *Tampa?*" I do the same, with the other hand.

She doesn't laugh or speak. Instead, she goes to the kitchenette, sifts through the boxes, and retrieves her jewelry box with a scowl. She opens it to take a brief visual inventory to see if I'm lying. When she realizes I could give two shits about her gaudy necklaces and ridiculous diamond rings, she snaps the lid closed and burrows into another box.

She plucks a few items out: a dress, a blouse, a stack of papers, and a couple of books. She dumps everything into one open box and plops it on the Italian hand-stitched comforter.

Her voice cuts through the silence like a butcher's knife.

"I know all about you, Ms. Blumquist. I know all about your parents and your brother. I know about Pleasant Oaks. I know about the

362

curse on your whole damned bloodline. You might think you have yourself a little *instant family* here with Eric and *my* daughter, but you don't."

"Tawny, *get out.*" Eric starts toward her like a bouncer, ready to eject the woman.

"I've got your number." She makes a face so smug I really think I might punch her. I've never hit another human before, but today she's fried my last damn nerve.

"You're poor trash, Ms. Blumquist. And you always will be. You hail from a fucking *trailer park* in Bridgeport that I wouldn't even drive by with my *car locked.* You can't keep a job unless you're sucking the boss's *dick—*"

Eric grabs her by the shoulders and yanks her toward the door. She snatches up her box just in time. With a crazed look in her eyes, she lunges back toward me. Eric wraps his arms around her just in time. "You stay away from Bella, you hear me? You will never be her mother. *You will never be her—*"

Eric shoves her out onto the patio and shuts the door. He looks back at me as he locks it, grasping his injured shoulder and wincing in pain. "Ow, fuck. Are you okay?"

My hands shake, but not out of anger.

Out of *fear*.

The crazed look of hatred in her eyes is giving me an instant flashback of the trauma my mother inflicted all of those years ago.

My body trembles as I'm enveloped by Eric's arms. He tries to comfort me, but I can barely hear his murmurs of apologies and reassurance over the tidal wave of horror that I'm experiencing all over again.

I can't stop thinking about the timbre of her voice and those eyes...

Those *cold, callous eyes.*

Just like those of the woman who brought me into this world and swore to protect my brother and me. The same person who promised to love my father through sickness and health.

The woman who destroyed my world like a detonated atom bomb.

I've been picking up the pieces ever since.

66

Eric

Kira is wearing sunglasses in my kitchen as if she's got a hangover. As Jacques plates up our omelets, I reach out and stroke her hand.

"I have something to ask, and I'm unsure how you will respond. So, please, just hear me out."

She nods solemnly. Her hand lays limply like someone in a coma.

"After I drop Bella off at mom's house today, I…"

I don't know how to say it. I suddenly feel like a chicken-shit.

Her face drifts over, and I can feel her eyes on mine, even through her glasses.

"I think we should go up to *Pleasant Oaks*."

"What?" She rears back like a defensive animal being jabbed at with a stick. "Absolutely not! Are you…" She stares at me for a moment, wounded, "Are you *serious?*"

"Yes." I can't believe she even just asked me that. "With this damn custody battle, I need to know what I'm dealing with here. I need full transparency. If something with your mother is going to be an issue, I want to get ahead of it. If there's something the lawyers and I can get in front of, I *will*. I can't lose Bella, Kira."

I cup her hand in both of mine now, rubbing so anxiously with my thumbs that I'm probably starting to irritate her skin… and *her*.

"...And I don't want to lose *you,* either."

Silence. She doesn't say a word. She just sits like she's been lobotomized, which is especially jarring, considering she's always so full of life.

The injury I've caused with my request lingers thick in the air, which is quiet save for ridiculous cartoon noises and the sizzle of eggs.

"Say something." I stare at the table again, picking at the smooth surface like I'm trying to tunnel through with my fingernails. "Anything."

My leg is restless. This stubborn silence makes my nerves feel frayed.

"I think it could help you, Kira. And I'll be there for you the whole time. If we're going to be in a relationship, I need transparency."

"*Relationship?*" she finally asks, as if the term is foreign. I can hear in the stuffy way she's talking that she's been crying.

"Are we…" She doesn't finish. She only stares at me, wrecked.

"*I mean,*" I laugh because the fact that we possibly weren't on the same page baffles me, "Yes, I assumed that's what this was. What did you think? That I was just having some kind of *fling*?"

366

She shrugs and touches the gold charger before her, fidgeting with the fine cutlery on either side. "People do it all the time."

"I'm not that kind of guy, Kira. I'm not built like that. Rob gives me shit about it all the time. I married Tawny straight out of college, and before that, I'd only been with two other women. Each for over a year, respectively."

I lean back in my chair and swirl my finger around a smooth knot on the wooden table in front of me. The entire thing was carved by chainsaw from a singular, gigantic trunk and polished so finely that I can see my frown reflected back in it.

"I like the idea of *building something* with someone. I'm sorry if I gave you the impression that you were just something *casual* to me. I never meant to make you feel that way."

"You didn't," she mutters. She reminds me of Bella right now when she's upset and unable to look at me. "I guess I just didn't realize you felt like that."

"Well, how do *you* feel? Am I just something casual to *you?*"

"I don't know."

She's quiet for another moment, lost in her stormy thoughts.

"Tawny was right, though," she finally says. "I'm a mess. I've never had my life together. I have all this emotional baggage. My family is…" she winces, but she reigns it in, "I've never had *any* sort of *serious* relationship before." She laughs, though her face stays somber. "I didn't even recognize that I was *in* one."

I grab her hand again, offering her silent assurances with my grasp.

"Financially, I've never had a pot to piss in. Now, I'm living in my boss's pool house."

"About *that*—"

"No, before you say anything, please… stop. I didn't say that so you'd ask me to move into the house. The pool house is amazing. It's honestly the nicest place I've ever lived."

That admission wrenches my gut. I know she means it, too.

I love this woman.

I want to give her the life she *deserves*. Not the one she *thinks* she does.

"It's just a *fact*," she finishes quietly.

I gaze into her dark aviators, hoping she can see my good intentions. "I really think we should go today. Who knows, it might be *good* to see her and catch up. Maybe you can squash your animosity because I'm sure whatever happened… you can work it out."

She sucks in a prolonged inhalation and finally laughs.

But it's not a funny-ha-ha laugh.

It's a *this is ridiculous* laugh.

"Fine," she finally says.

"— And by the *way*, Tawny was *wrong* last night." I take a sip of coffee to buy myself a moment to choose the right words. "About *everything*. She would say *anything* to cut another woman down. Always has. And while I refuse to disparage her in front of Bella, I will say, between us, she's always been so damn *petty*. She loves to go off half-cocked about things she doesn't understand. It was a *huge* problem for us during our marriage."

Jacques slides a steaming plate in front of each of us.

"Thank you, Jacques," we mutter in unison.

"Please, just think about this. If you don't want to go for your own piece of mind, then do it for Bella and me."

Before I can say anything else, she is carving her omelet with a fork and slathering her eggs with a batch of fresh homemade salsa. I watch her for a moment. Even though she is close enough to touch, she feels a mile away. I pick up my fork, suddenly far from hungry. There is so much that I still want to say. So much that I want to ask. But it's probably best to just let her eat.

***

"Hi, yes. We're here to see Lynne Blumquist."

Kira's voice sounds gravelly. Like she spent the night scream-singing karaoke in a smoky bar. I feel horrible for the pain Tawny has brought upon her.

No, *scratch that*, the pain *I* have brought upon her.

The rotund woman behind the desk with long gel-tipped nails spins a clipboard with visitation waivers around at us. "Once you each fill one of these out, you can take a seat in the activities room over there. I'll have an orderly bring her in for you."

We fill out the daunting waivers and *Release of Liability* forms, agreeing not to sue Pleasant Oaks if we are harmed on the premises. I suddenly have an uneasy feeling about all of this, and Kira's silence isn't helping.

Fifteen minutes pass, and I feel like I'm getting a root canal done. My leg is restless, bobbing so hard and fast that the bench beneath me squeaks like an old bed.

Kira sits beside me, and I'm honestly afraid to touch her. She was as quiet as Sernik on the thirty-minute drive. She hasn't said a word since breakfast. She just stares listlessly at the floor and spins the Ferris wheel on her necklace.

A woman with dirty-dishwater-blonde hair shuffles into the room in slippers. Her hair is pulled back in a messy ponytail. She's wearing pajama pants with cartoon bunnies and a light pink top. She's swathed in a large wrap-around knit sweater that could double as a bathrobe.

More than her physical appearance, I note the lost look in her eyes, as if her body is present, but her mind is far away.

Kira stands straight at attention as the woman enters. The male orderly that brought her waves, "I'll be in the hall if you need anything." He flashes us a brown thumbs-up and smiles before slinking out of the doorway into a seat in plain sight that we can see through the half-wall of windows.

Lynne offers a tired wave. "What's this about?"

Kira doesn't speak. I stand beside her and rub her back. Her arms fold in front of her chest, and I can feel her muscles tight as granite beneath my hand.

I finally respond, to buy Kira more time. "Hi, ma'am." I walk around the table and offer my hand to shake. "I'm Eric Salko. I'm afraid you don't know me."

She awkwardly holds my hand. It isn't a shake. I don't know quite what it is.

"Oh, okay," she says and then looks at Kira. "And *you* are?"

I watch a tear roll out from beneath Kira's glasses over cheeks, which are sunburn-red. I return to the spot by her side and touch her again.

She's shaking now, vibrating in her own hug, and clutching her arms tightly. I've never seen her like this. I didn't realize seeing her mother would affect her quite in this way, and suddenly, I feel horrible.

"Cat got your tongue?" Lynne asks.

"You *know* who I am… *Mom*," Kira growls, her voice like an animal's *stay-back* warning.

After a long moment of studying her from across the room, Lynne speaks. "Kira?"

She starts to come around the table, presumably for a hug, but Kira darts behind me and pops out the other side, giving herself as much distance between them as possible.

"You can stay right there. I don't want a hug or a handshake. I don't want anything from you. I fight hard every day to forget you exist so I can try to have some semblance of a normal life."

My gaze locks on Kira. I'm shocked that she said those things out loud.

"I understand your frustration with me, Ree-Ree. I do. But you're not seeing things for what they really are."

"Oh, shut the fuck up!" Kira clutches her ears, on the verge of screaming. "I can't hear that *bullshit* again!"

"It's not, Kira. I've told you a million times that man was not your father. He was a—"

"— *He was a Latvian secret agent sent to infiltrate our home.*"

Their voices chant it almost in unison, sending a chill straight through me. This conversation took a left turn fast enough to give me whiplash.

Kira is sobbing now, shaking her head. "I can't do this. Not again. I can't. We've been over this so many times before. Her brain is *broken*, Eric." The sound of my name snaps me out of the bizarre fugue state I've been thrown in. "She's diagnosed paranoid schizophrenic, among other things. That's why she did what she did. There's no telling her she's wrong. She really believes it, Eric."

She looks at her mother, a waif of a woman bearing an almost-uncanny older resemblance to herself.

"What does that mean? 'Why did she did what she did?' I'm afraid I don't follow."

"Tell him, Ree-Ree." The spindly mother prods. "Go on. Tell him what a villain I am for trying to protect our family and take us all home to glory so we could be with Christopher."

Kira shakes her head as if the whole thing is ridiculous and infuriating. She shifts her sunglasses up so that they are now a gold-and-black headband. Her eyes are crimson-rimmed, cheeks raw from dabbing and wet with fresh tears.

"My little brother, Christopher, the one with Tourette's, he got Leukemia. He was eight. I was ten. He declined quickly, and we kept getting turned down for treatment because our insurance was shit. We didn't have enough for the chemo and all the testing. They were estimating over thirty grand, which is thirty grand more than we had at the time."

She dabs at her nose and cheeks with the sleeve of her jacket and continues. "Chris died. Withered away fast. When he passed," she motions to her mother and flashes a look of pain and anger before returning her eyes to mine, "she had a psychotic break. She ended up here for a few weeks, which pretty much bankrupted my Dad. So, he signed her release and brought her home. We couldn't pay for the facility anymore.

We could barely eat. We were having to dumpster-dive just for food."

"Tell him why you really *hate* me, Ree-Ree." Lynne's gaze is piercing.

Kira swallows hard and continues. "Mom comes home talking about secret agents and Latvian spies and government conspiracies where people are scanning airwaves for our thoughts. She was convinced Dad was one of them and that he had infiltrated our family. My dad was a roofer with a ninth-grade education. No disrespect intended, but he couldn't have told you where Latvia was if he had a fucking *map* in front of him."

She spins in place and sniffles, "One day, I get home from school to see Mom in the kitchen with Dad's pistol. I have no clue how she found it. He had it locked in a safe. I kept asking him to pawn it for food money, but we were in a shitty neighborhood. He tried to get the gun from her, and she shot him three times." Her voice cracks. "In front of me."

I step toward her, wanting to offer comfort, but she dodges defensively. "Don't."

"Okay," I say calmly, hands up.

"...Then, she started accusing *me of* being involved in the whole conspiracy. I ducked under the dinner table, and she shot at me. Barely missed. She went to use the last bullet on herself, saying that she wanted to go on to glory and be with Christopher."

Tears are streaming from her eyes now. I want to hold her. I want to tell her that everything will be alright. I want to apologize profusely for ripping such an ugly wound wide open all over again.

"The gun was out of bullets. Hadn't been stored fully loaded, I guess. Cops came and carted her off. Dad's brother, whom I'd never met before, moved me up to Bridgeport. Took me in. After her diagnosis, the judge sent her here instead of prison."

Lynne laughs. "Pffft, Judge Lendger. You mean *Agent* Lendger..."

"See?!" Kira's eyes drift from me to her mother. After a moment, she shakily exhales and walks out of the room without uttering another word.

I offer a brief and cordial goodbye to Lynne and catch up to Kira in the hallway.

I try to stroke her back, but Kira pulls away, lost somewhere inside of herself.

I can't say I blame her.

The silence between us on the drive home is icy, so quiet it's loud again. All I can hear is the sound of springtime winds whipping past us on the highway and the practice of my future, formal apology playing on a loop in my head.

67

Kira

My long shower is so scorching it nearly blisters my skin. I almost don't want to leave it. I know I'll be limited to far shorter ones in the near future if I don't want to wear out my welcome.

As I dry and dress, I catch a glimpse of my puffy lids in the vanity mirror. I look like I've just been punched in both eyes.

I stuff the last of my necessities into my gym bag and seal up the last of the boxes I dragged in less than a month ago.

I sit on the bed with my laptop, a bed I'm going to miss splaying across on the rough nights ahead while I'm surfing on Remmy's lumpy couch.

I re-read the email I composed last night. I have re-composed about fourteen times since then. It's an email with both Rob and Eric in the 'Send To' slot with the regrettable subject line:

Resignation - effective immediately.

My finger is shaking as I click send and change the course of my future, pissing away the only job I've ever enjoyed and the only job I've ever had that paid well.

I can't bear to look Eric in the eyes, knowing I'm some cracked cup, shattered, re-glued, leaking my mess everywhere like a strainer with holes that can never be fully plugged.

Eric has enough going on in his life. He doesn't need my drama, too. Eventually, he will find someone who fits his lifestyle. Someone in the upper echelon of society. Someone who wouldn't think twice if he wanted to buy her a necklace in Paris. Someone who knows which fork to use at a six-hundred-dollar-a-head fundraiser. Someone whose shoe soles don't look like yapping puppet's mouths. Someone who has parents in Forbes magazine, not on a true-crime show about botched murder-suicides.

Eric deserves better.

So does Bella.

She deserves someone capable of being an actual mother to her. She deserves the love an acceptance Tawny robbed her of when she abandoned them both to play Jack Kerouac on the open road.

I love him enough to step out of the way so that he can find someone who can be everything he needs.

As I hear the whoosh of the email client sending my message, I have the overwhelming urge to be sick. I stay seated for a moment and allow the nausea to subside.

I rise, say a silent goodbye to the pool house, lay a folded, handwritten letter on the made bed, and then I lock up.

Moments later, I'm resisting the urge to bury my face in the steering wheel of my SUV and bawl my eyes out because the engine won't click over.

Tik-tik-tik-tik-tik-tik-tik-tik…

The battery is deader than Elvis.

It's time to call Remmy and tell him I need *yet another* favor: a ride away from here.

I'll just have to tow this piece of crap behind the Sprinter van when I come to pick up what little I have in a few days.

I almost want to laugh at how far down I've sunk in life, but I can't. I can't find any sliver of humor at this moment. I can't feel anything but the hard ground of rock bottom.

My car has broken down and given up.

And so have I.

68

Eric

I can't believe what I'm reading. I thought she needed time and space after our visit to Pleasant Oaks, so I left her alone the rest of Saturday and Sunday. I waited around like an asshole, checking my phone for texts every two minutes. Typing and then deleting. Rinse, lather, repeat.

But this morning, I felt sick when I saw her resignation email in my inbox. I came straight outside after reading it, only to find the pool house clean, bed made, and things packed back into the boxes they'd just come out of a few weeks before. Her books and toiletries were gone.

Her vehicle was in the rear driveway, leaking oil onto a piece of cardboard the whole time, so I never had a reason to suspect that she'd gone anywhere.

It's as if yet another woman in my life has up and just... *vanished.* The thought of this sickening deja vu infuriates me.

At least *this* one left a note.

I try to read through it, but the faint scent of her gardenia perfume on the pillows and sheets pull my focus from the devastating piece of paper in my hands.

The letter says she will be back in a week with a moving van to get her things. On its ruled lines, she apologizes for a myriad of offenses, so many things my head is swimming. I can't even keep track of everything she feels sorry for.

Knowing that she's left makes me feel like my heart has been ripped out of my chest. Like I can't *breathe*.

I just want to lay in this bed, hold her in my arms, and stroke her hair like I did the morning after we made love in Paris, watching the sun rise behind the Eiffel Tower from our penthouse.

She's gone.

I feel *foolish* for assuming she wouldn't be just another cloud of dust like *Tawny*.

The postscript of the letter is interesting. She mentions in it that she snooped (one of many itemized actions she apologized for) and that the camcorder under the bed contains footage of Tawny that might help my case in the custody battle. Things like Tawny yelling choice words at Bella in Anger.

She even made a small log of the clip numbers and what they contain on the back of the letter. This sort of organization would make me laugh if I didn't feel so livid right now.

I retrieve the camera from beneath the bed and head toward the door. I feel my anger percolating like a kettle, bubbling with ferocity. While I'm grateful for the tip, this whole thing makes me want to crush the camcorder in my hand by smashing it into the fucking wall.

Never in a million years did I think Kira would be the type to abandon me, too.

Somewhere, deep down, I feared this would happen.

I'm starting to think the problem is *me*.

I should just focus on what little time I may have left with Bella before she vanishes from my life, too.

Oh my God...

Bella.

How do I explain this to her?

How do I tell her that another woman she loved just split town without so much as a goddamned *goodbye*.

69

Eric

"Bella, sweetheart, not so close to the edge," I warn.

I try to force my tone to be pleasant, but inside, I'm seething over Kira's selfish decision to bail. Work-wise, it frustrates me. We were in the middle of designing several of our summer ad spots. She was flying through the new client packets with ease and helping me research a variety of electric vehicle stock projections. I have no clue where we are at with that stuff now.

But more than that, I'm pissed off about her leaving *me*... and leaving *Bella*.

"I don't see Howard yet," Bella pouts. "*Huh-huh*, do you think he's okay?"

I survey the lake in front of us, lost in thought. "I'm sure he's fine. He's around here somewhere. In the meantime, why don't you feed the other ducks?"

"Those aren't *ducks*, Dad, those are *swans*. And they're *mean* to Howard, and I don't wanna feed them."

"Fine. Then let's go home."

"No!" Her voice raises, and she turns to me, stomping her foot petulantly. "Give him some time to find us."

"Maybe he left." *Everyone always does, Bella.* "Maybe he's on to greener pastures." *Damn you, Tawny.*

Bella's look is one of worry and more serious concern than it should be for a duck. She cups a hand around her mouth and shakes her bag of frozen peas with the other. "Howard?! Howard, where are you?"

I wipe dew off the bench seat behind us, cast in full shadow by the blossoming trees all around, blocking out the sun. I feel like my relationship with Kira has been cast into the shadows, void of all of her warmth. She was a daily ray of sunshine through the gloom.

And now I'm in the frigid darkness.

I can't eat.

I can't focus.

I can't *sleep.*

I can't eat a damned nicoise salad without thinking of how she looked by the Seine, sun-kissed and glowing from being in Paris again. The *coq a vin* leftovers in my fridge piss me off every time I see them.

I can't stop thinking about her.

My hands grip the bench's wood so hard that my knuckles are bone white, arms flexed. I want to rip this thing apart when I think about her email.

My pool house is once again a free *Stor-It-All* unit for the women I've shared a bed with, women who leave behind their belongings just as fast as the man they *allegedly* care about.

383

I should have never told her I loved her in Paris. That was *stupid*.

I meant what I said, but saying it gave her the power to destroy me like this.

…To destroy what we *had*.

Maybe I shouldn't have pushed with her mother like that…

"Dad?"

"Yes, Ella-Bella."

"When is Kira going to be back?"

What the hell do I say to that?

Never. She bolted, just like your mom.

"I don't," the words are like ice, frozen to my tongue, "think she is, sweetheart."

Bella turns and stares at me. "What happened? Where did she go?"

I shrug. I honestly don't fucking know the answer to either question.

She shuffles back to the bench and sits next to me, watching the swans honk and flap, barking orders for her to feed them in their language. She fidgets with the bag.

"Did you call her?"

"Yes, honey. I called. I texted. I even sent an email." I sigh. "I think she just wants to be left alone." I nod toward the water. "Go finish feeding the birds, and then we can go home and let Sernik run around in his ball for a while."

She trudges with reluctance back to the water's edge. "Howard!"

She shakes the bag again as if it's some sort of dinner bell.

384

A moment later, I see her shoulders bobbing, head hung low. And then, a sniffle.

"Bella?" I start to stand. "Are you crying?"

She turns around. Her face is red, flooded with tears. "Howard's gone!" She throws the bag down on the ground and covers her face as she sobs.

I go to hug her, and she screams in my grasp, "Howard left! Everyone always *freaking leaves!*"

I pick her up and carry her back to the car as she cries and snots on the wide lapels of my suit, using them as a handkerchief.

I am fully aware that this isn't about a duck at all, and part of me agrees.

She's right.

Everyone does.

The drive home is serene as we listen to my phone's playlist through the Rivian's Bluetooth. But the moment John Denver's voice comes on, I flip the volume off and drive us the rest of the way in silence.

70

Kira

"This week is spring bulk trash pickup," Remmy mentions over the grapefruit we are splitting for breakfast. Each half sits on its own cheap paper plate. We dig and carve at them like we are on some juice-filled archaeological expedition with spoons that don't match.

I look out the living room window of his first-floor apartment. Bridgeport is a gross place, but this neighborhood is particularly slummy.

"Yeah, but the SUV's dead as disco at Eric's. That is if he hasn't had it *impounded* yet."

"We could see what we could fit in the back of my Accord. You always find *something* worth reselling when those spring-cleaning yuppies ditch their shit. Remember those birdcages you found and cleaned up? You sold those bitches for a mint."

I nod. Digging through people's trash to upcycle and resell is the last thing on my mind right now.

Two weeks ago, I was in the City of Lights shopping on the *Champs-Élysées*.

And now I'm discussing rifling through people's literal trash to make a buck.

My, how far I have fallen.

"I'm just saying, might be a good way to bring in a little income while you find a place," Remmy says. It's his polite way of reminding me that this place is far too small to sustain the both of us for any length of time.

"I have some appointments to go look at places with the Realtor today. She's picking me up in an hour."

"You have enough for first, last, and security?"

"I think so. I've been saving."

"What about your car?"

I fidget with my Ferris wheel necklace. The thought of having to sell it to afford a vehicle makes me sick to my stomach. But I know with where Zuzanna bought it, there was almost nothing in that store under five figures. One of the watches in there had a price tag of $126,000, so I shudder to think of what *this* cost.

I also shudder to think of what Bridgeport Pawn and Jewelers will give me for it…

It's not only a symbol of the last memory I have with my father, but it is also a symbol of the one time in my life I was lucky enough to have it all, even if I clearly didn't deserve any of it.

"I'll figure something out," I finally say.

Remmy loudly slurps the last of the squeezed juice out of his half and launches it across the kitchen toward the trash. It bounces out and lands on the wrinkled, ill-fitting vinyl flooring. "He shoots; he does *not* score."

"Go get ready for work. I'll pick it up. I'm going that way anyway." I scoop his paper plate beneath mine and head to the trash to toss all of the refuse.

I make my way back to the couch, which has been doubling as my bed for several nights.

I look at my phone and click open the gallery, scrolling through my photos from the last six weeks. It's a ritual I've participated in at least five times in the four days since I fled Greenwich with my tail between my legs.

I smile at the videos of Bella excitedly feeding Howard at the preserve. And of the burst of photos of Sernik in her splayed hands the first day he came home.

But the ones that bring me the most joy are the ones of Eric. Like a shot I have of him smiling at the kiosk while playing hands of high-stakes blackjack. Or the selfie of us dressed to the nines at *Le Moulin Rouge*. Or Zuzanna wiping his face after crepes. Him staring with bulging eyes at my giant pig's foot entree on an even bigger plate.

I scroll beyond my hire date and remember how dull my camera roll was before I met them. Most of my gallery is pictures of new sweater stock and Cassandra's finicky cat.

The Salkos brought a vibrancy to every day. And working for Eric, I felt like I had finally found something I was good at. Something that felt interesting and ever-changing. And appreciated...

I scroll back up and freeze, thumb hovering over my favorite photo, one I'd be devastated if I lost. It's blurry, but I remember the moment like it was yesterday. It is a photo of Eric sleeping at the hotel attached to the casino the night we broke all the rules.

He looked so peaceful, sleeping as the morning sun crept into the sky. I wish I could go back to those times. Before Tawny, before my mother.

I fan my face, trying to reel my emotions in. I switch to my messenger and look at the last text.

It arrived two days ago.

ERIC: Can we please just discuss this like adults?

I don't know what to say or how to respond. I don't know what there is to discuss.

We can never *be.*

We were foolish to allow it to last as long as it did.

I've started to text him back about fifty times, and every time, I delete it, hoping that he hasn't seen the three dots indicating that I don't know what the hell to say, except maybe…

Goodbye.

71

Eric

"Eric, no moon." That's my mom's way of saying don't frown or cheer up. I don't know why. Maybe something just got lost in translation somewhere, but it stuck. She always says it when I'm sad. "Why you no eat? I make your favorite," Zuzanna shakes her hand at a plate of steaming kielbasa and potato pancakes with sour cream and salmon atop them.

"I'm not hungry." I prod the food on my plate and look over to see my daughter scarfing hers down like a starved prisoner.

"He's not eating anything Jacques makes him, either," Bella says, ratting me out with a mouthful of potato. The little snitch…

I flash her a look, and she shrugs. *Sorry-not-sorry, it's the truth,* is what her reaction says.

"Bella, don't talk with your mouth full," I mutter, unable to hide the solemn tone from my voice.

"Eric, you must eat! You waste away. You too thin already." Mom takes a large sip of wine and looks me up and down.

"He's sad about Kira."

Now, I just stare at Bella and put my fork down. I don't like her sharing my private business like this.

But she taunts me, knowing she's adorable enough to get away with it. *"He wanted to smooch her. He wanted to —"*

"Bella, *stop*." My eyes flash something serious, and she goes back to horking down more food.

"I don't understand this." She waves her glass around now, swishing the contents. "You really like this girl, right?"

I offer a frustrated sigh. "She left, mom. She took off. It's... goddamned *Tawny* all over again." I look to Bella. "*Sorry.* When we get home, I will put five bucks in the swear jar."

"Kira no like Tawny." Mom shrugs. "Tawny... she ees selfish woman. She only care about herself. Everybody know that."

I grind my molars and gulp a mouthful of wine, allowing its burn to distract me from this useless conversation.

"Kira was nice girl. She take good care of Bella. She bring out of, uh," she has to think of the words, "her shell. She bring a little bit *you* out of your shell."

Mom eyes me suspiciously.

"You like her more than you say, I know. I saw the way you were in Paris together. She mean a lot to you. And I think you mean lot to her, too."

391

Even through her broken English, I find a sprig of hope in her words before stuffing it back down again and locking the thought away where it can't get to me.

"She's gone, mom. She doesn't want to be with me."

"Hey! I taught you better than *that*." My mom sounds half-angry, half-inspiring. She grabs my hand with her own. "In this world, you *fight* for what you *want*. You have to fight for what is *good*. No one said it would be easy, but love ees worth fighting for."

I take a bite of my food. My mother's an amazing cook, but everything I have taken a bite of these last few days tastes like flavorless cardboard. I chew it like I'm trying to crush my molars into dust.

"You say she coming back for her things in a couple of days."

"So?"

"And you going to see her again, right?"

I don't say anything. I only stare.

"Well," she continues, "make her know how much you care about her. You *fight* for her."

"Easier said than done, Ma." I fold my arms in front of my chest and pick a stray string off of the sleeve of my new suit jacket. "She's made up her mind. I'm not going to chase someone who doesn't want to be in my life."

"Oh, now, who look foolish? Eric, she *scared*. She *want* to be in your life. I see in the way she look at you... *and* Bella. Make the big gesture. Show her you care. If she still say no, then," she shrugs carelessly, "at least you say you tried!"

"What am I supposed to do, huh? Stand outside her window with a boombox in my arms and give her the Jerry Maguire 'You Complete Me' speech?"

"If there ees anything worth looking like *fool* over…" she turns to look at the photo of my smiling father on the wall. When she turns back, her eyes are glistening with tears threatening to fall from her soft brown eyes. "It ees *love*." She swallows hard. "If your father did not fight for *me* when it matter most, *you* would not be here."

After a long silence, Bella raises her hand, trying to hide a mischievous smile.

"Yes, you there in the pink shirt." I point to Bella.

"*Huh-huh.*" Her head twitches violently and returns to normal as if she has no inkling her body is at all betraying her. "I have an idea. But I don't want to say it out loud in front of everyone in case it's stupid."

"Everyone? It's me and *Babcia*."

Bella just stares at me.

"Alright, counselor. You may approach the bench." I wave her over.

What she whispers in my ear next is so ridiculous that only a ten-year-old child could come up with it.

The problem is…
I kind of love it.

72

Kira

My stomach is in my throat as I approach the gate in the rental van, chewing the last of my nails right off my fingers out of nervous habit. The sun is setting in a fiery spray of color overhead. Various vehicles are parked bumper-to-bumper along the roadside, glinting in dusk's vibrant palette.

Is Eric... having a party?

I don't remember any sort of function being on his calendar...

My confidence quakes further.

What if I'm interrupting? Should I come back? I should have texted.

Dammit.

I sit, engine idling, looking at the worn yellow tow straps in the passenger seat.

Just pull off the band-aid, Kira.

Get in and out. Less than an hour. It's not that much stuff.

Plus, the online video made hooking up the CRV for transport look easy enough.

I roll down my window and hear the faint waft of jovial music and the whir of machinery. It sounds strangely familiar, though uncommon for this serene part of Greenwich. I can't quite place it.

Behind the mansion, I see the faint flicker of lights.

What the hell am I about to interrupt?

I swallow hard and push the buzzer at the front gate. The ten seconds it takes to hear someone speak feel like *hours*.

Finally, the familiar warmth of Eric's voice oozes through the airwaves, sending a Pavlovian shiver through my body at the sound of it. "Kira?"

I miss it. I didn't even realize how *much* I missed it until I heard him say my name.

"*Yes*," my voice barely comes out. I feel like I have no control over it. It feels small and laced with cowardice.

"Kira, I'm glad you came. Before you get your things, I need to give you something."

I want to say a million things.

Instead, I freeze and utter nothing.

The box buzzes, and the gates sweep inward, allowing entry. I creep through, hearing the gas-guzzling engine hum over the faint sound of music and celebration drifting from somewhere beyond the mansion.

As I make my way down the drive, more lights come into view, and the musical sounds cease abruptly, leaving only the buzz and grind from some large, unseen apparatus.

It isn't until I pull up near the bumper of my SUV that I throw it into park and get out of the running vehicle, mouth agape with fascination and wonder.

I can't believe my eyes.

I soak in the spectacle before me. There's a horde of people, some gathered in casual spring attire. Others are in tuxedos carrying trays of food and drink in white-gloved hands. Some are young children I recognize vaguely from Bella's school.

Bella is in the front of the crowd, staring at me, buzzing with a look of nervous excitement. Zuzanna is behind her with tears in her eyes, hands clasped over her mouth.

Eric approaches the van I'm in with a smile. He looks like a million dollars wearing a bespoke charcoal suit and gold tie I've never seen him in.

But there is something in the distance that floors me. I'm frozen in this moment, riddled with shock.

Behind them all sits a full-blown carnival with a handful of rides. There's a small midway of balloon games in tiny trucks with colorful awnings. There's a small petting zoo with goats and ponies at the end of the strip.

I leave the van, still trying to soak it all in. Everyone is staring at me in silence. The scent of fried funnel cake wafts through the air, making my stomach flip.

I've barely eaten since I left this place. The thought of the finality of our relationship ending made me feel constant waves of nausea. The thought of Eric and I being over caused a wrenching pain so strong and lasting that food was the furthest thing from my mind.

Eric approaches warmly, trying to hide the smile on his face. "It's so good to see you."

The words are like molasses, sweet and thick, covering me.

Before I can figure out what to say, he speaks again. "Please, would you take a ride with me?"

I don't know what he's talking about. My head is swimming.

He offers his arm, and I take it, unable to offer anything more than an utterly stunned silence.

He leads me down the midway, and halfway down, I see *it* beyond the bunching of thick orchard trees.

It's a Ferris wheel.

He smiles with kindness in his eyes, and my whole body buzzes with every emotion under the sun. This must have cost a fortune.

I see a grouping of well-dressed people at the base of the ride, each with instruments ready, beaming at me through the dusky light. The luminous bulbs of the wheel light their grinning faces. Eric walks up the steps and holds a hand out for me.

I finally speak, wanting to choke on every word from the nerves. "Eric... I don't know what to say."

"You don't have to say anything. Just come for a ride with me." There is so much sincerity in his golden-ringed eyes melting me. "Please? One ride."

After a moment of contemplation, I take his hand and enter the open bucket with him. The man running the ride latches the door and nods at him. He engages the lever, and we ascend, whirling up the side.

I hear Bella holler a cheer from her spot next to Zuzanna at the machine's base.

Once we are at the top, like a maestro, the man working the ride motions the grouping of instrumentalists seated near the ride.

They begin to play.

I instantly recognize John Denver's melody, and tears well in my eyes. I cover my face, feeling the hot skin beneath my hands as the string quartet plays the most beautiful version of the song I've ever heard.

Eric gently takes my hands from my face and looks at me seriously as the notes of *Sunshine on My Shoulders* swell in the spring air.

"I can't believe you did this," I whisper, looking out over the people who have all gone back to enjoying their rides and midway games.

"I can't take all of the credit. Bella and Mom helped with some of the planning since I no longer have an assistant."

His eyes hold mine, and I am flooded with a sense of deep longing.

God, I have missed him. Missed lying in his strong arms. Missed the amazing way he always makes me feel. Missed his sexy smile, his infectious laugh.

Eric tilts his head and takes a deep breath. His hands tremble as they grasp mine, and my heart melts.

"I know things have never been easy for you in this world."

His honeyed eyes feel like they're looking straight into my soul, and suddenly, I don't know how I was ever able to walk away from this man.

"Until recently, I had no idea just *how* hard things were. You have gone through so much more than I could ever imagine and come out stronger. You could have let this world beat you down, harden you, rob your sense of humor... but you didn't. You became indomitable and funny and stayed caring. Like you were with Bella from the start. Like you were with *me* from the start."

"Eric, you did this for me?" I'm shaking now, watching the world spin behind him. "I don't—"

"What? *Deserve* this? Is that what you were going to say?"

I nod, tears pouring from my eyes.

I don't. None of this.

And even *less* so now that I tucked-tail and ran—

"Kira, before I met you, I couldn't *imagine* loving someone like I love you. I didn't think I would *ever* find someone who made me feel the way that you did. I," he chokes nervously on his words and rubs his neck, "I want to travel the whole *world* with you. I want to wake up next to you and watch you unapologetically eat the weirdest thing on every menu."

I laugh and clutch my face, watching all of the cherry blossoms fall like pink rain. Watching the topiary garden circle around.

"I want to build a *life* with you."

I wish I could capture this moment in time forever and live here in the bucket of this Ferris wheel for eternity.

"You deserve the world, and I... I want to give it to you." His eyes are misty now, too. "Bella and I miss you."

"I miss you both, too." I cover my mouth with a shaky hand. My breath hitches. I feel like I can't breathe. I clutch the spinning pendant around my neck and squeeze it for comfort. "*And* Zuzanna."

"Kira, she's the kind of mother you *should* have gotten in this world. I didn't know how lucky I was until we went to Pleasant Oaks. I know that day was horrible, but I never realized *just* how strong you really are until I found out all of that." He shifts in his seat and flexes his jaw to keep his own emotions at bay.

I look down at the swirling band and smiling faces of Bella and Zuzanna, watching us from the ground.

I finally gather the courage to speak.

"God, I have missed you."

"I missed you, too." He rubs my hand, and I see a smile forming on his gorgeous face.

The symphonic music swells, and more tears flood my eyes. "I love you, Eric."

I finally say it for the first time in my entire life, and I feel like a million pounds of weight have been lifted off my chest. I wipe away the tears streaming down my cheek, raining onto my blue jean jacket.

Eric moves next to me and caresses the side of my face. I am elated by the swell of emotions running through my trembling body.

I don't know what I did to deserve a love like this.

"Did you kiss yet?" Bella shouts from the ground through cupped hands.

Eric and I laugh for a moment.

"Not yet, Mouse," I yell over the side.

"What are you waiting for?" Bella squeals.

Eric smiles and presses his lips to mine.

Joy and electricity course through me.

I kiss him back.

With everything I have.

With everything within me.

He sees me not as the broken wind-up toy I *feel* like but as a woman. One *worthy of love.*

"*Please, don't ever leave me again,*" he whispers in my ear, begging me from the depths of his soul. "I felt so lost without you."

401

The Ferris wheel slows to a stop with us at the bottom, and Bella and Zuzanna join us in the bucket as if on cue.

Their entry gives the rest of the miniature carnival the cue to mingle again. The horde of people go back to enjoying the festivities and fried treats. Goats bleat.

The moment they step into our bucket, I grab Bella and hold her so hard I fear I might squeeze all the air out of her.

"Oh my God, Mouse, I have missed you."

"I missed you, too," she says with a smile, hugging my neck so tight I feel light-headed.

I don't want to let her go.

I want to be a positive force in her life. An example of strength and warmth. Something neither of our mothers could prove to be.

Zuzanna looks at Eric with a curious face and puts her thumbs in the air as if trying to ask: *did everything go well?*

Eric gives her a thumbs up.

Zuzanna wipes her eyes and wraps Bella and me both in her arms. "Awww, I so glad you back. Eric and Bella, they sad mess without you."

Then she points out toward the mansion. "Hurry, look! You don't miss."

We all turn in the bucket, and as the final sustained notes of my favorite song emanate up from the string quartet below, a grouping of well-timed fireworks pop in the distance, high overhead illuminating our world in color, if only for a split second at a time.

We watch the glittering sky from this whirling dream.

One I would never *dare* to wake from.

Epilogue

Kira

The restaurant is especially packed for a weeknight. Still, it's Eric's favorite Kobe steak within a fifty-mile radius of the house.

Zuzanna raises her glass of white wine to toast. "To Eric and Bella. *Congratulations!* I so happy this thing behind us now. *Nostrovia!*"

"I second that emotion," I say, raising my glass.

Bella raises her soda and twitches her neck, nearly sloshing dark liquid over the rim.

"Careful, baby," Eric says before laying a quick kiss on her blonde head.

"*Huh-huh-huh,* I want to toast, too."

"Alright, you go for it." Zuzanna motions to the rest of the table.

"Rub-a-dub-dub, thanks for the grub. Let's eat."

I laugh.

Eric cocks his head to the side. "Not a toast, but okay. You heard the woman. Let's eat!"

"*Huh-huh,* I don't know what we are toasting to."

I put my drink down and look at Eric. "May I take a crack at this one?"

He scoffs. "Pfft, be my *guest.*"

"Well, Mouse," I turn to her, "today, a judge told your mom that she can't take you away to Florida to go live with her."

Bella sighs with relief. "Oh, *good.* I don't think that Sernik would like *that* trip."

"No," Eric laughs at how well Bella took the news, "I can't imagine he would. God forbid."

Suddenly, Eric's eyes flash at me, and a smile touches his lips.

"What?" I ask, glancing back and forth between him and the plate of Rocky Mountain Oysters Bella ordered for me.

Eventually, I will learn my lesson.

But the giggle she makes when the "*weirdest food on the menu*" is put in front of me is worth it all.

"I know you speak French," he says.

"*Oui, monsieur.*" I smile.

"How's your Italian?"

I say a few words in a mock-Italian accent. "A-f*ettucini. Rigatoni. Arrivederci. Bellissimo.*" I blow a chef's kiss with my hand.

He chuckles.

I shrug, digging into the food in front of me. It's actually not half bad. Much better than the foot of a pig. "Unfortunately, that's about all the Italian I know."

"What about Greek?"

"Oof. It's all Greek to me." I take a sip of my wine. Bella laughs like a chipmunk at the dumb joke.

"What about you?" He asks Bella. "Can you speak any Italian?"

She shrugs. "I can say hello and count to ten in Mandarin."

"Well, Mandarin is not going to help you when we are in Italy, is it?"

The three of us look at him, confused. "You guys have a month to learn some before we go to Rome."

"Yay!" Bella celebrates.

"And I figured from there, we can do a few days in Glasgow."

"Scotland?" Zuzanna says, eyebrows raised as if to say *wow, I didn't know you had it in you.*

"What do you think?" he asks me, slicing into his steak.

"*Challenge accepted,*" I say with a sly smirk.

He fights the urge to smile at the dirty reference, piercing eyes sparkling beneath the string of lights overhead.

I love this man more than words can say.

My heart skips a beat as I look around and the reality hits me. I have finally found a home. I have a family. A mother who cares for me the way a mother should. A child that I would give my life for, if the situation ever called for it.

I have found love with a man who cares for me in ways I didn't even know I needed it.

As I look around this table, watching Bella turn forked bread rolls into a set of walking feet…

As I watch Zuzanna howl in joyous laughter at her granddaughter's antics…

As I catch the look of adoration in Eric's eyes as he locks eyes with me over the commotion…

I feel *whole* for the first time in my entire life.

As I sit back in the cushioned booth and look at the warmth and happiness I'm surrounded by, I can't believe this is real life.

About the Author

Odessa is an award-winning filmmaker and a cancer survivor who spent over a decade working in the film industry. However, storytelling has always had a spell over her.

Born in Wyoming and spending most of her adult life in Florida and Louisiana, she now lives on the beach in New England with her boyfriend and their two pups. When she isn't writing, she's usually tending to her massive vegetable garden or kayak fishing.

Odessa Alba is a romance pen name (an easy way to keep her genre fiction separate for readers.) She has published several horror novels under her real name, Erica Summers, and also writes cozy mysteries under the pen name Trixie Fairdale.

A Note From The Ogres

Even though this book was proofread thoroughly by professionals, beta readers, and ARC readers… mistakes happen. We want our readers to have the best experience possible. If you spot any spelling, grammatical, or formatting errors, please feel free to reach out to us at:

Rustyogrepublishing@gmail.com

Reviews

If you could take the time to leave an honest review after you've read this book, we would greatly appreciate it. We respect your time and promise it doesn't *have* to be long and eloquent. Even a few words will do!

As a small publishing house, every review helps others determine if this book is right for them and greatly increases our chances of being discovered by someone else who might enjoy it.

Call of the Wyl

A Standalone Destorian Fantasy Novella
Available worldwide in ebook and audiobook

What would it take to send your own brother to the dungeons?

Wyl bounty hunter, Brutus, is in hot pursuit of his elusive brother, Otis. With a bounty on his sibling's head (and Brutus in desperate need of fast coin) he must bring his own relative to justice. Along his mysterious journey, Brutus finds himself in the clutches of Brute Fest, a violent festival where black eyes and vicious brawls are celebrated. His trip takes an even more intriguing turn when he becomes enraptured by a rose-gold beauty named Violet. Captivated by the wild, new world around him, Brutus must make an impossible choice between love, money... and family.

The Ugly Sweater PARTY

A FORCED PROXIMITY ROMANCE NOVELLA

AURORA ALBA & ODESSA ALBA

The Ugly Sweater Party

By Aurora Alba & Odessa Alba

Available in paperback, ebook, & audiobook.

Ascending to a holiday party on the thirty-second floor of a Manhattan skyscraper, the building's only elevator breaks down, trapping grinchy curmudgeon "Nasty Nate" DuPont and the stubborn Director of Finance, Twila Henderson, inside. With bumbling maintenance workers en route and emotions running high, Twila and Nate struggle to stay civil. As hideously dressed co-workers mingle feet beyond their blocked exit, stuffed emotions bubble to the surface over the captive duo's seemingly forgotten past.

Bursting with heat and humor, this third-person steamy laugh-riot will leave you with an HFN that will warm your heart on even the coldest winter night. From the Alba sisters (authors of The Billionaire's Assistant & Call of the Wyl) comes a spicy standalone contemporary romance novella for fans of forced proximity, enemies-to-lovers, workplace romance, grumpy boss, holiday romance, & romantic comedy tropes.

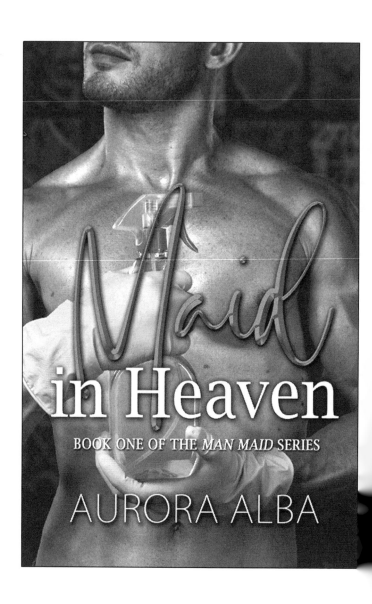

Maid
in Heaven

BOOK ONE OF THE *MAN MAID* SERIES

AURORA ALBA

Maid in Heaven

By Aurora Alba

For ages, men have openly lusted for women in skimpy French maid outfits. But what do women want? One desperate entrepreneur, desperate to pay off his daughter's mounting medical bills, has cracked the code. Sexy single dad, Will Jessup, has started to earn a decent living dusting the cobwebs off for Jackson Hole's horned-up housewives, offering a unique twist on a timeless service: scrubbing mansions spotless with his mouth-watering body clad in risque costumes.

Salty from her divorce and reeling from the loss of her career after a botched client call, Ava Quinn is now woefully unemployed and simultaneously overqualified for every finance job in Jackson. With a bit of help from her hilariously unfiltered bestie, Ava soon finds the frustratingly handsome maid in her home. In a strange twist of fate, Ava soon realizes that the male maid in the skimpy policeman's uniform with arresting cobalt-blue eyes could be precisely what she needs to clean up the mess she's made of her home... and her life.

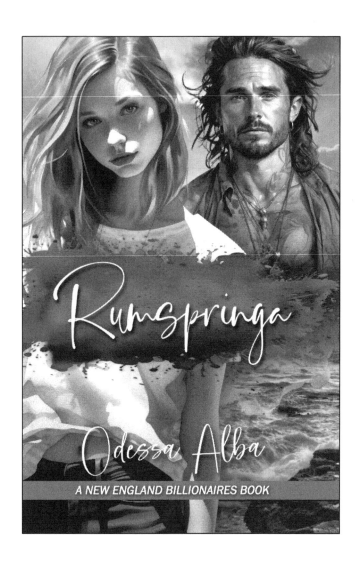

Rumspringa

Odessa Alba

A NEW ENGLAND BILLIONAIRES BOOK

Rumspringa

**Book two of the
New England Billionaires Series
By Odessa Alba**

Coming soon to ebook, paperback, hardcover,
and audiobook!

Made in the USA
Columbia, SC
22 November 2024

47344017R00257